ZUCCHINI
PIE

Granny's Recipe for Life

OTHER BOOKS AND AUDIO BOOKS

BY SUSAN AYLWORTH

Right Click

ZUCCHINI
PIE

Granny's Recipe for Life

a novel

SUSAN AYLWORTH

Covenant Communications, Inc.

Cover design copyright © 2013 by Covenant Communications, Inc.

Published by Covenant Communications, Inc.
American Fork, Utah

Printed in the United States of America
First Printing: June 2013

19 18 17 16 15 14 13   10 9 8 7 6 5 4 3 2 1

ISBN-13: 978-1-62108-351-1

For Patricia Kimsey—
sister, confidant, reader, helper,
travel companion, and dear friend—
with love.

For Jacob, Elise, Erin, Abby, and Eric.

For Caleb, James, and Corbridge,
Emma and Vaughn,
Adelaide and Sadie.

And always,
for Roger.

ACKNOWLEDGMENTS

DEEP APPRECIATION AND MANY THANKS are in order for my beta readers: Roger, Pat, Matt and Marie, Becca and Jonathan, Hugh and Nona, Sue, Carly, and the rest of you who read every word or just a little here and there and gave occasional suggestions and comments.

Thanks also to Samantha Millburn, Stacey Owen, and Kathryn Gordon at Covenant and to my friends in ANWA and LDS Storymakers who have encouraged the development of this story. Also, special thanks to everyone who shared their secret family recipes and to Becca for lending Tom your birthday.

I am indebted to actor and author Carrie Fisher, who gave us the great observation that "Resentment is like drinking poison and waiting for the other person to die." I have relied heavily on that observation not only in the creation of this work, but in my personal life as well. Thanks, Ms. Fisher.

I especially acknowledge my debt to my husband, Roger, and to Paul, Carly, and Adelaide, who shared my space and lived with my changing moods as I coped with the needs of the Burnetts. Thanks to you all.

Recipes

Potato and Sour Cream Casserole
a.k.a. "Funeral Potatoes"

1 can (10.75 oz.) condensed
   cream of chicken soup
¼ C. butter
2 C. sour cream
2 pounds precooked potatoes,
   diced or shredded

⅓ C. chopped green onions
2 C. shredded Cheddar cheese,
   divided
2 C. crushed corn flakes
salt and pepper to taste

Directions

1. Preheat oven to 350.
2. In a small pot, heat the soup, butter or margarine, and sour cream over low heat.
3. Combine potatoes, green onion, and 1 C. cheese in a large mixing bowl. Mix in the heated soup mixture. Season with salt and pepper. Pour into a 9 x 13 dish. Sprinkle remaining cheese over the top of the casserole and add crushed corn flakes over the top.
4. Bake 35–40 minutes or until heated through and cheese is bubbling.

Variations

Substitute cooked potatoes with frozen hash browns; cream of chicken soup with any other cream soup (mushroom, cheddar, potato); and corn flakes with flavored bread crumbs, crushed potato chips, or crushed crackers.

NOTE: Except where otherwise stated, all recipes, including variations and comments, are from the files of Karen Hendricks Burnett.

CHAPTER 1

Wednesday, June 13, Late morning

KAREN BURNETT

"ONE OF THOSE MORNINGS" DIDN'T begin to describe it. It had been a cacophony of verbal miscues, stumbling missteps, and unexpected phone calls, most of them demanding more than I felt I could give. This was shaping up to be what folks in my house like to call a "nibbled day." The phrase referred to a statement once made by Eric Sevareid, a network news anchor back when Tom and I were kids, about how working for the networks was "like being nibbled to death by ducks": no major wounds or arterial bleeding, just the little bruises piling up, one upon another.

I had finally completed the agenda for my presidency meeting and was just taking the casserole out of the oven when the cell phone in my pocket started playing. My first thought was to ignore it, but the music was "Pinball Wizard" from the rock opera *Tommy*, the ring tone for my husband, Tom. He often calls around midday just to check in, and I usually look forward to the chat. This time I looked at the open oven door and back at the hot casserole. Within a minute, that heat would be burning right through those flimsy oven mitts to my hands. I looked at the door to the garage, which I had carefully propped open less than a minute ago, and the open door to the backseat of my Hyundai, where a thick pad of old newspapers was waiting. The clock said 11:55, and I knew the sisters planned to start serving lunch just after noon. I live only three minutes from the stake center, but still . . .

Promising myself I'd get back to Tom after I'd made my delivery, I grasped the casserole dish, pushed the oven door closed with my elbow, and headed for the car, where I plugged the phone into the car charger. I wiped sweat from my brow with the back of my hand and hoped I wouldn't look too disheveled once I got there. As I started for the church, I had a feeling that I needed to speak to Tom ASAP, but it seemed an odd, random thought, so I dismissed it.

Sister Reedley, Relief Society president in the fourth ward, was directing traffic in the kitchen when I arrived. She said, "Hi, Karen. Thanks!" and sent me out to set the casserole on the serving table alongside the ham, Jell-O salads, rolls, and green bean casseroles furnished by other sisters from her ward. Almost immediately one of the mourners stepped forward to offer a blessing, and the lunch began, so I knew I'd arrived not a moment too soon. I was glad I'd hurried things along.

I didn't know this family or the elderly sister who had died—they're all from the fourth ward—but the gathering looked just like the dozen or more I had coordinated during the past year, and I felt great empathy for these grieving people. Who knew when our turn might come?

As I headed back to the car, the random thought returned that I needed to call Tom and quickly, only this time it was clearly a prompting—a somewhat urgent prompting—and I knew I needed to get to the phone and get back to Tom right away. I quickened my pace.

It was good to have repaid the favor I owed Sister Reedley. She had certainly come through for me a few weeks before when three sisters called in sick on the same day we had a big funeral lunch in our ward. I had needed to repay that favor, and I was just crossing it off my mental checklist when I saw Anna Campbell coming toward me. I grinned but thought, *Oh no*, at the same time and tried to think of a quick way to dodge her without seeming to, but it was too late; she had already spotted me. "Sister Burnett!" she called. "Glad I caught you!"

Anna Campbell is a sweetheart, one of the few elderly people in our ward who always has fun and happy stories to tell, and I always enjoy my visits with her, even the small, impromptu ones. I very much wished I could stop to visit today, since she always sends me away cheerful, yet I really didn't have time—not when I was so preoccupied by that prompting. Even on a day that was already so full of commitments—a presidency meeting, a last-minute request to accompany my daughter's summer choir rehearsal, serving dinner to the missionaries, attending the choir's concert at the mall, not to mention all the simple tasks necessary to put the just-finished school year behind us and get ready for a small family vacation—that prompting took priority.

That's when I realized I hadn't really been listening to Sister Campbell. I told Anna I'd call before the weekend and rushed back to the car. By the time I reached my Sonata, the music from *Tommy* was playing again, and I knew there must be an urgent need for Tom to call again this soon.

I rushed to grab the phone, but it had stopped ringing. That was when I saw that Tom had called four times in the last eleven minutes, and a feeling of dread dropped in my stomach like a brick.

Tom picked up before I heard the first ring. "Are you okay?" he asked.

"Yes," I answered. "Just busy. Why? What's happened?"

"It's Granny Adelaide. She's bad. Can you come to the hospital?"

"I'll be right there." Just like that, other commitments all leapt to the back burner. Granny Adelaide is Tom's paternal grandmother and one of my favorite people ever. In the twenty-some years I'd known her, I had seen her hospitalized exactly twice—once years ago when she had emergency gall bladder surgery and the other time two years back when she had a stroke, a minor one, but still disabling enough to keep her from crawling off the gurney when they hauled her away by ambulance. She'd had her remarkable one-hundredth birthday in April and, until this last month, had been healthier than most horses. If she was in the hospital, it was bad.

I was choking down worry as I called my first counselor and told her what was happening. As I knew she would, Larissa promised to put the presidency meeting on hold and to see that the missionaries were fed. I still needed to do something about the choir rehearsal, but that could wait. I turned toward the hospital.

As I drove, I remembered important moments in my life that featured Granny Adelaide. She had been the first of Tom's relatives to welcome me into the family—even before Tom had proposed. When Tom's mother, bitter and angry after her own divorce, seemed lukewarm about an upcoming wedding, it had been Adelaide who had called Tom's aunts and uncles, confirming addresses for the invitations and drumming up enthusiasm to support Tom and me in our new adventure. She even baked homemade carrot cake for the open house in Tom's home ward.

She'd been there when we brought Melissa home from the hospital, for the span after Melissa when I worried I might never conceive again, and for each of the babies who came after. She had often been the first to respond when someone in the family was sick or injured.

As I looked back over my years in the Burnett family, Adelaide seemed the one sure rock, the steady constant I could always count on. Nothing could ever be the same without her, and I shuddered as I thought of the sympathy I'd been feeling only moments ago with strangers who'd lost a relative. I hoped we weren't "there" yet. I parked the car near the hospital and headed for the room Tom had mentioned, praying Adelaide's solid presence would be able to stay in our lives a little longer.

I slid into the room at a half run to find it already filling up with family members. Our daughter Melissa and her husband, Jason, were seated next to Tom beside Granny's bed, along with Ruby, Granny's live-in attendant. Emily was there too, standing near them. Tom must have picked her up at the high school choir room. He looked up as I came in.

"Karen's here," he said to Granny, and I got my first look at Adelaide as she turned her face toward me. Her skin was pallid gray, her eyes rheumy, her flesh wasted. She looked worse than I had ever seen in a living person. She and Ruby had joined us for dinner just last Sunday. I marveled that so much had changed in a few short days, but her eyes still crinkled with warmth as she said, "Well, hello, sweetheart. Good to see you."

I felt my eyes filling with tears, but I couldn't help grinning right back at her. "Hello yourself, gorgeous. So what's a cute young thing like you doing in a place like this?"

She managed a weak grin. "Now, dear, I don't want you to get all upset or anything, but I'm pretty sure I'm dying."

I swallowed hard, the tears already starting. "Oh, Granny . . ."

"Oh, look at you. There you go crying, and I told you not to get upset too." She lifted her hand with some effort and wiped a tear from my cheek.

I couldn't respond over the lump in my throat. A tear ran down the other side of my face and fell onto the hospital bed, but I shook my head and attempted a smile as I took her hand.

"It's going to be just fine, dear," she said, her voice creaky with age and cracking with weakness. "It's time, really. Don't you think? I've had a full century; that's one hundred great years, and it's more than most folks get. Now I need to move on and let you young folks take over." I couldn't help thinking that it was only in the company of people like Adelaide that I ever felt young anymore. At forty-eight, I'm "middle-aged," which is accurate in this case since I have just under half of Granny's years.

"You'll get better. You always do," I said, looking to Tom and the kids to back me up. No one said anything, and I realized the doctor must have briefed them already.

"Not this time." Although her eyes still shone with warmth, Adelaide no longer smiled, and her voice was heavy with the weight of her message. I could hear my daughters sniffling. "I've just been waiting for you to get here, Karen. There's something I want you to do. Call it my dying wish."

"You know I'd do anything for you, Adelaide, but—"

"How's she doing?" I heard someone whisper from the hallway, and I looked up as Stephanie, our middle daughter, entered. Tom looked to Granny, then back at Steph, and shook his head meaningfully. I was grateful that Adelaide was turned toward us and couldn't see him. Steph's gasp caught in her throat, but she composed her face as she stepped forward to hug her great-grandmother. "Hi, Granny."

"Hello, darling," Adelaide said and reached out toward Steph, who quickly stepped forward to offer a hug and a kiss on the paper-thin skin.

"What can we do for you?" I asked Granny. "Is there anything that can make you more comfortable?"

Granny apparently had an agenda of her own. "I've already given Tom some directions about my funeral service," she said. Tom held up a white business envelope as Granny pointed in his direction. Granny's tone was as matter-of-fact as if she'd just handed him a grocery list. "He can handle that for me. What I need for you to do is more personal . . . and perhaps more difficult."

She paused, and I realized I was holding my breath. I think we all were. Granny had done well at setting up the dramatic moment.

"The funeral lunch will be happening right around the time of my wedding anniversary," she said almost as if she had already scheduled it, "and I want my whole family together."

"Oh, Granny," I said, starting to make some excuse.

But she went right on. "You may not remember it, dear, but I'm sure Tom does and many of the other relatives will as well. Way back in the earlier days of our family, we used to have a reunion every year on or around June twentieth to celebrate the day our family began, the anniversary of my marriage to Arthur. There were traditional recipes everyone prepared, and we always had a big picnic in the park. It was lovely."

"Well, of course it was," I said, "and we shouldn't have any trouble getting the family together again. We'll call Aunt Lenore and Aunt Shirley, Mary and Steve, and the cousins. Of course Brian won't be there," I said, referring to our son who had just entered the missionary training center in Brazil, "but the rest of us—"

Granny cut me off. "No, dear. I mean my *whole* family. The ones in Texas too."

I heard Tom choke and a look passed between us—his disapproval, my panic. "Um, Granny, I don't even know how to get in touch with those people." It was only a partial lie. Behind my husband's back I had exchanged some greeting cards with his sister Carrie over the years, but he didn't want to know about it, so I hadn't ever told him. And I really didn't have contact information for any of the others, no phone for Carrie either. I started to try to explain that. "I—"

"Don't worry about that, dear. Everything you need is right here in my purse." She leaned toward the bedside table. "Ruby, dear, can you hand me my purse?"

Ruby complied. Granny reached in with quivering hands and drew out another carefully prepared envelope. Family members all exchanged wry looks; Granny's organizational envelopes had long been a joke in our family, and I wondered how long she had been carrying these two—just in case. "This lists all the names and telephone numbers, as well as letting you know who's who."

"Have you stayed in touch with them all these years, Granny?" Melissa asked.

"Of course, darling." She smiled. "It's not as if I have so many grandchildren that I can afford to let a few drift away."

Melissa patted Granny's shoulder. "Oh, Granny! That really sounds like you."

Granny turned back to me. "So take the envelope and give them each a call, won't you? I'd like them to come for the funeral and, of course, the family lunch. What I need you to do is to dig up some of the old recipes—you know, the family reunion dishes that Tom and Steve and Mary remember from when they were little, back when the family was still together. That's what you need to serve when the family is all together again."

My throat constricted, but I croaked out, "Okay, Granny. I'll try."

"Nope, no trying," Adelaide said. "I need your promise, Karen. Do this for me."

"Of course, Granny, but I—"

Tom cleared his throat, and I looked up, my eyes pleading with him not to say what I felt sure he was planning to. I saw him change his mind even as he opened his mouth. "Of course we won't need any of this," he said. "You're going to be just fine, Granny. We'll have you home in your own place again in no time." Was this the same man who had shaken his head at Stephanie just moments before?

"That's right, Granny," Melissa said, faking brightness. "Jason and I are planning on having you around to tell old family stories to our kids."

Jason and Steph and Emily all nodded, murmuring agreement, and Ruby said, "We'll have you home soon."

But Adelaide sighed. "Remember some good stories to tell them about me, darlings." Then she used one shaky hand to cover a yawn.

"Granny . . ." Tom stepped forward and took her hand. "Granny, don't ask us to do this. You remember what he did, how he hurt us all . . ."

Granny gave him her sweetest look. "Sweetheart, let me remind you that the *he* you're referring to was your father and my son."

"I know, Granny, but—"

"What your father did was wrong, Tommy." She stroked his hand, and I saw my husband soften at her use of his pet name. "It was wrong, and he spent the rest of his life paying for it, but he's gone now, and so is your mother. There's no reason to perpetuate their problems, and you have family you really should get to know."

"But you can't expect us to welcome that woman—"

"*That woman* is the mother of the sisters and brother you have never met. It's time to put the past behind you, Tommy. If you can't do it for yourself, do it for me." She took his hand in both of hers. "Please? For me?"

Tom swallowed hard but was saved from answering by a timely intrusion as a nurse in bright scrubs stepped into the room. "If you'll all step out now, I need to wheel Mrs. Burnett down the hall for some tests."

"Sure. We'll go down to the waiting room," Tom said. He dropped a kiss on Granny's cheek as he left. "Love you, Granny," he said. "We'll be right back."

Each of the children either kissed Adelaide or gripped her hand. Ruby stroked her cheek, and I followed suit, gently stroking her arm. "See you soon, Granny," I said.

"Not yet," Granny said to the nurse as she gripped onto me. "I need your promise, Karen. You're the only one who can do this for me. Promise me you will."

"You know I can't make them come," I began.

"Of course not. Just promise me you'll do your best. That's all I could ever ask."

I took a moment before I responded, but Granny's sweet look could have melted marble. "I promise," I answered, leaning down to peck her cheek.

"See you soon," I said as I joined the others in the hall.

"See you, Granny," Tom called over my head.

"Good-bye, my dears," Granny answered, the words pregnant with meaning. We all stood still, watching as the nurse rolled her away.

"She'll get better," Tom said as Granny disappeared around a corner. He looked as if he thought it might happen simply because he demanded it.

"I don't know, Dad," Stephanie said. "I've never seen her like this."

"She'll get better!" he insisted, and the kids exchanged pointed looks.

We got to the lobby and found seats. I started to ask Emily if anyone had made arrangements for someone to accompany her summer choir program, but my question was interrupted by the reappearance of the brightly dressed nurse. "Mrs. Burnett will be in tests for a little while," she told us, "and after that, she'll probably be too tired for company. If you'd like to come back later this evening, say, after seven or so? She might be rested enough to visit with you then."

We looked around at one another, realizing we had been dismissed.

Ruby was the first to stand, followed quickly by Tom. "All right, then," he said. "We'll be back."

"Have a good evening," the nurse said, and we filed out of the hospital toward the parking lot.

"She'll get better," Tom said as we stepped outside. "She has to."

"I hope so, honey," I answered. The envelope in my purse felt as heavy as lead.

Classic Meatloaf with a Twist

1 C. finely chopped onion
1 celery rib, minced or chopped very fine
1 Tbsp. minced garlic
1 ½ C. carrot, grated or finely chopped
½ C. finely chopped scallions (can substitute green onion)
2 tsp. salt (use 1 ½ tsp. if using Italian sausage)
1 ½ tsp. freshly ground pepper
2 tsp. Worcestershire sauce
⅓ C. minced fresh parsley leaves
½–1 tsp. red chili powder
1 ½ pounds very lean ground chuck
¾ pound lean ground pork sausage or Italian sausage (a mix of sweet, spicy, and hot is great!)
2 large eggs, beaten slightly
Catsup or sweet chili sauce for topping

Directions

1. Grind, grate, or chop vegetables.
2. Mix all ingredients until thoroughly combined.
3. Shape into loaf and fit into loaf pan.
4. Top with catsup or sweet chili sauce (Heinz makes a good one).
5. Bake approximately 1 hour at 350 or until loaf is firm.
6. Pour off extra oils.
7. Slice and serve with catsup and chili salsa on the side.

Variations

You can experiment with different meat mixtures, including wild game. Make a more savory, less spicy meatloaf by exchanging the chili powder for ground sage, or give it an Asian tang by exchanging soy sauce for Worcestershire and finely chopped cilantro for parsley. Use chili salsa for topping instead of catsup, or use plain tomato sauce for a less spicy, less sweet flavor. For a delicious sweet sauce, combine 1 small can of tomato paste with ¼ C. maple syrup.

CHAPTER 2

Wednesday, June 13, Early evening

EMILY BURNETT

WHEN WE GOT HOME FROM the hospital, Mom started the oven and popped in the meatloaf and the potato casserole she had already made. I hope I can be half as organized as she is when I have a family. It's really pretty remarkable how she gets so much done. Anyway, she got it all going in seconds, and then she said, "Can you keep an eye on this for me, honey? Your dad and I need to talk for a little bit."

I thought, *Yeah, I'll bet you do,* but what I said was "You got it, Mom, I've got it covered. Do you think you'll still make it to my choir concert tonight?"

She paused and gave me one of her sweet, sad looks that always means she's going to have to let me down and she doesn't like it. "You should still be able to go, sweetie, though I doubt if your dad or I can be there. I know he will want to go see Granny again as soon as they'll let us." Then she smoothed her hand over my hair. "I hope you're not too disappointed?"

I couldn't help smiling at her. "Yeah, I'm disappointed," I told her, "but it's okay." I said it because it was the right thing to say, even though I didn't really mean it. I don't think Mom gets how important this concert is. Ms. Nguyen had some lady call her up from the mall to tell her about this special event they were having in June and to ask if our high school choir would sing. When she realized the time came after we were out for the summer, Ms. Nguyen asked for volunteers to do this special summer choir.

Within the next few weeks, Ms. Nguyen will be picking the singers for the Senior Honor Choir next year, and everybody knows that she'll be giving special consideration to those of us who volunteered for summer choir. If I ended up having to miss tonight . . . Then I thought of something. "Mom? Granny's really sick, isn't she?"

She patted my arm. "I'm afraid so, honey."

Dad said, "Are you coming, Karen?" and Mom gave me her sad smile again as she followed him into the office and shut the door.

I felt so many things all at once just then—selfish and worried and guilty and even a little bit angry. What can I say? Life is unfair. I'd really been looking forward to this concert since our end-of-term concert four weeks ago, and having something come up to keep my family from hearing it just seemed . . . well, unfair. Still, didn't I have to be a pretty awful person to feel sorry for myself when my great-granny was really, really sick? I was just wishing she didn't have to get so sick right *now*.

I said a little prayer for her then set the table for dinner, adding places for Melissa and Jason, who wandered home from the hospital with us and then into the TV room with Stephanie. Talk about unfair! I thought about getting my sisters to come help me in the kitchen, but I was feeling pretty sad and I kind of liked just being by myself for a while.

I finished setting the table, and then I made a cabbage-and-apple slaw, just the way Mom taught me, and got some frozen peas out to warm in the microwave. Maybe if dinner was over in plenty of time, some of the family would still be able to come to hear the concert. Maybe I'd still get my chance to show Ms. Nguyen that I deserved honor choir after all.

I have always loved music. Mom says I've been singing since I was a baby. She likes to tell people that my first solo was when I was two and sang, "Up, Up in the Sky" for one of her Sunday Relief Society lessons. I don't remember that, but it doesn't surprise me. I absolutely *love* to sing! Offhand, I can't think of much of anything that I like better, which is why honor choir next year is so important. I have this total career plan, starting with Senior Honor Choir and moving on to majoring in music at college, and well, one day I want to sing with the Tabernacle Choir. Hey! It could happen.

Ms. Nguyen, our choir teacher, is awesome. She loves to sing as much as I do—and she's *so* smart! She's pretty too, which is why we have more boys in the choir this year. When they saw the new choir teacher, guys started transferring in—even the ones who used to say choir was for losers.

She's has us singing some complicated songs for this special three-week summer choir gig; she calls them "pieces." My favorite is a five-part madrigal. Five parts! Mr. Peavey, the cross-country coach who directed the choir last year, was lucky if he could get us to do two-part harmonies, usually just soprano and alto with three or four guys singing the melody an octave lower. But Ms. Nguyen knows how to present things, and she found this really super awesome five-part madrigal that used to be sung by traveling minstrels in Europe. Finally, we get to sing some decent music!

There's a little, short three-bar alto solo in it, just before the second verse, that I get to sing all by myself, and I just adore the part at the beginning of the chorus when the alto voices move against the whole notes in the other four parts. Well, it's probably my favorite of any choral piece I've ever sung. (Solos, of course, are the very best!)

We have some other great pieces too, including some of the really famous old composers like Bach and Dvorak and another super-awesome madrigal by Orlando Gibbons. Ms. Nguyen says he's like the great-granddaddy of all madrigal composers, and she really knows her stuff. She showed us some super complicated pieces with twelve and sixteen parts that she hopes to have us—that is, the honor choir—work on next year. Super cool. So much better than with Coach Peavey!

Just thinking about the music made me feel better. I was humming to myself as I finished dressing the slaw and warming the peas. That was when the phone rang. I answered it and a business-like voice on the other end asked for Mr. Thomas Burnett. I knocked on the door of the office.

"Daddy?"

Mom opened the door. "What is it, Em?"

"There's a phone call for Dad. It sounds important."

Mom turned back into the office, a worried look on her face. There was some murmuring, and then she asked me, "Do you know who it is?"

I shook my head.

From inside the office, I heard Dad say, "I'll take it."

I went back into the kitchen to hang up the phone, but before I put it down, I held the receiver to my ear, just to be sure Dad had answered before I hung it up, and that's when I heard him say, "Oh no. When?"

I felt my heart jolt, but I couldn't stop listening. "Just a few minutes ago," the voice on the other end answered. "Would you or your family like to see her before we call the funeral home?"

Funeral home. My hands shook as I dropped the phone, and I heard an awful noise. It took me a second to realize I was the one making it, and in that moment, it occurred to me that there were worse things than having my family miss my concert.

I had never known anyone who died before.

Incredible Sourdough Dinner Rolls

In this recipe, the sourdough starter is used just for flavor. A recipe for making the starter follows.

1 C. sourdough starter
1 ½ C. warm water (around 110°)
1 Tbsp. yeast
1 Tbsp. salt
2 Tbsp. white or brown sugar

2 Tbsp. olive oil
4–5 C. flour (can be ½ white and ½ wheat)
Melted butter

Directions

1. In a large metal or glass mixing bowl, combine starter, water, yeast, salt, sugar, and oil.
2. Stir in flour, ½ to 1 C. at a time, until dough is sticky but manageable. Use only as much flour as needed.
3. Place dough in a bowl and cover. (Consider spraying the dough with vegetable cooking spray to prevent crust from forming.) Let rise in a warm place until double in size.
4. When dough has doubled, punch it down and knead for 5–10 minutes, stretching the gluten to improve dough texture. Then use lightly floured hands to form into rolls.
5. Place in a lightly oiled 9 x 13 pan. Let rise until doubled.
6. Bake approximately 20 minutes at 375.
7. Five minutes before removing from oven, brush with melted butter. Or, for a shiny finish, brush with egg wash made of egg whites and water. Serve warm.

Makes 12–20, depending on size.

Sourdough Starter

2 C. all-purpose flour
2 tsp. granulated sugar (optional)*
1 packet (2 ¼ tsp.) active dry yeast

2 C. warm water (105–115°)**

Preparation

1. Mix the flour, sugar, and yeast together in a clean and sterile

container that holds at least 2 quarts. (Use only glass, glazed ceramic, or crockery to hold your starter. *No metal or plastic.*) Gradually stir in the water and mix until it forms a thick paste (don't worry about any lumps as they will disappear).

2. Cover the container with a dishcloth or a breathable wooden lid and let sit in a warm (70–80°), draft-free place. NOTE: Temperatures hotter than 100° or so may kill the yeast.

3. The dishcloth or breathable lid lets wild yeasts pass through into the batter. The mixture should bubble as it ferments, foaming up substantially.

4. Place the container on a washable dish. Spilled starter is tough to clean.

5. Let it sit out for 2–5 days (usually about 3), stirring it once a day. The starter is ready when it develops a pleasant sour smell and looks bubbly.

6. Once your starter starts bubbling, feed it daily.

7. Stir, cover loosely, and store it on your countertop or in the refrigerator.

* Adding a little sugar will help jump start the process. Yeast rises by feeding on the sugars in flour and expelling carbon dioxide. Don't overdo the sugar.

** Avoid chlorinated water as chlorine can stop the development of yeast.

Maintenance

1. Daily remove (use or throw out) 1 C. of starter. Replace with 1 C. flour and 1 C. water. Stir well, but don't worry about lumps as they will disappear. If you have a large amount of starter, you can use 2 C. for a big recipe and replace with 2 C. flour and 2 C. water. Remember it's preferable to use distilled water or other water without chlorine, but tap water can work if the chlorine is minimal.

2. If you are going to be away or unable to feed and care for your starter, keep it refrigerated. When you return, the starter will have separated. (The liquid at the top is called *hooch* and is about 14%–17% alcohol. The alcohol cooks away during baking.) Stir the hooch back into the starter mixture, let the starter warm to room temperature, and begin the daily feeding process again.

CHAPTER 3

Wednesday, June 13, Late evening

KAREN BURNETT

I POURED GLASSES FULL OF chilled lemonade, moving strictly on autopilot. We had put away all the food that Emily and I had prepared for dinner because no one felt like eating, yet we all knew we needed something. I warmed some of the sourdough rolls leftover from last night's dinner and asked Steph to whip up some lemonade. Tom said a quick blessing, and we all began to eat, silently, everyone moving as if caught in slow motion.

The scene at the hospital was surreal. Since I became our ward Relief Society president a couple of years ago, I'd seen death, yet it never failed to amaze me. When we visited with Granny that afternoon, she had looked about as ill as anyone I've ever seen. Then, when we went back to the hospital that evening, she was no longer there. No, they hadn't yet removed Granny's body, but *Granny* was no longer there. I don't know how anyone, especially any health professional, could see that change over and over and over again and still have any doubt that there is an eternal spirit, a life source that departs when death comes. The body didn't even look much like Granny anymore. Still I felt her warmth, her humor, and I knew she wasn't far away. I hoped she wasn't getting too big a kick out of her final joke on us.

I kept waiting for the other shoe to drop when I heard what Tom would have to say. When things stayed quiet in the kitchen, the tension taut as a stretched rubber band, I went to the family computer and began writing in my daily journal.

We lost Granny today. I will miss her intensely. Yet even as I say this, I realize I am not hurting for Adelaide. She went easily and peacefully, and we know she was ready. The nurses said she came back from her tests and said, "Tell my family I love them all," then closed her eyes and went to sleep. About an hour later, her monitors went flatline. Since they had a standing DNR order, they didn't attempt to resuscitate her but just went into the room to be certain it wasn't an equipment failure. When they knew she was gone, they noted the time for her death certificate and called us.

No, I'm not hurting for her, just for us. None of my daughters has seen death before. Well, there was the death of Tom's mother, Judith, but that had so many layers and ramifications that we managed to keep the kids a couple of steps removed, and since they had never known her well, they weren't really as rocked by it as they might have been with a grandmother they were close to. Melissa had a high school pal who was killed in an accident, and she went to the funeral, but except for that, this is a new experience for our children. They're all suffering. Of course, we haven't told Brian yet.

I'm glad Melissa has Jason. He will be a steadying influence for her while she is getting through this first experience. He has lost all of his grandparents and a few others who were close to him. Not that grief becomes less painful as you endure it more. It's just that after a few experiences, you learn you can live through it—whether you want to or not.

Stephanie, our Stoic Steph, is being the strong one as always. Except for a sniffle here and there, she doesn't seem to be hurting the way everyone else is. She's the one who is calmly going about comforting everyone else and helping Tom and me make plans. She even offered to take Em to her concert, although Emily said she was too distraught to sing, which tells me how badly this has shaken her. I hope Steph's stoicism isn't a form of denial that will come back to haunt her later.

I'm most worried about Emily. Well, and Brian. He said good-bye to Granny before he left, and both of them realized that it was probably a final good-bye, but he's only been in the MTC some three weeks. He will be wondering why it had to happen this way and why he couldn't have been here with the family. Knowing my son, he will feel guilty that he isn't here for us. We talked with the mission president. He will break the news to Brian, and he is making arrangements for Brian's district leader to give us a call. We will give him details and assure him we're okay, and the DL will pass the word along to our son. We hope that will help.

There's no question of him coming home. He wouldn't even consider it, but he will want to feel like he's participating with the family, even from a distance.

Emily is another matter. She's barely sixteen and that girl lives to sing! The fact she chose not to sing and hasn't mentioned it once in hours lets me know how much this death has really rocked her. The sound I heard come out of her when she dropped the phone was unlike any noise I've ever heard a human being make. If a short lifetime full of great illusions had all been dashed at once, I don't think it could have sounded much worse than that. Emily has hardly spoken since then. I will have to keep a close eye on her. She's quiet, but she feels intensely, bless her.

When it really comes down to it, I'm also worried about my husband. Sometimes I know Tom even better than he knows himself, and he hasn't realized yet just how hard this is hitting him. When his father left, Granny Adelaide was the one who was there for him. When his mother ceased to do much mothering, it was Granny who took over. And even when he lost his mother, he always had Granny. Now I fear he will suffer through the pain of his mother's incapacity and death as well as the pain of his father's betrayal all over again as he mourns the passing of his beloved Granny. I wish I could do anything to make it easier for him, but I doubt very much if I can— other than my prayers, of course, which he always has. It's just something he'll have to experience. I know we weren't promised life would be easy, but sometimes it seems like too much all at once—especially when the hurt is happening to people I love so much.

He called his high priests group leader, Brother Wright—Tom serves as his counselor—to tell him we wouldn't be helping with the ward building cleanup scheduled for tomorrow evening, but other than that, he seems almost to be in denial, as if none of this is really happening. I wonder how long it will be before he can express what he's thinking and feeling.

I've barely begun the process of contacting family members. I've already spoken with Bishop Anderson, and he thinks we can have the funeral next Wednesday, June 20. It seems fitting that Adelaide and Arthur are being reunited so near their wedding anniversary. Besides, that will allow time for people to come from wherever—even Texas. As I've looked over the notes Adelaide entrusted to me, it's been surprising to realize how closely she's kept in touch with all the family members out there. It seems that even her vacations over the years, when she took a break with Ruby as her travel companion, have often taken her to Texas. She's been nearly as involved with the Texas Burnetts as she has with us—and she lives right here! It seems the rest of us will be playing catch-up on a reconciliation that Adelaide began long ago.

I will need to notify the rest of the family. I've called Tom's sister Mary, and she will call their brother Steve. She also volunteered to call his aunts, Lenore and Shirley, and Shirley will handle calling her kids, Tom's cousins. The tough part will come tomorrow when I start on Granny's list, calling to invite the people in Texas. She may have known them all, but they're strangers to me.

Well, that's not completely true. It's not as if I don't know them at all. I received announcements when his sister Carrie was married and when Michael graduated high school and, later, college. I sent greeting and gift cards signed from both Tom and me, although I never bothered sharing more than a mention of the announcements with Tom. He has always been hypersensitive about the baby brother and sister he lost when his father abandoned the family with the little ones and their babysitter. Tom always said he could have understood that desertion better if he hadn't chosen to take the babies with him.

Who can guess what he and Rocio were thinking? I expect by then she had become so attached to the two little ones, so used to raising them as if they were her own, that she almost felt they really were. Maybe he couldn't talk her into going without adding the little ones to sweeten the deal. Or, more likely, he knew that my late mother-in-law still couldn't handle the kids any better than she could when they were born. After all, it was her mental state that caused Tom Sr. to bring Rocio on board in the first place, whether my Tom wants to hear it or not.

Who knows? All I'm sure of is Tom has never forgiven the departure. He refused to have another thing to do with his father till the day the man died. Even past that, really, since he refused to attend the funeral or even to be notified of the pending services. He hasn't spoken to Carrie or Mikey since his dad took them away, and as far as I know, he doesn't even know the names of his half siblings, the kids that Tom Sr. and Rocio had together after he divorced Judith and married the younger woman. I've exchanged a few Christmas cards with some of them, and I have their names in my genealogy records, but other than that, I can't say I know much of anything about the Texas relatives. Calling them tomorrow is going to be an interesting challenge.

Then there's that other business, digging up old family recipes and trying to re-create the kind of family reunion picnic they might have shared together in the old, presplit family days. I've got to hand it to Granny Adelaide: she always did come up with the interesting approaches.

Of course, I still have some of the recipes Judith, my mother-in-law, handed down when I first joined the family, back when she was still reasonably put together, and I can ask Mary and Tom's aunts if they are aware of any special recipes from their family reunions. Maybe Steve can remember some too, although I know he doesn't cook and his wife barely cooks anymore. I wouldn't expect him to bring anything. Still, if I could get him to describe some favorite, remembered dishes that could help a lot.

"Mom?"

I looked up to see my youngest standing there. "Hi, Em. Are you doing okay?"

"Yeah. I guess." She didn't look okay.

I tried to give her a reassuring smile. "What's up?"

"Daddy and Jason are kinda hungry. Is it okay if I rewarm the meatloaf and the other dinner food?"

"Sure, honey," I answered. "Give me just a moment to finish this journal entry, and I'll be right there to help you."

Emily patted my shoulder. "It's okay, Mom. I've got this." She smiled at me, and I reminded myself that as young and as often self-absorbed as my baby girl can be, she is a sweetheart and often much more mature than her years.

"I'll be right there," I promised. Then I added a final line:

I know Heavenly Father blessed us to have Adelaide all these years, and I'm sure He is blessing her now by taking her home. I know she must be having a blissful reunion with her eternal sweetheart. Nor has she left us comfortless: her legacy of warmth and love will last for some time to come. I only hope I'm up to the challenge she has left for me. It isn't the old family recipes that trouble me most. The question is what recipe can you use to glue a broken family back together? Adelaide hoped she had found it, but I'm the one left to see how it turns out.

I clicked the Save button and closed the file, knowing I had finally hit on the source of my greatest worry.

Temple Oatmeal Cookies

The best recipe ever, from the LA temple kitchen

2 C. butter-flavored shortening
(NOT margarine)
2 C. brown sugar, packed
1½ C. granulated sugar
5 eggs
1 Tbsp. vanilla

1 Tbsp. cinnamon
2 tsp. salt
1 tsp. soda
5 tsp. baking powder
4 C. all-purpose flour
8 C. whole rolled oats

Directions

1. Preheat oven to 350.
2. Use a mixer to cream shortening, sugars, and eggs. Add vanilla, cinnamon, salt, soda, and baking powder. Slowly add flour.
3. Remove from mixer, and slowly stir in rolled oats 1–2 C. at a time.
4. When dough is complete, form into large disc shapes and place on vegetable-sprayed cookie sheets.
5. Bake until barely browning on edges and high spots, about 10–12 minutes. Better to underbake than overbake. Cool on tray for 5–7 minutes. Remove to newspaper-covered counter for complete cooling.
6. Makes up to 5 dozen, depending on cookie size.

Variations

Replace 1 or 2 C. of oats with shredded coconut. Add 1 C. raisins or butterscotch chips. You may also add 1 C. chopped nuts. For "loaded" cookies, use the coconut and then add 1 to 1 ½ C. butterscotch chips, the same amount of chocolate chips, and a cup of nuts. Delicious!

CHAPTER 4

Thursday, June 14, Midday

THE BURNETT FAMILY HOME

Even from her quiet home office, Karen could smell the vanilla, cinnamon, and butterscotch. The aroma was mouthwatering, and she had to remind herself she wasn't hungry. It was easy to confuse appetite with hunger, especially for someone who, like Karen, tended toward comfort eating.

In some ways it felt odd—disrespectful, almost—that the girls were baking cookies for a family funeral, but Adelaide's last wish had been that they bring the family together with all the usual recipes they had once shared at summer picnics, and these cookies had been part of that.

But, then, at least some of Tom's cousins would be coming this week, and those families included little children who knew nothing of Granny or funerals but still felt the excitement of a summer picnic. The family had talked it over and decided to go ahead with as many of the family traditions as possible. Now, as she smelled the warm cookies just removed from the oven and heard her daughters laughing and teasing, she was grateful Granny had given them permission to enjoy their preparations. Certainly Adelaide had wanted it this way.

She stretched, yawning. The family had been slow to get started this morning—no one had slept well—but there was so much to do that some efficiency seemed necessary, so Karen had turned the more enjoyable tasks over to Steph and Emily while she began working through Granny's Texas list, calling all the relatives there. So far she had made six calls and left messages on six answering machines. She hadn't wanted to deliver the news over a machine, so she had simply explained who she was, told them she had important family news, and asked them to return her call.

She decided to call her brother-in-law Steve next to see if he could recommend any old favorite recipes and found herself leaving another message. Frustrated, she pulled out the envelope Granny had left with Tom and a yellow pad to begin the work of trying to plan the funeral service. Granny's plans were both extraordinarily detailed (mostly about what she *didn't* want) and somewhat vague (especially when concerning what she *did* want), which made the prospect of carrying them out rather frustrating as well. "Ah, Granny, Granny," Karen sighed, and then she smiled in spite of herself.

*   *   *

In the kitchen, Emily and Steph were faring far better with their task.

"Do you think this batch is done?" Emily asked, momentarily stepping away from the oven window so Stephanie could check.

Steph peeked in at the cookies. "They sure smell good," she said, wiggling her eyebrows.

Emily grinned. "I know they smell good, goofy-face. I asked if you think they're done yet."

"Maybe not yet," Steph answered, "but not more than a couple of minutes. I'll watch them for a while. You can check through the other recipes and decide what to make next."

"Sounds good," Emily said and started leafing through the other recipes in her mother's file. After a quiet moment, she asked, "Do you think Daddy's okay?"

Stephanie paused, considering her answer, and then said, "Yeah, as okay as any of us, I guess. I know he didn't sleep well."

"No," Em answered. "I don't guess any of us did."

*   *   *

Tom, who really hadn't slept well, had left soon after waking that morning. "I need to go for a run," he'd said to Karen. "I'll be back in time to help with arrangements. Do you think you can go with me to the cemetery this afternoon?" He had waited for Karen's nod as she looked away from her phone call. Then he had set his exercise watch and jogged out the door.

He was on his fourth mile now, trying to come to terms with Granny's last request. He hadn't slept well at all the night before, due largely to disturbing dreams of Granny Adelaide. He had barely dropped into sleep before she had been there beside him, haunting and taunting him. They stood at the side of a steep precipice that dropped into nothingness hundreds of feet below. The opposite side of the canyon sat nearly on the horizon, shrouded in distant mists, and Granny had stood there expecting him to leap it.

"It isn't much I'm asking, Tommy," she said. "Just jump across and land safely on the other side. You'll do it for me, won't you, Tommy?"

And when he responded that he couldn't do it, that it was so far no ordinary human could possibly do it, she had smiled sweetly and said, "You can, Tommy. Do it for me."

He had jerked awake with a gasp that had disturbed Karen, causing her to moan in her sleep. It seemed a long time before he dropped into sleep again, and when he did, Granny was again beside him.

They stood at the bank of a river where roiling floodwaters raged by, carrying uprooted trees, boulders, cars, and even houses. Awed by the river's power, Tom had stared across at the far side, probably half a mile away, knowing that no human being could safely cross that intense torrent. Yet Granny had been insistent, requiring him not only to swim the river but to carry her across on his back. "Do it for me, Tommy?" she had asked him again and again. "You'll do it for me, won't you?"

The second time he had forced himself awake, he had pushed himself up and out of bed. Then he had walked around the house, making himself think of other things and waking himself up so completely that it was nearly morning before he finally slept. Even then he hadn't slept well.

Did Adelaide really understand what she was asking? His father's desertion had been the defining moment of his childhood, the event that had forced him into adulthood far too early. To let go of all that carried him through these past decades would be like forgetting who he was. Surely even Granny could see that? Yet even as he thought the question, he could see her still smiling at him: "Do it for me, Tommy," she said, and he knew her vision was far different from his own.

* * *

Karen had planned enough funeral services that she'd assumed she could knock this one out with no problems at all, but it wasn't really working that way. She paused, sighed, and put her pen down, realizing she would probably have to meet with and talk to more family members before she could piece the whole thing together.

Granny had asked for three "very short" talks. The first was to be a personal history, given by a family member, although Granny hadn't suggested who. She had, however, included an itemized list of ideas to cover—a century of full, rich living condensed into less than a page of bullet points. The second talk was to be by another family member (again, Adelaide had been disinclined to suggest which) relaying some "fun and funny family tales." This too was followed by a list of suggestions. The final talk was to be doctrinal, what Granny had called "a brief overview of the plan of happiness," given by a local priesthood leader. Each talk was to take no more than fifteen minutes. The rest of the service was to be filled with music.

Adelaide had been both vague and specific about that as well. "For the opening and closing, choose hymns everyone likes," she had written, "but please, skip the clichés. No 'O My Father,' no 'God Be with You Till We Meet Again.' Some choral numbers would be lovely, and please, get together as many of my great-grandbabies as possible to sing 'I Am a Child of God.' I'll be listening for that one!"

Surely Adelaide *would* be listening. Karen found herself chuckling as she read; she wanted this program to be pleasing to the woman who had meant so much to them all. She'd have to see how many of the great-grandchildren she could round up. Maybe even some of the relatives from Texas would like to participate—if she could ever get any of them on the phone. Sighing again, she stepped away from her desk and decided to take a break.

She was just coming out of the restroom when she heard the phone ring and was grateful when she heard Emily answer it. As she finished washing her hands, Emily called from the hallway, "There's a call for you, Mom."

Karen stepped around the corner, still drying her hands on a towel. "Who is it, honey?"

"At first I thought it was one of those phone sellers, you know, because she asked for Mrs. Karen Burnett. So I asked, 'Who is calling, please?' and she said her name is Carolyn Juanarena. Do we know anybody with that name?"

"Carolyn . . ." Karen furrowed her brow in concentration. "Carrie! It's your dad's sister, Carrie. I'll take it in the office, honey."

Karen jogged to the office and picked up. "Carrie?"

"Hello, Karen. Good to finally 'meet' you."

Karen smiled. "You too. I'm afraid I have bad news, though."

"It's Adelaide, isn't it?"

"Yes. I'm sorry. She passed away last evening."

Karen heard a sharp intake of breath and a slight pause. "I knew she couldn't last forever, but she always seemed like one of those unstoppable forces of nature . . . Was it . . . was it an easy passing?"

"Yes, very peaceful. She was ready."

Karen teared up as she described their last visit with Adelaide and the call from the hospital, and then the two women talked for a while. Even as she chatted, amiably answering questions, Karen couldn't help thinking how easy and natural this was, as if she and Carrie had been talking regularly throughout these past twenty-five years. When she invited Carrie to the services, Karen wasn't at all surprised to receive an enthusiastic response. Carrie even volunteered to talk with other family members, encouraging them to come as well.

"I doubt if my husband can get away," Carrie was saying. "He has a small but active restaurant here in Seguin, and it gets busy right around the time school gets out, what with everybody taking summer vacations and traveling through. I'll come, though, and I'll probably bring one or two of the children with me. I'll talk with the rest of the family as well to see if any of them would like to travel with us."

"That would be great," Karen answered and then asked Carrie about her family.

Before she concluded the call, she had a list of Carrie's four children and their birthdays, as well as an e-mail address, a cell phone number, and Carrie's promise to send family and school pictures by e-mail before she joined them the following week.

"I don't know your area at all," Carrie said as they were winding down. "Can you recommend a good place to stay?"

"Stay with us!" Karen said and then realized she'd need to retract a little. "Well, not with us, really. I wish I could invite you to stay here, but we've already committed to having Tom's aunts, Lenore and Shirley, and some of the other family as well. I've talked with Ruby Dashov, though. She was the caretaker who'd been living with Granny for the past ten years or so. Because she had Ruby, Granny was able to stay in the old family home, and there's plenty of room there. Ruby said she'll make up all the spare rooms. There should be space for anyone you want to bring, and there are sleeping bags and lots of floor space for little ones. We can make room for all of you. Just let us know."

"Okay, I'll get back to you," Carrie answered.

"And, Carrie? It's been good talking with you. I wish we'd done this long ago."

"Yes. I feel the same way."

Long after Karen hung up, she still felt the warmth of that phone call. Whether Tom wanted to see his youngest sister or not, Karen couldn't help feeling she had found a soul sister, a friend she could know and love. She realized she was actually looking forward to Granny's funeral service. Maybe this wasn't going to be so bad after all.

Blackberry-Spinach Dinner Salad

This is a great way to use fresh blackberries. Serve with cooked, cooled beef or chicken strips for a complete dinner.

3 C. baby spinach, rinsed and dried
1 pint fresh blackberries
6 oz. crumbled feta cheese
1 pint cherry tomatoes, halved

1 green onion, sliced
¼ C. finely chopped walnuts (optional)
½ C. edible flowers (optional)

Directions

In a large bowl, toss together baby spinach, blackberries, feta cheese, cherry tomatoes, green onion, and walnuts. Garnish with edible flowers. Serve with individual dressings chosen to taste, or toss with a berry vinaigrette.

Variations

This recipe is open to all kinds of variations. Substitute other kinds of berries. Add water chestnuts for crunch. Use candied walnuts instead of plain or consider tossing in some pine nuts. Replace the halved cherry tomatoes with halved seedless grapes or just experiment using whatever is fresh and in season.

CHAPTER 5

Thursday, June 14, Midafternoon

KAREN BURNETT

THE ENTIRE FAMILY—EVERYONE BUT Tom, who was back at work—had gathered. Emily and I worked quietly in the kitchen, tossing a simple salad for dinner. The rest of the family sat in the family room, carefully sorting through old photographs, choosing some to set out in the foyer during Granny's service.

We had talked with President Bettencourt from the missionary training center in Brazil that morning. He said Brian was training way out in the jungle, but he promised to arrange a call from the district leader at four o'clock that afternoon. The district leader would receive the specifics about what was happening at home so he could pass them along to our missionary. We could then catch Brian up on the news in our regular letters and e-mails. It was nearing four o'clock, and we were waiting for the DL to call.

My excitement about talking with the Texas relatives had lasted right up until I'd gotten Michael—no longer Mikey—on the phone that morning. He had used some language I wasn't used to hearing and asked in the same unpleasant tone why I thought he'd be interested in having anything to do with Tom when Tom had wanted nothing to do with him—not just now, but throughout his life. Then he slammed down the phone before I could speak.

Okay, I thought as I put the salad in the fridge and joined the family, trying not to show how much Michael's verbal assault had shaken me. *Maybe it isn't all going to be as easy as talking with Carrie, but I have to keep trying.* I had already decided not to mention that call to Tom unless he asked me directly. Why borrow trouble?

So far I hadn't gotten through to Rocio, nor had I reached Marco, Christina, or Amanda, Tom's half siblings born to his father and Rocio in Texas. Michael's call had shaken me badly enough that I'd promised myself to take the evening off unless one of them called me back. It surely wouldn't hurt to wait one day to talk to the rest of the folks in the Texas family.

I looked through the photos the kids had chosen, thinking of how easily the funeral preparations had gone so far. Tom and I had visited the cemetery that morning only to learn that Granny had laid all the groundwork for us—so to speak—thus making arrangements for her burial quick and easy. We then drove straight to the funeral home where we replayed almost the same script, finding once again that Adelaide had taken care of almost everything. A quick telephone visit with our bishop confirmed the time and place of the funeral service, and we were good to go, so Tom went back to the office. Now I prayed I could find the stomach for dealing with the rest of Granny's plans.

"I'll get it!" Emily called, jumping up as the phone rang.

I looked up. It was only 3:40. "Looks like Brian's DL is a little early," I said to no one in particular.

But it wasn't the call from Brazil. "It's for Dad," Emily said, holding the phone toward me. "It's someone named . . . Rocio?"

I thought of the look that came into my husband's eyes whenever he heard that name: something like a cross between panic and homicidal mania. "I'll take it, honey," I said. I took the phone from Emily's hand and walked into the office, closing the door behind me.

"Hello? Rocio? I'm Karen Burnett, Tom's wife."

There was a short pause. "Hello, Karen. May I speak to Tom, please?"

"He isn't here just now. Besides, I don't think that would be wise."

There was a short pause and then, "Tom doesn't want to speak to me?"

I considered making up a pleasant half-truth but opted for honesty. "No, ma'am. I'm afraid he doesn't."

"Well, I'm not surprised." Rocio's trace of an accent over her perfectly correct English charmed me. "Listen, Karen, I understand Tom's reluctance, but Adelaide was an important person in my life. I want to honor her, and I'm hoping that past differences won't prevent that."

I swallowed hard and made sure to temper my tone as I answered. "We'll be happy to have you, Rocio. Please tell the other family members we want them to come as well. The memorial service really isn't about us—any of us. It's about Adelaide, and we hope all the people who loved her will feel free to come and celebrate her life." I took a deep breath and added, "Please join us."

I bit my lip, wondering how I was going to explain this to my husband. Well, he had been there when Granny Adelaide charged me with this responsibility, hadn't he? He knew what I had to do. And it was also the right thing to do, last request or not. Still . . .

"Thank you," Rocio answered. "I look forward to meeting you soon."

"Um, yes. Uh, me too."

I hung up the phone, wondering what I had just done and how badly things might go as a result. Moments later the phone rang again, and I looked up at the clock. Four o'clock on the dot. I went back to the family room and put Brian's district leader on speaker.

Great-Aunt Joan's Pumpkin-Date Bread

A fine fruit bread, great anytime

2 C. pumpkin (canned or cooked
  and mashed; NOT pie mix)
4 eggs
1 C. vegetable oil
1 C. water
3 ⅓ C. sifted all-purpose flour
3 C. sugar
2 tsp. baking soda

½ tsp. baking powder
1 ½ tsp. salt
1 tsp. cloves
1 tsp. cinnamon
1 tsp. nutmeg
1 C. dates
1 C. chopped walnuts

Directions

1. Mix pumpkin, eggs, oil, and water in large bowl until well blended.
2. Sift together dry ingredients (flour through nutmeg) and add to the first mixture.
3. Hand beat until mixture is smooth. Add dates and nuts.
4. Pour batter into greased and floured loaf pans. (Makes 2 medium loaves or 3 small ones.)
5. Bake at 325 for about 1 hour. Cool in pans for 12–15 minutes before turning out.

Variations

You can substitute raisins or other chopped dried fruit (prunes or apricots perhaps) for the dates or other nuts for the walnuts. Try using rich Saigon cinnamon and doubling it to 2 tsp. For a more cake-like flavor, add 2 tsp. real vanilla.

CHAPTER 6

Thursday, June 14, Evening

KAREN BURNETT

IT WAS JUST AFTER SIX WHEN the front doorbell rang. I'd spent a couple of hours trying to deal with an unexpected need in the ward and was feeling exhausted and out of sorts, so I was surprised—and a bit panicked—to see Aunt Shirley standing there. She gave me a one-armed hug and a big kiss on the cheek then filled my arms with the dozen or so fragrant pumpkin-date loaves she was carrying in a brown paper bag. The bread is Aunt Shirley's signature treat, made from her mother-in-law's recipe. June isn't exactly fruit bread season, but I was grateful to see it anyway when I thought of the large, hungry crowd we were expecting.

"It's great to see you," I told her. "We didn't expect you yet."

"I hope you don't mind my coming early," Shirley answered. "I just couldn't make myself stay away any longer."

That was when Emily saw her and screamed, "Hey, everybody! Aunt Shirley's here!" Things got a little crazy while Steph and Melissa and Jason came running, all eagerly trying to greet her at once.

In truth, had it been almost anyone else, the arrival of an early houseguest would likely have sent me into meltdown. Even before Adelaide's passing and the special requests that went with it, I'd felt more than a little stretched with the responsibilities and emotions of the past few days. In fact, *overwhelmed* seemed a limp and pallid word. I was trying to run faster to keep up and just kept falling further behind all the time. But Shirley was like her mother, Adelaide, in that she always gave more than she required. Having her around would be a blessing. Seeing her with my daughters, soothing and cheering them, I relaxed.

"Do you want me in Melissa's old room again?" Shirley asked as we closed the door.

"If you don't mind."

"Mind?! I love it! Melissa always had the best room in the house," she said, winking at my married daughter, who grinned back. Steph and Emily groaned obligingly.

"I'll go back for my suitcase," she said, turning toward the car, but Jason spoke up.

"I'll get it, Aunt Shirley," he said, loping out to her car while my daughters and I escorted Shirley into the family room.

"You've got yourself a good man there," Shirley said to Melissa, who grinned again and said, "I know."

"In fact," Shirley continued as we sat together on the family room sectional, "if you haven't already chosen someone to offer Mother's personal history at the funeral, I'm thinking Jason is the perfect man for the job."

"Jason?" Melissa spoke first. "I mean, he's a great guy, but . . ."

"Mother told me about her plans to have someone give a history, so I've had time to give it some thought," Shirley answered. "Jason seems perfect. He's family, but he's only been part of the family for a few months—unlike the rest of us who've known Mother our whole lives, or like you, Karen, for your whole adult life. He loves and respects her and will be able to give the history in a meaningful way, but he doesn't have as many memories as the rest of us, and he isn't as likely to dissolve into tears and be unable to finish. I think he'll make a fine showing of it."

Melissa swallowed hard when she answered, "Good point."

"I know *you* wouldn't be a good choice," Steph said as she watched Melissa tearing up again. Melissa had seemed unusually emotional lately, and a death in the family wasn't making that any easier.

"Me either," Emily answered. "And I don't think Dad would be good at it. He gets pretty emotional about Granny Adelaide."

Tom had gone to the office as quickly as he could manage it, first thing this morning, telling us he needed to get a few things done so he could take time off for the funeral, but I secretly suspected he was finding it easier to deal with work than with the serious emotional issues raised by his grandmother's death.

"So what do you all think?" I asked, polling the group. "Shall we ask Jason?"

"Sounds like Jason is it," Melissa said as her sisters and I agreed.

"I'm what?" Jason asked as he rejoined us.

I took up the cue. "Jason, would you be willing to give Granny Adelaide's personal history at her funeral?"

"Me? Don't you think it should be someone who's known her longer?"

"Actually, we just took a poll, and we agree you're the perfect fit," Melissa said, patting the couch beside her.

Jason shrugged. "Okay," he said. He took the space next to his wife and put a protective arm around her. "If that's what Melissa wants, that's what we'll do."

Shirley grinned at Melissa. "Like I said, you have a good man there."

Melissa grinned back. "The best."

"Now," Shirley said, "how's the rest of the program going?"

I was just getting out the notes I had made on the funeral service when Tom came through the kitchen door. "Hey, everybody, I'm home," he called, then looking around, he added, "Aunt Shirley, great to see you!"

"You too," Shirley said, getting up to give Tom a hug. He hugged her the way a drowning man would grab a lifeline.

Then my husband looked at the empty dining room table. "What's for dinner?"

"Dinner?" I asked, faking my best blank look. "Oh, I knew I forgot something!"

The kids snickered and Tom looked obligingly embarrassed.

"We're having a spinach and blackberry salad," I answered with a smile, "and I'll add some strips of Tuesday's leftover beef roast on the side. It's all ready. We just have to set it on. Emily, get Jason to help you set the table, okay?"

"If you have a few minutes, I'll whip up some biscuits," Aunt Shirley offered.

"Sounds great to me," I said. I didn't think we really needed the biscuits, but I didn't want to discourage Shirley, who was always ready to help.

"Do you still have your sourdough starter?" she asked.

"Um-hm. Shorty is right there on the counter, in the crock-pot," I answered.

"Shorty?"

Karen grinned. "The girls and I decided that anything we have to feed and care for daily is a pet and should have a name."

Shirley chuckled. "Great! Let's put Shorty to work. I've got the perfect recipe." She hurried her biscuits along and within half an hour, we were sitting down to eat.

Planning continued easily through the evening. When we'd all eaten our fill, Aunt Shirley managed cleanup. I watched her, thinking I should take notes. She did it all without offending anyone—delegating tasks, taking a large share of the responsibility but never too much, keeping everyone's efforts coordinated, and leaving my kitchen cleaner than I usually expected.

It occurred to me that most Relief Society presidents (not to mention Young Women leaders, Primary presidents, and priesthood leaders) could learn a lot from Aunt Shirley. Maybe she practiced what she had learned at home from her mother, or maybe she'd benefited from her years of church leadership. One way or another, she had her delegation skills down pat. She was always productive and effective, and she helped others to be productive and effective too.

Along the way she inspired and uplifted the people around her— even to the point that Emily hummed and sang as she worked, the first music we'd heard from her in two days—and everyone loved Shirley for it. Certainly I could find worse role models. In fact, I realized I was usually somewhat like her when I was really on my game. That got me thinking about how far *off* my game I'd been these last couple of days.

That got me thinking about Adelaide again—about the family she'd raised and the sorrows she'd seen and the whole of her productive, beautiful life. She had been one of the greatest builders I had ever known, and a blessing to so many people . . .

Just as my thoughts turned in that direction, Shirley asked, "Have you decided what to do about music at the funeral service?"

"I, uh . . . No, not really," I answered a bit lamely, and then I showed her the detailed-but-vague plans Adelaide had left for us, hoping Shirley could pull another rabbit out of her hat.

She did. Stepping up behind Emily, she laid a hand on her shoulder. "How about turning all the music over to our songbird here?"

I grinned at her. "An inspired choice," I answered. "Emily, will you take on the challenge of handling the music? You heard what I read to Aunt Shirley, right?"

Em nodded.

"Well, okay then!" I said. "Find some of Granny's favorite hymns, get some special numbers . . ."

"I'd love to! Can I sing?" Em asked, her face lit with enthusiasm.

"I'm sure Granny would love that," I answered, while Shirley smiled over Emily's shoulder. I gave her a grateful look.

By the time we all retired that evening, Aunt Shirley had helped us put our family in order. The funeral service had been sketched out using Shirley's suggestions and Adelaide's plans. Emily was eagerly working on the music, and Tom was busy deciding who would give prayers and who among Adelaide's progeny would be listed as pallbearers and honorary bearers.

As we said good night and settled in for the evening, I came to a realization: Despite how "together" I kept telling myself I was, I had been deeply shaken by Adelaide's death and by her final commission to me. Though I kept telling myself I was fine, I was *not* fine at all, and that Shirley had seen through so many of the gaps in my planning only emphasized that fact. I needed Shirley's calming presence as much as anyone in the family, maybe more than most.

It was Shirley herself who reminded me of this during a few quiet words shortly before we rested for the evening. I was thanking her for all her help and explaining that I'm usually more on top of things when she said, "Karen, stop running so fast."

"What?"

"The world is spinning around you, and you're trying to run faster to keep up. You need to give yourself time to grieve and worry right along with the rest of us."

"I . . ." I had intended to defend my actions. Instead I said, "You've just lost your mother, and yet you seem so much more together than I am. Why is that?"

Shirley smiled gently. I almost saw Adelaide in it. "Yes, I'm grieving, just as much as any of you, but you're also worried. I know because I'm worried too—about Tom and how he's reacting to all this, about your daughters, about Brian in the mission field . . . I can be a step removed from all those worries, but they're right in your face." Then Shirley sighed. "Remember the general conference talk a while back about airplanes that encounter turbulence?"

I nodded. "President Uchtdorf gave it. He said to slow down. Focus on what matters most."

"Exactly." She patted my hand. "Delegate Relief Society to your counselors for the next week or two. Let the rest of us help with what has to be done here at home and for the funeral service. Read your scriptures;

say your prayers. You know, focus on the basics. You need time to get through this, just like all the rest of us. If we all focus in and help each other—"

"That was what Adelaide had in mind, wasn't it?"

Shirley grinned, and I felt about 100 percent better.

Later that evening I realized how a loving Heavenly Father had blessed me by sending Aunt Shirley a little earlier than expected. Of course, she too was grieving—after all, she had just lost her mother, and that is *never* easy—yet she had a spirit of peace about her that our family very much needed. The deep, calm peace that came from knowing our eternal purpose and our loving Father's plan was usually at the center of our lives. I had briefly allowed grief and worry, the turbulence in my life, to steal it from me, and I was glad to have it back. Shirley had brought it with her.

Shirley's presence had also reminded me of how grateful I was to have known Granny Adelaide. There had been serious trouble in Tom's family, and it had left lasting, deep wounds and painful scars, but somehow Granny's love had transcended it all. Now if I could only carry through with her final plan to bring the family together, maybe that healing love, Adelaide's reflection of the Savior's love, could bring peace and wholeness to her son's broken family. As I prepared to retire for the evening, I prayed that it might.

Aunt Shirley's Perfect Sourdough Biscuits

3 C. all-purpose flour*
2 tsp. granulated sugar
4 tsp. baking powder
½ tsp. baking soda
1 tsp. salt
½ C. chilled butter, margarine, or
  shortening in ¼-inch pieces

2 C. sourdough starter, at room
  temperature*
8–12 Tbsp. warm water (½ to ¾
  C.)
Melted butter

Directions

1. In a large bowl, sift together dry ingredients. With a pastry blender
   or two knives, cut in butter or margarine until particles are the size of
   small peas. Mix in sourdough starter. Sprinkle in water, 1 Tbsp. at a
   time, tossing with a fork until all flour is moistened and pastry dough
   almost cleans side of bowl. Note: You want the ingredients to barely
   bind together.
2. On a lightly floured surface, knead dough gently a few times until it
   forms a cohesive mass. Gently roll dough to approximately ½-inch
   thickness. Cut with a floured 2-inch biscuit cutter and place onto
   greased baking pan. Place close together for soft-sided biscuits or an
   inch apart for crisp-sided ones. Brush with butter. Cover and let rise
   in a warm place (85°), free from drafts, about 1 hour.
3. Bake 15–20 minutes in an oven preheated to 425 until tops are a
   light golden brown. Remove from oven and immediately remove
   from baking sheet. Serve warm.
4. Makes 20 biscuits. Serve with butter, honey, jam, jelly, or apple butter.

* The thickness of your starter determines how much flour needs to
be used. If you think the dough is too moist, add additional flour, a
tablespoon at a time. If too dry, add additional warm water a tablespoon
at a time.

CHAPTER 7

Thursday, June 14, Late evening

EMILY DAYLE BURNETT

I'VE NEVER LIKED MY MIDDLE name. I know it's a family name, but nobody ever told me much about the Dayle whose name I got stuck with. I've heard people say that girls should always have middle names they can complain about (isn't that like in a movie somewhere?), but what kind of name is Dayle, anyway? I hate it. Usually I just pretend I don't have a middle name unless someone pushes me about it. Thank goodness for Aunt Shirley! I know a little more about my name now, and I think I might even learn to like it—well, live with it, anyway.

After dinner was over, I took a glass of milk and a couple of Aunt Shirley's awesome biscuits to the upstairs hallway outside my bedroom, where we have the family computer set up. I opened the high school website and clicked on the choir directory. Ms. Nguyen is more than just smart and pretty. She's really organized too. We've never had a directory for the choir members before this year, but we have one now. And she keeps it up to date.

While I was looking up Ms. Nguyen's number, I was thinking about how I'm super glad that Aunt Shirley came early and even gladder she suggested I plan the music for the funeral. I loved my great-granny Adelaide, and I want to do this for her. Besides, I love, love, love the music we sing in church! True, it isn't always the most fun music and some of it is really old-fashioned. (I always kind of snicker at "In Our Lovely Deseret." I mean, do Church members in *Japan* have to sing that?)

Still, our hymns are mostly sweet, sacred music that have such a nice feeling, and I'm sure I know all of Great-Granny Adelaide's favorite hymns because I used to sit next to her in sacrament meeting almost every week. Planning the music is giving me something important to do to remember her. I want to do the best job I can.

I punched in Ms. Nguyen's phone number and held my breath since I felt fairly certain she'd be out of town for the holidays, probably hanging with her family. When the phone had rung three times, I felt pretty certain that Ms. Nguyen wasn't there, so it surprised me when she answered.

"Hello, Ms. Nguyen? It's Emily. Emily Burnett? I thought you might be taking a vacation now that summer choir is over."

"I'll be leaving in a few days to see my family, but I'm here until then. What can I do for you, Emily?"

Ms. Nguyen already knew about my great-granny dying since that was the reason I had missed our concert, and she was happy to hear that I was planning the music for the service. She assured me I'd do a great job. "I hope you're singing," she added with a smile in her voice. Wow. How cool is that?!

"I plan to," I told her. "I thought it would be sweet if I could sing with some of the other kids from choir—maybe even find enough people to do the cool madrigal we prepared for summer choir."

"Oh! That Orlando Gibbons piece would be perfect. It's the sound of it that works so well. You know what I mean, Emily. It has that eerie but ethereal sound like the best of the Renaissance music. It would be lovely."

"I like it, but it needs a really strong high soprano," I said. "You don't happen to know which of the choir kids are in town this week, do you?"

"Sydnie Adams has as strong a soprano as you're likely to find. I'm pretty sure I heard her say she'll be around."

"Great! I'll call her. Do you know who might be here to sing the other parts?"

We talked for a few minutes with me making notes as fast as I could and Ms. Nguyen volunteering to play the accompaniment herself, which I thought was awesome. Then we ended with a plan for me to round up the singers and call her back with a time when we could rehearse at her place on Saturday afternoon.

It took me three tries to get Sydnie. She's pretty popular, so I was surprised I could reach her that quickly. She said yes, she would be in town, and yes, she'd love to sing at our funeral. She asked where the service would be, and I took a deep breath before I told her it was scheduled at our stake center. Sydnie goes to this other church that preaches against ours, and, well, I just wasn't sure if she'd have a problem with coming to the Mormon building, but it didn't seem to bother her. I told her about our Saturday rehearsal, and then she suggested I call her cousins, Anthen and Caden Adams, who were also in summer choir.

"They'll be in town too," she explained, "and if you get them both to come, you'll have the men's parts covered. Wait! Let me call them. Anthen owes me a favor."

"That would be fantastic!" I answered.

"I'll get back to you in a few."

I thanked her and then called the Matthews twins, looking for a second soprano. I asked to speak to Abby or Erin, not knowing what I'd do when one twin agreed to sing and I only had a place for one. I got Erin, who said she'd be happy to sing. Then she resolved the other problem by asking if Abby could sing the second soprano part with her. Neither of them is into showboating, and they can blend well in a choral group. I told her that'd be great.

Sydnie called back right after I hung up with the twins and said she had set it up with her cousins, so then I called Ms. Nguyen back, and just like that, we had our group together, complete with an accompanist and a rehearsal time on Saturday.

I was on a roll, so this seemed like a good time to choose the opening and closing hymns. I started by just flipping through the hymnal, writing down the numbers of the hymns Granny Adelaide loved. That gave me a list long enough for a couple dozen funerals, so I started narrowing down. I quickly eliminated sacrament hymns. Then I cut songs that seemed too cheery. I had it down to about twenty when I saw Aunt Shirley coming up the stairs.

"Looks like things are going well," she said, puffing a little as she reached the top. It occurred to me then that, even though she's a generation younger than Great-Granny, Aunt Shirley is getting kind of old too. "How are you doing with the music?" she asked.

"It's good," I assured her and told her about my progress with Ms. Nguyen. "I've been going through the hymns, but I've still got too many songs and I'm not sure which ones to pick."

"Did you look in the back for the hymns most appropriate to funerals?"

I guess you learn something new every day, right? "I didn't know we had a list like that."

"Here, let me show you." She reached for the book.

I pulled up one of the hallway chairs for Aunt Shirley, and she showed me the list under "Funerals" in the topics section. I was happy to see how many were on the list I had already made. That cut my list to about twelve. Then Aunt Shirley and I got it down to eight, but at that point, I was kind of stuck.

She looked at her watch, touched my arm, and said, "Well, Emily Dayle, I'm thinking we should set this all aside, sleep on it, and come back to it tomorrow."

I grimaced. "I don't like that name much."

"Emily?"

I frowned harder. "No, Dayle. Why'd they stick me with that, anyway?"

"You know you had a great-aunt named Dayle, right? She was my oldest sister who lived and died before I was ever born."

"I know it's a family name, but I don't know anything about her."

"Well, maybe it's time someone told you," Aunt Shirley said and settled back.

We talked for nearly an hour longer, and I learned a lot about my great-granny and the family she'd raised. I knew my great-grandfather had served a mission to the central states, but I hadn't realized that he was called after he was married. Great-Grandpa Arthur Burnett got his call just before their first baby was due. He wanted a son, and so he said the name would be Dale, after a friend he loved, and Granny agreed. When the baby came late, just two days before Great-Grandpa was to leave, they didn't have a back-up plan, and so they named her Dale anyway, but they added the *y* to make it look more feminine.

"What happened to her?" I'd heard that Great-Aunt Dayle had died, but I didn't know anything about how or when.

"Smallpox," Aunt Shirley answered. "It's almost been eradicated in our day, but it was fairly common then. She was only a toddler when it came around. She died about a month before your great-grandpa got home from his mission. My mother always told me how grateful that she was that my dad had a chance to lay hands on Dayle's head to give her a father's blessing before he left. It was one of the few times he ever got to see her."

"Why'd they do that?" I asked. The thought of what those people went through suddenly seemed just . . . well, awful . . . and really unfair.

"Excuse me? Bless her, you mean?"

"No! Why did the Church call a father to leave his family and go away for years at a time like that? It seems so unfair."

Aunt Shirley smiled. "It seems unfair to us now because we live in a different time and this hasn't been the practice for a great many years."

I shook my head. "It was unfair even then."

"My parents didn't think so." Aunt Shirley had a faraway look, almost as if she could remember that time before she was born. "They knew they were being asked to sacrifice, but from their point of view, there was nothing more important they could sacrifice for than sharing the gospel with others."

I thought about that. "I guess I just don't have that kind of faith."

"You will." Aunt Shirley patted my hand. "Hang in there. You will."

She looked at her watch again. "Oh my. I didn't realize it was after ten. What do you say we sleep on this too?"

It surprised me to hear it was so late already. I liked talking with Great-Aunt Shirley. "That's good," I said. "We can talk again tomorrow."

I helped her find towels and stuff in the bathroom, and then I sat up for a little while, writing in my journal about the day. After a while, I turned off the light and tried to sleep, but it wasn't happening. I kept thinking of Granny Adelaide and the sacrifices that she and her husband and so many of the early Church members had made and wondering if I'd ever have that kind of faith.

Finally, I slipped out of bed and said a second prayer. I thanked Heavenly Father for sending me to a good family. I told Him that choosing the right music was important to me and that I'd be praying about it the next day. Then, although it surprised me even to think it, I thanked Him that my parents had named me for my Great-Aunt Dayle and that Aunt Shirley had told me a little more about her.

By the time I climbed back into bed, I was really feeling good about things. I knew that Dayle's name in the middle of mine could stand as an example of the faith I wanted to have someday. I felt better about the music too, since I felt I would find hymns that would please both Granny and me. In fact, I could almost imagine that she was close by, watching me while I worked on it. It felt really peaceful, really nice.

Amish-Style Baked Oat Breakfast

1 ¾ C. quick oats
¼ C. granulated sugar
¼ C. packed brown sugar
½ tsp. salt
1 ¼ tsp. baking powder

1 tsp. cinnamon
¼ C. melted butter
1 egg
½ C. milk
1 ½ tsp. vanilla

Directions

1. Combine dry ingredients in large bowl.
2. Add wet ingredients and mix thoroughly. Spread in a greased or sprayed 9 x 13 baking pan.
3. Bake at 350 for about 25 minutes or until golden.
4. Let cool for a few minutes and then cut into portions.
5. To serve, crumble each portion into a cereal bowl and add milk.

Serves 8–12, depending on hunger levels.

Variations

You can substitute ½ C. white or brown sugar for the two sugars in the recipe and play with the cinnamon and vanilla to taste. This is great served with fresh fruit!

CHAPTER 8

Friday, June 15, Early morning

KAREN BURNETT

THE KITCHEN WAS ALREADY FILLED with the scent of Aunt Shirley's baked oatmeal by the time I got up. In fact, it smelled a lot like the delicious cookies the girls had made and frozen for the family reunion.

There were a few unguarded moments when I watched Shirley working in my kitchen before she knew I was there, and I realized this busyness is one of the ways she copes. A psychologist I know calls it "overfunctioning." Since that's usually my way of dealing with crises—trying to run faster and do more—I readily identified. It's how I attempt to get some control over any uncontrollable situation that arises, and it doesn't usually work any better for me than it does for others. Still, I can't help falling back into the pattern, and I recognized it as soon as I saw it in Shirley. I also knew she had taken time for scripture study and prayer, just as she recommended to me; the calm, centered peace around her told me that.

The night before I had been merely grateful to see her, knowing I could use her help. Now I felt I understood her, woman to woman, in a way I had never known her before. Watching her work warmed my heart, but it also made me feel a bit like a spy, intruding on her privacy.

"Good morning, Aunt Shirley," I said, stepping into the room.

"Oh, good morning, dear." She gave me a sunny smile, too bright actually, considering she surreptitiously wiped a tear. "Breakfast is almost ready."

"I know. I could smell it clear down the hall. Smells delicious!" Then I stepped closer and put my arm around her shoulders. "You miss her terribly, don't you?"

"Every day," she answered, dropping the bright pretense. "Probably for the rest of my life." I hugged her, and she hugged back, hard, while we each shed a few more tears.

"I miss her too," I said as we held each other. "There weren't many like your mother."

"None." Shirley shook her head. "She was one of a kind."

For a moment, we just stood, arms around each other, commiserating. Then I broke the spell, picked up some bowls, and started setting the table. "Did she tell you about her last request to me?"

Shirley gave me a subtle grin. "You mean her plan to save her son's family?"

"Um, yeah. That one. I see the answer is yes."

"Oh, she talked to me about it, all right. I tried to persuade her that it wasn't likely to work, but she insisted on trying anyway. You know the old saying: nothing ventured, nothing—"

"Gained," I finished with her. "I've got to tell you, it isn't going so well so far."

"Tell me all about it." Shirley picked up the milk and followed me to the table, so I told her about Carrie's call and then about my talks with Michael and Rocio. I shared the excitement about meeting Carrie soon, the trepidation I felt about meeting Rocio, and the combination of fear that I had offended and a fair amount of offense taken from my brief chat with Michael.

Shirley just nodded. "I can't say any of that surprises me, except perhaps that Rocio is willing to brave the hurdle of meeting with this group. She's got to know she won't be well received here."

"Yeah, I'm pretty sure she knows that," I answered. Then I looked at the clock. "We've got a few minutes before I need to call everyone to breakfast. Can you tell me more about what happened with Tom Sr., Judith, and Rocio? My Tom won't talk about it, and I've sort of been operating in the dark. Anything you can share will help."

Shirley pursed her lips. "I can't say I know a lot. Much of it we had to infer after the fact, but it became clear to all of us early in their marriage that Judith wasn't well and Tom was becoming increasingly frustrated. He told Mother once, in front of me, that Judith had experienced some mild psychological problems before he married her. Apparently those problems were intensified by the shifting hormones that accompanied a pregnancy, so she became increasingly worse every time she carried a baby. She'd get a little better between births, but never very well, and then she'd start another pregnancy and suddenly become much worse again, and every low got lower."

Shirley looked around nervously, almost as if she felt she was betraying a confidence—although anyone she might have betrayed had been gone for years. "He told Mother that he had begged her to quit after the third child—"

"Ohhhh. That would be Steven, right?"

"Steven, yes, but Judith said that as a Mormon mother she had an obligation to bring children into the world—"

"That's a common problem," I interrupted. "I've seen many women conflicted over that one."

"Me too," Shirley answered, "especially among the older generation of sisters, but we both know that counsel was never intended to cause women to jeopardize their own health—or sanity. Mother tried to talk with her after Steven was born, but Judith essentially told her that it wasn't a mother-in-law's business to pry into such a personal decision and that she'd have more children if she wanted to. By the time Judith had delivered Carrie, her doctor had diagnosed her with some fairly serious ongoing problems—including schizophrenia." She paused, watching for my reaction while I struggled to keep my expression neutral. "Her doctor told her she needed to be on medication, but she wouldn't take it because—"

"Let me guess. She was planning on getting pregnant again, and she knew the medicine wouldn't be good for the baby."

Shirley nodded. "Yes. At least I think that was how it went." She paused.

I struggled to control my response. "I had no idea things were that bad."

"They got pretty bad," Shirley agreed. "In fact, once—"

"Yum! What smells so good in here?"

We both looked up with a start. We had become so engrossed in our conversation that neither of us had heard Tom enter the room. Shirley recovered quickly, "It's Amish oat breakfast," she answered, then she looked up at the clock, "and it should be ready just about now."

"Well, it smells wonderful," Tom said. "Thanks, Aunt Shirley." Then he picked me up and whirled me around. "Good morning, beautiful."

"Good morning, yourself," I said, straightening my dress. Shirley was bringing the oat dish to the table. I turned back to my husband. "Tom, will you please call the girls?"

Tom stepped to the stairs. "Stephanie! Emily! Breakfast!"

Shirley and I exchanged a wry smile. "We'll finish this later," she whispered to me as Tom turned back toward the table.

"Later," I whispered back.

*   *   *

I thought about Tom's parents and the struggles that had finally destroyed their marriage while we ate our breakfast and did some quick cleanup. Obviously I had known there were problems, but the level and intensity of them was surprising, especially since Tom had always given the impression that his mother's illness had begun with his father's desertion. Between the delicious oatmeal and the unsavory conversation, Aunt Shirley had given me plenty to digest.

I spoke little while the family chatted quietly over the meal. Then the girls went upstairs and Tom left for work. Shirley and I were alone again during cleanup.

"I asked Steph and Emily if they'll take over the cooking this evening. That will give us some time to work on other plans."

"Sounds good," Shirley answered. Then she dropped her voice into a whisper. "About our earlier conversation, do you think maybe you and I could take a walk together?"

"I think that would be a great idea," I answered. "Buster needs a walk anyway." Buster, the beagle, is Brian's dog, the canine best buddy he's had since his tenth birthday. Although I hadn't wanted to get a dog, Buster has been just plain fun to have around, and true to his promise, Brian did most of the caretaking. By the time Brian was ready to accept his mission call, I had grown so fond of his little buddy that it was no burden to take over his care. "I've got a few things I need to take care of this morning," I told Shirley, "but maybe we can take Buster out this afternoon. If that doesn't work, I'm sure there will be time tomorrow. Does that work for you?"

"That will be fine," Aunt Shirley answered. Then she said, "I've been thinking about Mother's funeral service. Have you given yourself a role in it—other than helping us dress her?"

I paused, collecting my thoughts. "Honestly, Aunt Shirley, I'm not sure I'll even be able to attend."

Shock appeared on Shirley's face. "What are you talking about? Of course you'll attend! You wouldn't want to miss Adelaide's funeral."

"I've only started accumulating family recipes," I scrambled to explain, "and I don't see how I can possibly have this meal ready for everyone after the service if I'm not in the kitchen—"

Shirley dropped the pan she was holding. "Oh, for heaven's sake! What do you think the Relief Society is for, anyway?"

"But I'm the president. I'm supposed to be the one taking care of others—"

Shirley stared at me, clearly astounded. "Let me get this straight," she said. "You are the ward Relief Society president, but you don't have a testimony of the organization's *purpose?*"

I must have looked as shocked as she did. "Of course I have a testimony! It's not that. Both of my counselors have already volunteered to help, but this is all happening at a very busy time of year. Many of the sisters are still out of town on summer vacations, others have house-guests; everybody's kids are out of school, and they'll all be carrying on the business of their own families. I just can't ask the sisters to drop their own plans to help me with something like this."

Thank goodness for the twinkle in her eye as Shirley said, "You would deny them their blessings as members of the kingdom?"

I had to smile. Shirley can certainly drive a point. "Oh, come on, Aunt Shirley. I'm not trying to deny anyone anything, but this isn't like asking for ham and funeral potatoes. We'll be coming up with all kinds of special recipes, some of them different from anything I've ever tried before, and to ask the sisters to help me—" I glanced at the clock and found the excuse I needed. "Look, I need to leave in just a couple of minutes. Our presidency meets on Friday mornings, and I promised I'd let them know about our plans for Adelaide's service."

"Then ask *them* about the funeral lunch," Shirley directed. "And remember, dear," she laid a gentle hand on my arm to soften her words, "one of the first covenants we make as members of Christ's kingdom is to mourn with those who mourn. Let your sisters help you, just as you'd help them. Delegate. Focus. Slow down." She gave my arm a gentle squeeze.

I took her hand and squeezed back. "I'll ask the presidency about it," I promised as I went to get my things, although I still couldn't see myself intruding on other sisters' families the way Shirley seemed to expect.

But I didn't get a chance to ask the presidency about it at all since Larissa Mackey, my first counselor, asked me about it as soon as I saw her, even before our meeting had officially begun. "I've been thinking about the funeral lunch," she said as we greeted each other. "I've got a sign-up sheet ready to pass around with the roll this Sunday—"

"No, no, wait. You don't understand," I explained as I looked over the sheet she handed me. Then I told her about Granny Adelaide's final request and how the funeral lunch would be made from special family recipes, most of which I hadn't even gathered yet. I found myself saying the same things I had said minutes before to Aunt Shirley, except that Shirley had managed to place enough doubt that I stumbled over some of the concepts this time.

Larissa took my explanations about as well as Shirley had. She listened to every word I said while skepticism grew on her features. She was frowning hard by the time I said, "And that's why I can't ask these sisters to help me."

"Help *you*?" she said, carefully emphasizing the last syllable. "Dear Sister Karen, it sounds like you're overfunctioning again."

"What?" I suddenly wanted to kick myself for sharing that little detail. "Larissa—"

But Larissa was smiling, calmly shaking her head from side to side. "This isn't about helping you, Karen. It's not about asking the sisters to serve you. It isn't about *you* at all. Some of our Relief Society sisters have grown up in this ward. A few have lived here since the wards were reorganized and others have been here their whole married lives. For some, Adelaide Burnett is as much a fixture in this ward as the pipe organ— maybe even more so since our ward met in another building for a while."

I grinned at that and her expression softened further. "Really, Karen. There's hardly a woman in this ward who hasn't received one of Adelaide's hand-crocheted baby blankets or handmade birthday cards or personalized Christmas ornaments or handmade Easter commemoratives or—"

"I see your point." I looked again at the sign-up Larissa had prepared. "If I just had maybe three or four kitchen helpers to keep things warm while I—"

Larissa took the clipboard out of my hand. "Not *you*, Karen. Let *us* do this, not for you, but for Adelaide." She laid her hand over mine. "We all love her. Let us do this."

"Okay," I said. "You can pass the sign-up sheet, but the sisters need to understand exactly what this is all about—"

"I'm conducting Sunday. I'll be sure to explain." She moved the clipboard away almost as if she thought I'd snatch it back.

"Explain what?" The voice from the back of the room announced the arrival of Charis Tenney, my second counselor. Kerry Roth, our secretary, was with her.

"Come on in and we'll tell you all about it," Larissa answered. Then, looking to me, she said, "Shall we get started?"

Still feeling conflicted, I pulled my chair up at the table.

Naan (East Indian Flatbread)

1 package (.25 oz.) active dry yeast
1 C. warm water
¼ C. white sugar
3 Tbsp. milk
1 egg, beaten

2 tsp. salt
4 ½ C. bread flour
2 tsp. minced garlic (optional)
¼ C. butter, melted

Directions

1. In a large bowl, dissolve yeast in warm water. Let stand about 10 minutes, until frothy. Stir in sugar, milk, egg, salt, and enough flour to make a soft dough. On a lightly floured surface, knead for 6–8 minutes or until smooth. Place dough in a well-oiled bowl, cover with a damp cloth, and set aside to rise. Let it rise 1 hour until the dough has doubled in volume.
2. Punch down dough and knead in garlic. Pinch off sections of dough about the size of a golf ball. Roll into balls, and place on a tray. Cover with a towel, and allow to rise until doubled in size, about 30 minutes.
3. During the second rising, preheat grill to high heat.
4. At grill side, roll one ball of dough out into a thin circle. Lightly oil grill. Place dough on grill, and cook for 2–3 minutes, or until puffy and lightly browned. Brush uncooked side with butter, and turn over. Brush cooked side with butter and cook until browned, another 2–4 minutes. Remove from grill, and continue the process until all the naan has been prepared.
5. Serve with hummus and baba ganouj (recipes follow).

Yummy Hummus

1 clove garlic

1 can (19 oz.) garbanzo beans,
half the liquid reserved

4 Tbsp. lemon juice

2 Tbsp. tahini (sesame seed paste)*

1 clove garlic, chopped

1 tsp. salt

black pepper to taste

2 Tbsp. olive oil

Directions

1. In a blender, chop the garlic. Pour garbanzo beans into blender, reserving about a tablespoon for garnish. Place lemon juice, tahini, chopped garlic, and salt in blender. Blend until creamy and well mixed.
2. Transfer the mixture to a medium serving bowl. Sprinkle with pepper and pour olive oil over the top. Garnish with reserved garbanzo beans.

* Available at Middle Eastern and natural foods stores.

Baba Ganouj

2 1-pound eggplants, halved lengthwise
¼ C. olive oil
¼ C. tahini (sesame seed paste)*
3 Tbsp. fresh lemon juice
1 garlic clove, chopped

Directions

1. Preheat oven to 375. Generously oil rimmed baking sheet. Place eggplant halves, cut side down, on sheet. Roast until eggplant is very soft, about 45 minutes. Cool slightly. Using spoon, scoop out into a strainer set over bowl. Let stand 30 minutes, allowing excess liquid to drain from eggplant.
2. Transfer eggplant pulp to processor. Add ¼ C. oil, tahini, lemon juice, and garlic; process until almost smooth. Season to taste with salt and pepper. Transfer to small bowl. (Can be made 1 day ahead. Cover and chill. Bring to room temperature before serving.)

* Available at Middle Eastern and natural foods stores.

CHAPTER 9

Friday, June 15, Early afternoon

STEPHANIE BURNETT

I SLID INTO THE BOOTH at my favorite frozen yogurt shop, looked at my watch, and noted it was a couple of minutes fast according to the clock on the wall. A girl in an apron came by to remind me to place my order at the counter, and I told her I was waiting for someone. Just then I saw Jessica at the entrance and jumped up with a grin.

Jess held out her arms for a hug as I drew near. I was grateful. It had been a while since we'd seen each other, and well, I wasn't sure how happy she'd be about this meeting.

We hugged and then turned to the counter. "Order whatever you like," I told her, quickly adding, "My treat."

Jess looked wary. "That's not necessary, Steph. I can buy my own yogurt."

"I know you can, but you're the one doing me a favor. Let me get this for you."

Jessica gave me a long, appraising look, but then she smiled. "Okay," she answered. "Thanks."

We placed our orders and went to the booth I had chosen. It was the one we always preferred, back when we came here as a group of roommates, back when Jessica and Megan, Allie and I all lived together and occasionally came here for a cheap outing, back before . . .

"We heard about your grandma," Jessica said, derailing my thought train just when it might have crashed on its own. "Are you doing okay?" The expression on her face had a whole subtext written in the worry lines.

"Yeah," I said. "It was my great-grandmother actually, my dad's Granny Adelaide. We'll all miss her something awful, but she was more than a hundred years old. We couldn't keep her forever."

"No, I guess not," Jess said. Then she added, "This wasn't your grand-mother who had the, uh, problems?"

"No. That was my Grandma Judith, my dad's mom. She's been gone for a long time. In fact, I don't remember much about her—except for the problems."

"That's what I thought, but Allie said—" She cut the thought off quickly, looking away, looking chagrined.

I swallowed. "How is Allie?"

"She's good. She said to tell you she's sorry about the loss in your family."

I gave Jess a long, *long* look. "Did she really say that, Jess, or are you just being diplomatic again?"

Jess gave me an earnest smile. "She really did, Steph. She said she wanted you to know that she's sorry about your grandma and she hopes you're . . . doing okay."

"I am," I answered, and then I realized I had been rubbing my fingers over the raised scars on my left arm, between my wrist and elbow. I sighed and dropped my arms to my sides. "I'm sad, but I'm okay."

"Glad to hear it," Jess said. Then she turned her attention elsewhere. "I brought the recipes you asked for." She took them out of her purse—three note cards, one each for naan, hummus, and baba ganouj. "Here you go."

"Thanks so much," I said, taking them, looking them over. "We'll have lots of family in town for the funeral, and these will create some-thing different for everyone to snack on, something other than the usual chips and dip."

"Everybody always loves the naan," Jessica said. "Of course, Mom learned how to make it when she and Dad were serving their mission in Australia. There was a small group of Christians who had migrated there from Lebanon, and they brought their Middle Eastern dishes with them. Some of them converted, and Mom worked with the Lebanese sisters in the Relief Society."

"These should be fairly authentic, then."

"Absolutely authentic!" Jess answered brightly.

I read through the recipes. "Do you know of any place around here that sells tahini?"

"I don't," she answered. "The only time I made these foods for our apartment, I brought some of the more unusual ingredients with me from a visit to see the folks. There are lots of Middle Eastern markets in the East Bay."

"Yes, I imagine there are," I murmured. "Would these recipes taste okay without the tahini, do you think?"

"I think probably so. You could also ask around, maybe at the health food stores." She named a couple of other places that might carry her secret ingredient, and I made notes on the back of my shopping list.

The girl at the counter called my name, and Jess and I went up to get our frozen yogurt. I gladly paid for both. We took our orders back to the booth and sat companionably, slowly savoring the sweet treat. It took a minute before I spoke again.

"Jess, how is everyone doing—really?"

She smiled. "Everyone is *really* doing fine. In fact, we miss you. Nyla is a good roommate, but since she got engaged, we never see her. Meg and Allie and I were just talking a couple of nights ago about how much fun we all used to have together before—" She cut the thought off, no longer smiling, looking away again.

"Before I lost my mind and started hurting people?"

Jessica sighed. "We know you didn't mean to hurt anybody, Steph."

"But I did, didn't I?"

Jess didn't answer.

"Is Allie healing okay?" To my chagrin, I realized I was rubbing my scar again. I carefully folded my hands.

"She's healing fine. Her cuts weren't nearly as bad as yours," she answered. "Have you been . . . okay since then?"

I couldn't help the wry smile. "If you're asking if I've had any more wigging-out episodes since I moved home, the answer is no. I seem to have been totally sane for these past few months."

She swallowed hard but didn't take the bait. "Did you ever see the doctor, like we talked about?"

"I thought about it, and I promised myself that if it ever happened again, I'd go right away, but my focus so far has been on trying to keep it from happening. I'm taking fewer classes this semester, to reduce the pressure, and I'm trying to be more self-aware. If I feel myself sliding a little, or if I feel the . . ." I paused, looking for the right word. "If I feel the darkness closing in, I take a little downtime, all alone. I usually listen to some Tabernacle Choir CDs—you know, soothing, spiritual music that helps me fight the . . . the dark side of the force."

"So it's you and Yoda, forget the doctors." Jessica summarized for me.

"Yeah, that's about it." I licked mountain blueberry off my sugar cone. "But it's been enough so far," I added.

"That's good, then," Jess said. She swallowed again, finishing the last of her yogurt. "I hope you don't mind, Steph, but I need to run. I have a couple of appointments this afternoon . . ." She stood.

"No problem," I said, standing to hug her. "It's been great to see you."

"Yeah," she answered. "Great to see you too. Glad you're doing well."

"I am," I answered, trying to reassure her. "I really am."

"Good to hear. Well, see you."

"Yeah, see you, Jess." I stood, watching as she walked away. She was almost to the door when she turned back. "You really need to stop in and visit sometime, Stephie," she said, using a pet name I hadn't heard in a while. "Everyone would get a kick out of seeing you again." Bless her, she looked like she meant it.

"I'll consider it, Jess. Thanks."

She waved and walked away, then I sat down to finish my cone. I hadn't really talked with any of my former roommates much since I'd moved out suddenly a few months before. It hadn't been easy to talk to them at all, even when I ran into them in the halls at church meetings in our singles ward. It had been good to visit with Jess again and to hear that Allie was doing okay.

I had never meant to hurt Allie, or myself, either. After it had happened, I'd had to take everyone else's word about exactly what *had* happened since I didn't remember it clearly. They said I'd just "lost it" when I accidentally dropped and broke a glass bowl in the slick dishwater, and I'd started throwing pieces of it around. Allie had walked into the room to see what all the shrieking was about and a piece of broken glass had clipped her upper arm, slicing into a small blood vessel and leaving our kitchen drenched in scarlet. I moved home the following day.

You know how people use the expression "I just saw red" when they're trying to excuse themselves? Well, I had seen black, and that was all I saw when I tried to recall the incident. The blackness had been slowly moving in around me for days, and when it had reached fullness, it had taken over, driving me to do things I couldn't even picture myself doing.

I'd never told anyone about it, not even my parents, and my loyal roommates had kept my ugly little secret. Still, I knew now—and I knew they knew—that I did, in fact, take after my Grandma Judith, the one who had the "problems." I knew I'd be wise to plan a career and to look to a future alone since it'd be very unwise to marry, inflicting the family brand of looniness on a hapless husband. I also knew now that I must never, ever pass the genes I carried to any future generations of crazy Burnett women.

Jess was the only one who understood that part of the secret, the reason why I now choose never to have more than two dates with the same guy, even if he asked again—no, *especially* if he asked again. If I wasn't ever going to marry, there wasn't any point in leading some sweet guy along, giving him hope for things that would never happen between us.

I finished my yogurt, cleaned up the booth, and headed for the stores Jessica had mentioned. Even if we didn't end up using the naan and the spreads that went with it for the picnic, these would give me something fun to introduce the family to sometime soon. I sighed. Time to play the role of the sane-and-happy daughter once again.

Delicious Chili Salsa

Bottle this salsa in summer when you have plenty of extra tomatoes; use it all year long. This is one salsa recipe that does not overwhelm with vinegar flavor.

10 C. chopped tomatoes
1 large, chopped onion
¼–½ C. fresh green chilies, minced (jalapeños are good!)
½ head (6–8 cloves) finely minced garlic

2 green peppers, chopped
1 Tbsp. cumin
1–1 ½ tsp. salt (to taste)
Lime juice (for bottling)

Directions

1. Chop all the vegetables and combine in a large soup pot.
2. Cook until the mixture reaches a slow boil.
3. Measure 3 Tbsp. lime juice into each sterile pint jar.
4. Scoop boiling mixture into canning jars. Affix sterile lids.
5. Process 30 minutes in a boiling water bath.
6. Remove bottles. Label them when cool.

Variations

You can play with the flavors in this recipe, but don't reduce the lime juice as that helps to maintain the salsa's acidity. "Five-Alarm Salsa" needs more chopped chilies (try 1 C. habañeros!). You can increase or decrease the garlic, peppers, cumin, and salt to taste. This is a delicious, non-vinegary salsa, excellent for all kinds of recipes or for eating with corn or tortilla chips.

CHAPTER 10

Friday, June 15, Late afternoon

EMILY BURNETT

"The key to an easy meal of red beans and rice is Mom's homemade salsa," Steph said as I stepped into the kitchen.

"That's what you've always said," I answered and started opening the cans of beans and diced tomatoes that Steph had waiting on the counter. Mom had assigned us dinner, and I wasn't surprised to find Steph working on red beans and rice. I was surprised at the recipe she'd chosen: she was making the style Dad liked best—where the beans and rice are cooked separately—and not her own favorite, the cook-it-all-together method.

When she first graduated from high school, she had tried living on her own for a while. She had a job as a teller in a local bank and was taking classes at the college, building credits before she transferred to the state university. Melissa and Jason had just gotten engaged and things were kind of crazy at home, so I guess Steph just decided it was time to move on and move out. She met some friends in the singles ward, and they got an apartment together.

For a while it was a kick. I'd go visit at Steph's some weekends when she didn't have other plans, and we'd stay up late watching cheesy chick flicks and making brownies or caramel corn. She didn't much like the regular chore of cooking every day though. For a while Mom kidded her about all the rice, beans, tomatoes, and salsa that kept disappearing from our cupboards, and I think she was relieved when Steph finally gave up and moved home. Steph said she didn't want to pay rent or cook anymore, but I always wondered if there was more to it than that. She seemed awfully tense when she first came back, and she hasn't had much to do with her former roommates since then.

When I asked her if she was okay, Steph laughed and said it was all about her diet. She claimed it was easier to move home now than to have to take off the fifteen pounds first-year students typically gained—the dreaded freshman fifteen. She liked the thought of shedding it while it was only seven or eight instead. Mom joked that it was easier not to have to replace all the makings for red beans and rice. I know it was easier on me when Mel moved out since I still had one sister around.

"How much rice do you think we'll need?" I asked as I lifted the five-pound bag.

"I don't know," Steph answered. "We usually cook a couple of cups if it's just the four of us. Add Melissa and Jason, Great-Aunt Shirley, and maybe Ruby, and we're up to double; then you'll have to double that for the water before you cook it—"

"Double and double again . . . let's see. Do you think eight cups will be enough?"

"Sure. Sounds good," Steph called from the back hallway. Then she went to the storage shed to get a pint of Mom's salsa. I got out a huge soup pot and measured eight cups of dry white rice. I put in a little salt, about a tablespoon or so, and then I carefully counted out sixteen cups of water. It looked like an awful lot. I put it on the back burner and started it cooking.

"Whoa!" Steph stepped back into the kitchen just as the pot started to boil. "Don't tell me you have that whole thing full of rice!"

"Well, rice and water."

"You're kidding! How much are you cooking?"

"Eight cups, just like you said."

"Eight cups of *water* or eight cups of *rice*?" Steph lifted the lid. "Oh no! You're cooking eight cups of rice, aren't you?"

"Wasn't that what you said to do?"

"You're joking, right?" For just a second, Steph looked like she thought I'd lost my mind. "Really, Em? Really?"

"You said eight cups," I repeated, weakly defending myself. Even I was beginning to see what a dumb mistake I'd made.

"Eight cups of *water*, Em. Only four of rice. We've got enough rice here to feed your whole high school varsity football team. Maybe the JV as well." She stared at me, her brow furrowed, and then her face began to crumple and she chuckled.

"The whole ward, anyway," I said.

"The whole neighborhood." Steph was laughing harder.

"The whole state! I'll call the governor."

"Maybe all of Ch-China." Steph could hardly speak, she was laughing so hard. "And they *like* rice!"

"The whole w-world," I blurted, laughing even harder than she was.

It was so stupid. We were both just laughing and laughing until the tears rolled down our faces, until we had to hold on to each other just to stay standing, until we almost burned the rice because we couldn't stop laughing long enough to turn down the heat. We laughed and laughed until we finally got control of ourselves, and then we looked at each other and started in again.

I don't think laughing has ever felt so good.

Some-Like-It-Hot Tacos

Directions

This recipe is made in separate parts: Make the spicy slaw first and let it chill in the refrigerator while you are preparing the chili beef. Heat the tortillas and grate some cheese. Serve them all separately with sour cream and salsa on the side, and let your guests stack their own tacos at the table.

Spicy Cilantro-Jalapeño Slaw

½ head cabbage, thinly sliced
½ head red cabbage, thinly sliced
1 whole jalapeño, halved
   lengthwise and thinly sliced
½ C. whole or soy milk
½ C. mayonnaise

1 tsp. white vinegar
1 Tbsp. sugar
¼ tsp. salt
¼ tsp. cayenne pepper
2 C. cilantro leaves, barely
   chopped

Directions

1. Prepare the cabbage, red cabbage, and jalapeño by cutting each in half, turning each half on its side, and slicing very thinly.
2. Mix the next six ingredients (milk through cayenne pepper) in a small bowl. Add to vegetable mixture and toss, coating veggies thoroughly.
3. Lightly chop the fresh cilantro leaves and toss them into the mixture. Cover and refrigerate. Use within the next two days.

Chili Beef

A Burnett family favorite

3 ½–4 pounds beef roast
1 can (28 oz.) red chili sauce
   (NOT enchilada sauce)

1 large onion, cut in large pieces
1 tsp. salt

Directions

1. Empty chili sauce into a 4-quart (or larger) saucepan or slow cooker.
2. Add beef and bring to a low boil. Turn down to a simmer and cook 4–6 hours or until beef falls apart at the touch of a fork.

3. Remove and shred the beef. Remove as much extra fat as possible during this process. Put the beef back into the sauce, add the onion and salt, and cook until the onion is transparent. Serve hot.

Serving Suggestions

1. For "Some-Like-It-Hot Tacos," serve the shredded chili beef with warm tortillas; grated cheddar, cheddar/jack, or pepper jack cheese; sour cream; and salsa. Add spicy slaw at the table.
2. You can also serve the chili beef over salad greens, with sour cream and guacamole on the side to make a spicy salad, or serve the chili beef over spicy slaw.
3. Make up another batch of red chili sauce and roll the chili beef into enchiladas. Serve over rice or cornbread with cheese and other condiments. Use your imagination to think of a dozen other ways.

Variations

You can substitute fresh pork for beef to create "carnitas." A similar recipe (though not shredded) can be used with chicken, turkey, or other poultry. You can also substitute green chili sauce for the red, though it may look less appealing and be more bitter.

CHAPTER 11

Friday, June 15, Late afternoon

KAREN BURNETT

IT WAS LATE IN THE day before I reached Carrie. I'd tried several times before I went to my presidency meeting, and I'd been trying since I'd gotten home, but all I'd been getting was a busy signal. When I finally got through, after Aunt Shirley and I returned from our walk, it rang four times before a recorded greeting answered: "Buenos dias! You have reached the home of Carrie and Carlos. If you wish to reach Carlos, Juan Carlos, or Sara, leave a message after the beep, or you may call Los Hombres Restaurant at 830-555-1212. If you wish to reach Carrie, Candi, or Sofie, please leave a message. We'll get back to you in just a few days. Have a great summer!"

A few days? What? That's when I realized that if Carrie was driving, she must already be on her way. I dug around on my desk; I knew I had her cell phone number somewhere. Once I found it, the call went quickly. Carrie answered on the second ring.

"Hello? Karen?"

"Hi, Carrie. Sounds like you're on your way here."

"Yes. We got an early start." In the background, I heard a young person's voice grumble, "A *very* early start."

I smiled. "So you're cruising right along, I guess. Where are you now?"

"Well, we passed through Las Cruces a while back and should be in Tucson within the next few minutes, so we're making good time."

"Then you'll be here by . . . when? Tomorrow evening?"

There was some mumbling in the background, and then Carrie answered, "We won't drive straight through, but we'll make it to California before we stop. We want to see some family members in Southern California, and they're a little off the beaten path, so we'll probably arrive at your place sometime late tomorrow evening."

"Wow, that's fast!"

Carrie hesitated. "Uh, that assumes you'll be ready for us by then?"

"Oh, no problem! We'll organize the bedrooms at Granny's early tomorrow. Things will be all ready."

"Are you sure you have room for all of us? We can get a hotel, you know."

"I think we can accommodate everyone at Granny's house. She has four bedrooms and three baths, plus there are sleeper sofas in the living and family rooms. So, how many of you are coming? You weren't sure last time we talked."

"Tina's husband, Jeff, has a twelve-passenger van that he uses for Scout outings and temple trips and such," Carrie said, "and we're filling it up. As I told you, my husband can't get away from the restaurant this time of year, and I left our two oldest, Juan Carlos and Sara, home to help him, but I'm bringing my two younger girls, so I have Candi and Sofie with me . . ."

"Candi and Sofie," I repeated, writing it down. "Okay, so that's three of you . . ."

"Then Tina and Jeff are here with their three boys—"

"So that's five more, total of eight . . ."

"Plus Mandy and her husband, Terry, have their two little ones—"

"Four more, total of twelve. You really are filling up that van!"

"You ought to see it! With all twelve of us, plus our luggage . . . Let's just say it's way more than full."

"Yes, I'd say so!" Then as I thought about what she'd said, a thought registered. "Carrie? If Tina's and Mandy's husbands are coming, maybe they would like to be on the program? We could use them both as pallbearers, if they're willing, and we also need a closing prayer for the service . . ." I paused, wondering if I'd overstepped. But Christina's husband drove on temple trips, right? So he must at least be a member of the Church. I was kicking myself for putting the family in an awkward position when Carrie covered the phone and mumbled something. I could hear more mumbled responses.

"Jeff says he would be happy to pray," Carrie answered, "and both Jeff and Terry will be honored to be among Granny's pallbearers."

"Great!" I said, relieved that it had gone that well. "We want to list honorary pallbearers too, and I think it would be sweet if the little boys in your group wanted to walk behind the casket together. Can you tell me the names of the boys who might want to be included?"

Carrie listed Tina and Jeff's three little guys—Jacob, Isaac, and Eric—and Mandy's youngest, Thomas. That named tugged a little at my heartstrings, and I couldn't help wondering what my husband would think when he realized that one of the half sisters he'd never met had named a son for the father they had shared, the same father whose name he also bore. Well, it was time and past time. Tom would just have to cope.

"There's more," I said to Carrie, trying not to think of what Tom would think. Then I asked who would like to be included in the singing when Granny's younger progeny presented "I Am a Child of God." There was more murmuring inside the big van and then Carrie said to include all the boys she had just listed plus her daughters—Candi and Sofie—and Amanda's daughter, Sammie. I dutifully noted all the names and repeated them back, making sure to ask if I had the spellings correct. When I did that, Carrie gave me the girls' full names—Candelaria, Sofia, and Samantha.

It had been a good conversation and I was feeling positive about these relatives, so I didn't know whether I should stick my neck out with the next question, but just to be certain, I asked it anyway: "I don't suppose Mikey and Marco might be coming later?"

A pregnant silence followed, underscored by some mumbling I couldn't quite make out in the family van. Then Carrie said, "First, just so you'll know, Michael hasn't been called Mikey for years. It's Michael, and Michael is all he answers to."

"My apologies," I answered quickly.

Carrie's voice softened. "I don't suppose you could have known," she said. "It's just . . . he's really quite touchy about it." I heard mumbled assent behind her, and she chuckled drily. "Another thing I guess you'd better know is that our Michael is really quite touchy about a number of things, so no, I don't think he will be coming to this service. Marco won't either."

"I'm sorry. I really didn't mean—"

"It's not your fault, Karen." Carrie sighed. "There are a number of people whose fault it might be, but it isn't yours. Not even a little bit."

"Well," I said, "um, thank you for that."

There was some more awkward silence, and I could hear children's voices.

"Uh, listen, Carrie, can I give you directions to Granny's house?"

"No need. We have a GPS, and we have Granny's address. It's still the same one where she lived forever, right?"

"Yes, the same one. That's why there's all that room. She and Grandpa Arthur built it for their own family and then kept it so everyone could visit. Well, I guess if you have the GPS, you're all set, then." I somehow felt that we hadn't quite covered everything, that there was something more I needed to do before I let them go. "I guess we've about covered it," I said aloud, hoping Carrie would contradict.

She did. "Oh, Karen, one more thing. May we have your address too? And can you tell us where you meet for church and what time your meetings start?"

"Oh, of course!" It thrilled me to think they'd be joining us for church. I rattled off our address and how to get to the stake center. Carrie and I talked a little about whether to try to meet for breakfast but agreed that it might put too much strain on everyone's families. I promised to leave breakfast fixings at Granny's house, and we agreed to meet at the stake center just before the start of our eleven o'clock sacrament meeting.

"Okay then," Carrie said. "I guess we'll see you Sunday morning."

"See you then," I responded. "Drive safely!"

I was just about to click off when Carrie asked, "Karen, are you still there?"

"Yes?"

"I thought of something else I wanted to tell you." There was a loud sound behind her, a man's voice, and then Carrie said, "That is, my *dear* brother-in-law Jeff reminded me of something I had intended to tell you." I could hear someone, presumably Jeff, laughing.

"Go ahead," I prompted.

"Remember how you sent a message around to everyone, asking if we remembered any recipes our mother used to prepare for Burnett family reunions?"

"Yes, but surely *you* don't remember . . . I mean, that was a long time ago."

"Well, yes and no. There was a recipe that Judith, that is, our mother, always made that the kids all loved. It was an easy one, and Rocio learned to make it by watching our mom. Then later, Mama Rocio tweaked it a little and made it for us sometimes."

"Okay," I said, not wishing to comment on the ways Carrie had referred to the two mothers in her life. I found both the references and their inferences meaningful. "Do you remember how to make it?"

"Oh yeah. I make it all the time for my kids. We call it 'Some-Like-It-Hot Tacos.'"

"I have that recipe!" I answered, happily surprised. "Granny Adelaide used to make it too, and she taught me how."

"That sounds perfect," Carrie said. "I'll help if you want to make it for the reunion."

"That sounds perfect," I echoed. "See you Sunday."

"Sunday," she repeated as the phone clicked off. I looked at how much progress we'd made in only a few minutes and wished Tom had made this phone call himself. At the same time, I couldn't help wondering if we'd made more progress because he hadn't. Despite the lift I felt after talking with Carrie and hearing how much of the family was coming, I couldn't help feeling that there were still some impossibly high hurdles to leap if Granny's plan was going to work—my own husband being one of the tallest—and I didn't seem to have much energy left for leaping hurdles.

Berry Grapefruit Salad

Bibb lettuce
Watercress
2 avocados, seeded, peeled, and
  sliced
2 C. grapefruit sections

1 C. fresh raspberries
½ C. fresh blackberries or
  blueberries
Prepared sweet vinegar and oil
  dressing

Directions

Line serving platter or individual salad plates with lettuce and watercress. Arrange avocado and grapefruit over greens in a tight pattern. Scatter berries over the top and sprinkle with dressing.

Sweet Vinegar and Oil Dressing

2 Tbsp. red wine vinegar
¼ C. cooking oil (olive oil does
  not work as well)
2 Tbsp. brown sugar

4 drops Tabasco sauce
½ tsp. salt
Dash of black pepper

Directions

Mix oil, vinegar, and sugar thoroughly. Add remaining ingredients and mix again. Chill. Mix once more before using. Drizzle while still well mixed.

CHAPTER 12

Friday, June 15, Early evening

KAREN BURNETT

MELISSA AND JASON ARRIVED SOON after I got off the phone with Carrie, and Tom came in soon after. He bustled in and began putting things away and fussing with details. He seemed more himself than he had in a couple of days.

I was so grateful the girls had taken care of dinner. It wasn't long before they served up some of Steph's red beans and rice, cooked in Tom's favorite style. Emily had gathered berries from the garden, the first of the summer's harvest, and had used them with the last of the winter's grapefruit to make an attractive salad. The mix of bitter and sweet was a nice contrast to the spicy beans.

Over dinner we all got to hear the story of how many cups of rice to cook, and the resulting laughter broke some of our shared tension. It was good to see my family laughing again, even if we all knew it was just a temporary break from the sorrow.

"I guess we'll have to throw away some rice," Steph said as we began to clean up. There was still a huge bowl of it, nearly filled to the top, and more in the cooking pan.

"Oh, don't do that," Aunt Shirley answered. "Here, let me package up the leftovers. I have a recipe or two for that extra rice that everybody will love."

"What kind of recipes?" Em asked.

"Well, rice pudding for one."

"Pudding?" Jason cut in, his lip curled.

"You don't like pudding?" Shirley asked as she stacked the dirty plates and took them to the sink.

"I guess it's a generational thing," Melissa said, casting her husband a look. "I don't know many kids—" She caught Jason's look. "Er . . . people our age, who seem to enjoy pudding very much."

"Maybe that's because you've grown up in a world where pudding came ready-made in the grocer's dairy case or in a box you could mix up in five minutes without cooking. When you eat good, old-fashioned rice pudding—especially the kind I make—you might just change your mind."

Jason looked skeptical, but Melissa said, "We can always give it a try." Shirley grinned as she carefully packaged many cups of cooked rice into plastic refrigerator containers, and we began the process of cleaning up the kitchen.

Tom helped clean the table and put away food. Then he said, "Did I tell you about the frozen lasagna I brought home?"

"No," I answered. "Is it in the freezer?"

"Yep. I put it there as soon as I got home. I thought it would help with dinner tomorrow."

"That's very thoughtful, honey. Thanks," I said, giving him a quick kiss.

"I'm trying to be useful," he answered, kissing me back.

Then he explained he had some work to do for his high priests group, and he excused himself to go into the office. "I also have some fun planned for later this evening, if you don't mind," he said.

I assured him I was ready for some fun, and I thought the family would be too. He said he'd be back in a little while and hummed as he went into the office. I decided not to break the mood by telling him about my talk with Rocio—yet.

"The poor little guy could use a good walk," I said as I stroked Buster, partly because it was true and partly for the benefit of anyone who might overhear us. "Too bad it's getting dark out already."

"I'm sure he needs a walk," Aunt Shirley answered, "and I could use one too, but we can both make it till tomorrow."

"We'll look forward to tomorrow, then," I answered.

*   *   *

After the dinner dishes were loaded and washing, Aunt Shirley and I sat down to coordinate our plans and start putting the menu together for the funeral/reunion dinner. To do that, we needed to get more recipes and to find out who was coming. I picked up my cell phone, Shirley got hers, and with the house phone positioned between us, we started dividing up the relatives and making calls.

As I looked at the family records, I couldn't help being reminded that Granny Adelaide had experienced a hundred years of often very difficult living. It was amazing to me that she was always so positive, such a builder. Her first child, her daughter Dayle, had died as a toddler while her husband was serving a full-time mission. Their second child and firstborn son, Robert, or Bob, had grown to adulthood but had been drafted and killed in the Korean War before he married. My late father-in-law had been their third child and the first to have a family.

Since their fourth child, Lenore, had never married, Tom and Shirley had been the only two of their five kids to give their parents grandchildren. Then Adelaide had lived long enough to experience the deaths of both her husband and her only surviving son. For a moment, I was staggered by the pain and the losses she had suffered and amazed all over again at the positive energy she always shared with others. Her life was a sermon on faith and reliance on the Lord. I only prayed I could demonstrate some portion of that faith over the coming difficult days. I started calling.

An hour later, Shirley and I compared notes. She began by announcing, "Lenore is coming. She and I shared a bed as children, so we can do it again. I'll put her in Melissa's old room with me. Thank goodness Melissa had a double bed."

"Okay," I said, "or we can put her in Brian's room. I sort of saved that for her."

"I thought we'd put my son Scott in there if you don't mind. He and his wife, Alicia, will be driving up from Thousand Oaks. Their children are mostly grown, so they're only bringing the youngest, Alexis. She's fifteen and very easy to please. To quote Scott, 'That girl can sleep anywhere.'" She smiled.

"I remember how teenagers sleep," I said somewhat wistfully. My own sleep hadn't been that great lately. "Okay. That's fine. The big lounge chair makes into a pretty comfortable bed. I think Alexis should be comfortable there."

"That's settled then," Shirley said.

"Do you think Alexis might want to be added to the group singing 'I Am a Child of God'?"

"I didn't think to ask that. Maybe for the program we should just put something like 'sung by Adelaide's great-grandchildren,'" Shirley suggested. "Then, if there are last-minute additions or deletions, we won't need to worry about program changes."

"Oh. That's so obvious. Why didn't I think of that?"

Shirley smiled and put her arm around me. "Don't worry, dear. You have plenty to think about."

That comforted me—a little. Though I couldn't help hoping I'd get back more of my brain function as time went on. Although I only shed tears a couple of times a day now, I was still preoccupied by the grief of Granny's passing. I guessed we all were.

Shirley must have read my mind. "Cut yourself some slack, Karen," she murmured, her face close to my ear. "You're grieving just as we all are, and you're still doing everything Granny asked you to do. You'll see. This is going to turn out better than you ever imagined."

Over the grapefruit-sized lump in my throat, I managed to choke out, "I hope so."

"Feel confident," Shirley said. "You're getting help from the other side."

I thought about that and guessed she was right. We had been getting help. Now, if only someone—from one side of the veil or the other—could just get through to Tom . . .

Shirley must have seen that in my expression. "Even Tom will come around," she said, answering my thought. "Just watch. You'll see. He's doing better already."

All I could croak out was, "Thanks, Shirley. Thanks for everything."

"Don't mention it," she said. "Now. Back to business."

She told me her sons, Rob Jr. and Kevin, were driving up from their homes around Modesto. She gave me the names of their children who might serve as pallbearers or honorary pallbearers and said they wouldn't need places to stay since her daughter Brenda still lived in the south end of the county and had a big place. Her children's families would all drive up together for the service on Wednesday.

"Is there anyone else we should contact?"

"I've heard from a couple of distant cousins," Shirley answered. "They're making their own housing arrangements, but they will be here for the service."

"Then we should invite them to the family prayer meeting and the lunch."

"I already have." Shirley was just a little sheepish. "I hope you don't mind."

"Not at all," I assured her. I summarized my conversations with Mary and Steve and told her their housing had been arranged. Then I said, "If we've got the people all taken care of, I think the next item on the agenda is the food. I got a couple of recipes from Mary. She and Bill will be here Tuesday. They've arranged to stay with Steve and Cathy across the river, but she says she'll be around to help."

"I got a few more recipes people could remember," Shirley said. "I'll give them to you, but I think we need to get the program for the funeral home finished first. Are we missing anything?"

"Just the hymns Emily still has to select. Well, and the names of the pallbearers. We could take the program to the funeral home and call those in later."

"Then we ought to deliver what we have," Shirley said, anticipating my plan, "though I doubt they'll be open this late on a Friday."

"I think they are," I answered, checking my watch. "It's not quite seven thirty now. When I spoke with our counselor yesterday, she said they had a viewing this evening. She told me to stop in anytime before ten. Let me get my purse, and I'll be ready to take this program over."

"I'll come with you," Shirley said.

We put ourselves together and headed back into town. It was good to have the program ready, with all the slots filled in except the hymns, and I was glad we were getting it delivered. Somehow, bit by bit, the pieces of this puzzle were all coming together.

Tom's Gourmet Popcorn

Make one style for a small family group or both for a big gathering.

Directions

1. Start with 18 C. air-popped popcorn. Divide in two.
2. Follow each of the recipes below for half of the corn.

Sesame-Sweet Popcorn

3 Tbsp. butter
1 ½ Tbsp. liquid honey
½ tsp. salt
¼ tsp. cayenne pepper

2 Tbsp. toasted sesame seeds
1 tsp. sesame oil
9 C. popped corn

Directions

1. In small saucepan over low heat, melt together butter, honey, salt, and cayenne; stir to combine well.
2. Stir in sesame seeds and oil. Drizzle over popcorn and mix well, adjusting salt to taste.

Chili-Cheddar Lime Corn

3 Tbsp. butter
1 Tbsp. chili powder
3 Tbsp. minced or grated onion
¼ tsp. salt

1 Tbsp. lime juice
9 C. popped corn
1 C. finely shredded old cheddar
   cheese

Directions

1. In small saucepan over medium-low heat, cook butter, chili powder, onion, and salt for 3 minutes; stir in lime juice.
2. Drizzle over popcorn and top with cheese; mix well.

CHAPTER 13

MELISSA BURNETT KINGSLEY

JASON AND I HAVE ONLY been married a few months, but I'm blessed that he knows me well. Since we first learned that Granny was ill and it was serious, Jason has understood that I need to spend time with my family. It isn't just the loss we've all suffered. He knows how concerned I am about both my mom and dad.

Dad's never been very open about his background. As the oldest of the kids, I can remember times when Grandma Judith's weird behavior created nearly intolerable situations for my parents. That was later, after Dad was an independent man with children of his own. I can only imagine what it must have been like when he was twelve years old and left alone to deal with her. Suffice it to say, he hasn't been very eager to talk, but I've known for years that it was Granny who held him together during that time, and I've known for years that everything would come to a head for him once Granny was gone.

The fact that her dying wish has put him in the position of confronting his demons is both good and bad. He is going to have to deal with it sometime, just as we all have to face our own demons one day, but losing his childhood support system at the same time has put enormous stress on the dad I love.

You'd hardly know it from the way he acted this evening though. He behaved as if life had never thrown him a single curveball.

"Hey, everybody!" he called as he came back into the family room from the office. He barreled into the room, a perfect storm of upbeat, happy energy, waving something over his head.

"Whaddya have there, Tom?" Jason asked. My husband was pointing at the thin, bright red box Dad was holding.

"I made a quick stop on the way home," Dad said. "I've got our favorite movie!" When he named it—a comedy our family has probably seen six times in the past year—Em cheered, Steph groaned, Jason turned his back to Dad and rolled his eyes at me, and Dad said, "Now don't everyone get too excited. We don't want to overheat the house."

That was when I noticed what was off about Dad's delivery. Everything he said was too bright, too cheery, too old-school Dad. It was as if there had been no death in the family, no loss, no sad moments of any kind. Dad was in denial, big-time.

I started to say something, but Mom and Aunt Shirley had come through the garage door just in time to hear Dad's little speech. With her intuition in full gear, Mom seemed to know exactly what I planned to say. She cut me off before I could speak.

"Great! Come on, Mel. Let's clean these boxes of photos and such off the couch so there will be room for everyone."

I decided to take my cue from her. I said, "Come on, Jason. You can help me carry things." Jason, bless him, followed me puppy-dog style from the room.

Dad pulled out the movie as we were returning. I looked at the pleading expression on Jason's face and was just about to say that I thought we should be leaving when Dad said, "I have something special to go along with the movie tonight."

When no one responded, Mom asked, "What's that, honey?"

"Gourmet popcorn!" Dad announced with a flourish.

Jason's ears pricked up. His expression brightened. "Chili-cheddar lime corn?" he asked. Then he turned to me, his statement almost an apology. "Hey, babe. You know that's my favorite."

"Chili-cheddar and sesame sweet corn—both!" Dad declared.

"Make room on the couch, Em," my husband declared. "Mel and I will claim the places next to you."

For the next twenty minutes, we set up the movie, got it ready to play, and waited anxiously while Dad popped corn, mixed spices, grated cheese, and generally played the role of entertainer, host, and specialty chef. While he worked, Mom mixed up a fresh batch of lemonade, and Em dug out some plastic bowls and paper cups so we could all enjoy our treats in front of the TV without creating any unnecessary mess.

Before long we sat in front of our "favorite" movie, laughing in all the right places while we munched on two flavors of gourmet-flavored popcorn and drowned the salty tastes in lemonade. We might have been drowning our sensibilities as well, for all they showed.

Everyone seemed to be taking their cues from Dad. From the time he got home until Jason and I made our farewells after the movie ended, no one said a word about Granny, no one used the word *funeral*, no one behaved as you'd expect from the recently bereaved. It was as if we'd all made some kind of chilling pact that for one brief evening we'd pretend our world had not been completely turned upside down.

Dad was charming and very much present, the popcorn was fantastic, and even the movie was fun—again. It might have been a lovely evening if the pleasantness hadn't felt so forced.

Coconut Rice Pudding

¼ C. butter or margarine, melted
3 eggs, beaten
3 C. milk
1 C. sugar
2 tsp. pure vanilla

¾ tsp. ground nutmeg
½ tsp. salt
2 ½ C. cooked rice
¾ C. raisins
¾ C. flaked, sweetened coconut

Directions

1. Use butter to grease the bottom and sides of a 9 x 13 baking dish. Set it aside.
2. In a large bowl, combine eggs, milk, sugar, vanilla, nutmeg, and salt. Mix thoroughly. Stir in the rice and raisins, and mix again.
3. Transfer to the prepared baking dish and bake, uncovered, at 325 for 30 minutes. Sprinkle with coconut, then bake 10–15 minutes longer or until baking thermometer reads 160°.
4. Serve warm with whipped cream or nondairy topping. Refrigerate leftovers.

Variations

Make this dish appropriate for the holidays by mixing some sweetened, dried cranberries in with the raisins. You can also add 1 Tbsp. lemon zest to the egg-milk-sugar mixture and 1 tsp. lemon zest to the coconut added during baking. For lactose intolerant guests, substitute almond milk and nondairy topping.

CHAPTER 14

Saturday, June 16, Early afternoon

EMILY BURNETT

I MUST HAVE BEEN REALLY tired when I went to sleep after the movie Friday because I slept in late on Saturday morning. It was almost seven thirty before I woke up at all. (I know most of my friends don't think seven thirty is late, but then again, they don't all get up for early morning seminary either!) When I finally did wake up, the first thing I noticed was the smell of something delicious coming up the stairs from the kitchen—like cinnamon and vanilla and coconut. I wandered down in my pj's and was surprised to find Great-Aunt Shirley taking big glass pans full of coconut-covered rice out of the oven.

"Rice pudding?" I guessed.

"Exactly," Aunt Shirley answered. "What do you think? Does it look edible?"

"It looks and smells amazing. Can we have it for breakfast?"

"That will be up to your mother, but I can't see any reason why not. We certainly have plenty."

"I'll say!" She'd made about a ton of it, given all the leftover rice we had.

"I'll go see if Mom has any other breakfast plans," I said.

Luckily she didn't, so Mom and Steph and Aunt Shirley and I all filled big bowls full of warm rice pudding, topped it with whipped cream, and stuffed ourselves full of rich, yummy, coconut goodness. It was great! Even Jason said so later, when he had some to top off his lunch. Aunt Shirley was really right about this pudding: it's about as different from the pudding I'm used to (and don't like) as lightning is from lightning bugs. I thought I could become a pudding fan after all.

When I told Aunt Shirley, I thought she'd say, "I told you so." Instead, she just winked and offered me the recipe. I got out a note card and wrote it down.

This was the day when we had planned to discuss the final program for Great-Granny's funeral. The rest of the program's slots had been filled and the program taken over to the funeral home, but I still had to come up with the opening and closing hymns. Although I'd thought about the music a lot, I hadn't made any decisions yet, and I told my mom that when she asked me about it as we were cleaning up after breakfast. "You'll need to make some choices soon, honey," she said. "The funeral home wants the full program soon so they can start printing it on Monday."

"I know. I'll come up with something good before dinnertime," I promised. I only hoped I could think of something good by then. If not, I'd just have to point my finger at the funeral list and see what I got, and I knew I'd be really disappointed in myself if that's the way things turned out.

After breakfast we picked up Melissa at her apartment, and then all the women in the family went over to Granny Adelaide's to help Ruby get the place ready for company. We changed sheets in all four bedrooms, scrubbed the three bathrooms, swept and mopped floors, and vacuumed every rug; then we kept the laundry room busy, packed with load after load of sheets and blankets, washcloths and towels, with more for Ruby to do when we left for the day. I suppose Ruby could have done it *all* herself, but it seemed like an awful lot of work even with five of us helping. I was glad we hadn't left it all for her. Besides, it was kind of fun when we were all working together.

There was one bad moment, though, when I went in to strip the sheets from Granny's bed. Ruby had changed them the previous Wednesday, so Granny had only slept on them for a couple of nights before she went to the hospital. Still, the sheets smelled like her—like the little old-fashioned sachet packets she liked to put into the drawer with her nightgowns, like the scented talcum powder she always wore on her face and body, like her skin and hair. I smelled those sheets, and I missed Granny so much it hurt—I mean, physically *hurt*, like a throbbing ache in the middle of my chest. For a little while I just sat there on the side of Granny's bed, holding those sheets to my face and breathing in her scent, using the pillow case to dry my tears. It was tough taking those sheets to the laundry, knowing they would never smell like her again. The work mostly wasn't so bad though.

I overheard Mom and Great-Aunt Shirley talking with Ruby about what she would do next, and I was pleased to hear that Ruby has plans and a place to go, so she will be able to move on. We have all been so glad that Granny had Ruby's help. In fact, Ruby has been Granny's paid helper and companion for most of my life, so she almost seems like family to me. When you add that up with the fact that these past few years haven't been a really great time to look for a job, especially if you're getting up there toward retirement age, well, let's just say I was really glad for Ruby. I hope she won't forget all about us when she moves to SoCal.

We got back to the house after one o'clock, and Jason joined us for lunch and then took Melissa home with him. I finished my lunch in a rush and asked Mel and Jason to give me a lift to my rehearsal with Ms. Nguyen and my friends from choir. It wasn't far out of their way, so they said they'd be happy to do it.

Rehearsal went great! Sydnie made it clear she was only singing in a Mormon church because of me, but I decided that, under the circumstances, that was good enough. I can't guess how to make her feel better about the Church, but having her willing to sing is a good step. It even kind of felt good that she'd make an exception because she cares about me. Someday maybe I can turn that into a chance to share the gospel.

In the meantime, the boys stayed focused (something they don't do that well or that often), and we put the madrigal together the way we wanted it to sound. Then we arranged to meet at the church for a brief run-through a little before the family prayer meeting on Wednesday. After the other kids left, Ms. Nguyen got out some solo numbers she had used for funerals in the past. That was when an interesting thing happened.

"I'm not sure I know what kind of music to pick for a Mormon funeral," she said as she pulled out a stack of sheet music. "If this were a Christian service, I'd suggest something like 'In the Garden,' but I don't know what sorts of music would be appropriate for non-Christians."

At first I thought maybe this was some kind of weird joke. I waited for the punch line, but then I looked at her face and realized she was serious.

"Um, Ms. Nguyen, this isn't a non-Christian service. We have some different beliefs from other Christian religions, but we are definitely Christians."

"Really? I heard that Mormons don't believe in Jesus Christ, that you worship a man named . . . Joseph Smith? Or something like that?"

"Oh no!" I shook myself a little, glad I'd been listening in seminary and hoping I could get this answer right. "The full name of our church is The Church of Jesus Christ of Latter-day Saints," I said, emphasizing the Savior's name. "We believe Jesus Christ is the Creator and Savior of the world. This is *His* church, not the church of Joseph Smith."

"But I heard . . . well, I guess I heard wrong," she said. "Tell me about it."

So I said a little prayer inside, asking that I could remember what I'd been taught, and then I told her some of what we believe—that Adam and Eve were taught the gospel of Jesus Christ when they were put upon the earth and they taught their children that Christ would come someday, that most of the earthly religions created over the ages were derivations of the doctrine taught to our first parents and that they all looked forward to the coming of Christ in what we called the meridian of time. I pointed out that Christ had brought His gospel to the earth during his ministry in the Old World and had sent His Apostles and disciples out to teach it to everyone, but then a Great Apostasy occurred.

"Men like Martin Luther saw what was happening to the church in their time and realized it no longer practiced all the same things that Jesus had taught. They saw a lot of corruption among men who should have been godly, and they realized too much emphasis was being placed on worldly wealth and power and not on things of the Spirit. They tried to fix it all through reform, but the only way it was really going to be fixed was through a full restoration of Christ's doctrine from the Savior Himself.

"That was why God and Jesus came to Joseph Smith, to restore the gospel of Jesus Christ the way it had been when Jesus was on the earth. We honor Joseph Smith as the prophet of the Restoration, but we don't worship him," I finished, feeling good about what I'd said. "We worship Jesus Christ and that's what makes us Christians."

"That's very interesting," Ms. Nguyen said, giving me a thoughtful look.

"If you'd like to know more, I can always have the missionaries—"

"Oh! Um, no thanks. I mean, that won't be necessary, but thanks for giving me some background I didn't have before. It's good to know what some of my Mormon students believe. So . . . have you chosen your opening and closing songs yet?"

I didn't really want to change the subject, but I realized I had said about all I could unless she wanted to know more, and it had felt good to be able to say that much and know I had it right. Since Brian left on his mission, I'd been praying for more chances to share the gospel. I might not be a full-time missionary, like he is in Brazil, and I might not yet have the faith I hope to have someday, but I still want to help.

"I haven't picked the songs yet," I told Ms. Nguyen. "I just haven't decided which hymns will be best."

"Well, why don't you tell me about your decision process?" she suggested. "Which songs did you start with and how are you narrowing them down? Maybe if I hear what you're doing, I can suggest some ideas." So we sat down together.

I told her all about what I'd done so far. "I keep looking at those songs and thinking of certain ones that I know Great-Granny liked, but I can't help remembering what she wrote to my dad, how she didn't want anything cliché. She even named a couple of hymns that are commonly sung at funerals as examples of ones she *didn't* want us to use. Unfortunately, she didn't give any examples of the kind she'd like, so I'm not getting much past that."

"Who are you going to have play them for you?"

"Uh-oh. I hadn't thought of that," I said and felt a moment's panic.

Ms. Nguyen patted my shoulder. "Don't worry, Emily. If you can choose the hymns and get me a copy, I can play those for you as well as the others. It makes sense, since I'm going to be at the piano anyway."

"There won't be much time for you to practice—" I began.

"No, but I've played piano for a lot of years. I think I can manage. Now let's choose a solo for you and give it a couple of practice runs. Then when we're done, I'll give you a lift home, and you can lend me your copy of the hymnal. We'll choose the hymns for opening and closing so I can practice them over the next few days, and then I'll give your book back to you after the service."

"Okay," I answered. "Sounds good!" We began to work our way through her stack of sheet music while I quietly wondered how that was going to make it easier for me to pick hymns. We hunted for a while, and I found all kinds of music that I've never heard before and that didn't sound much like Church music to me. Then we came across a piece that gave me warm shivers. It was a medley of "Nearer, My God, to Thee" and "I Know That My Redeemer Lives." Since the hymns are both so familiar, and I know they were two of Great-Granny's favorites, I thought it might be good, but it seemed a bit sketchy to do an arrangement by someone I didn't know anything about, who wasn't a member of our Church.

"Can you play this through for me and let me get a sense of it?" I asked.

Ms. Nguyen did, and it was beautiful. I'd never heard this arrangement before, and I thought it might be new to most of the people at the service as well. It was a sweet high-alto solo in the range where my voice shines best, and I thought it would be great as a final tribute to Granny Adelaide. "I think this will be perfect," I told Ms. Nguyen.

"Great! Let's run through it a few more times," she said and began playing the introduction.

An hour or so later we finished our rehearsal—the madrigal ready to go, the solo ready, and an understanding that Ms. Nguyen would learn to play "I Am a Child of God" in order to accompany the group of grand- and great-grandkids we hoped to get together to sing for Granny. I thought that if I only had the opening and closing hymns picked out, I'd be ready to roll. I said something like that as we got into Ms. Nguyen's car so she could drive me home.

"You say your Church is about restoration," Ms. Nguyen said thoughtfully, and I nodded, glad I had been able to make that part clear. "Did your granny have any favorite hymns that were about the Restoration?"

A warm thrill ran through me, and I realized that was exactly the clue I needed. "Yes," I said. "Yes, I think she did."

"Maybe you can choose a couple of those?" Ms. Nguyen prompted.

By then I was grinning all over. "Yeah, I think I can. Thanks, Ms. Nguyen."

"No problem," she said and gave me another encouraging smile.

When we got to my house, I invited her to come inside while I found my hymnal. I introduced her to Mom and Steph and Great-Aunt Shirley, and then I left her in the kitchen with them for a minute while I ran upstairs to get our hymn book. I could hear them asking about her work at the high school and how she was enjoying teaching music in our district; I could hear her telling them how much she had enjoyed working with me and my friends in choir. I even heard her tell my mom, "Call me Wendy, please," which I thought was funny since I'd never even thought about Ms. Nguyen having a first name, and if I had, I never would have thought of Wendy.

Mom was just telling her how much our family appreciates her helping with the music at Great-Granny's service when I found the book and made note of a couple of page numbers. I came down the stairs and handed the hymnal to my teacher.

"I put a sticky note on the front page," I told her. It shows you the numbers for the opening and closing hymns and for the one you'll be playing for the children."

"Excellent. Thanks, Emily," Ms. Nguyen said and started saying her good-byes.

"No, thank *you*," I said at the same time both Mom and Steph said it, and we all laughed.

"Really," I said. "You're the one who is doing us a favor. Thanks so much."

"Happy to help," she answered. "I love music, and I enjoy seeing it help good people. I'll see you all Wednesday morning."

"Right. See you!" I said as I closed the door behind her.

"Well?" my mother said as I turned around.

"Well what?"

"Ah, come on, Em," Steph said. "You know we've been waiting to hear which songs you picked."

"Oh *that*!" I said, and then I grinned at them. "I think Granny will like them: 'The Spirit of God' for the opening and 'Come, Come Ye Saints' for the closing."

There was a long pause.

"Well, they aren't the cliché funeral hymns that Granny asked us not to choose," Mom said. "What made you decide on those two?"

"It was Ms. Nguyen who suggested it," I answered, and then I told them about my brief missionary encounter and how Ms. Nguyen had seemed to accept that we believe in the restoration of Christ's Church. "That's when she said maybe Granny would appreciate our using some of the hymns of the Restoration," I explained, "so I picked two of Granny's favorites."

"I think those are excellent choices," Mom said.

Steph's eyes glittered, and for a moment I thought she was going to say something mean or teasing about the hymns I'd picked. Instead she said, "Great choices, Em. I think Granny will be happy."

"Thanks, Steph," I answered, and I felt a warm glow. Even though I was still feeling really sad about Granny, just knowing we wouldn't see her anymore, I was thinking that, overall, this had been a pretty great day.

Emily's Zippy Zucchini Pie

4 eggs
¼ C. canola oil
½ tsp. salt
½ tsp. black pepper
4 C. shredded zucchini

¼ C. chopped, seeded jalapeño pepper
¼ C. finely chopped onion
½ C. shredded cheddar/jack or pepper jack cheese
1 deep-dish unbaked pie shell

Directions

1. In a small bowl, beat the eggs, oil, salt, and pepper.
2. Add the zucchini, jalapeño, and onion; stir to coat.
3. Stir in cheese.
4. Pour into pie shell.
5. Bake at 375 for 18–20 minutes or until toothpick comes out clean.
6. Let stand for 10 minutes before cutting and serving.

Serves eight.

Variations

For a less zippy pie, eliminate the jalapeño and add 2 tsp. dill weed. You can also use a mix of squashes including zucchini, yellow crookneck, or any other summer squash varieties. Replace chopped onion with green onions, leeks, or scallions. Try different flavors of cheese. This is an excellent way to get non–vegetable lovers to enjoy the season's freshest produce.

CHAPTER 15

Friday, June 15, Late afternoon

KAREN BURNETT

EMILY CAME IN BUZZING WITH excitement, so pleased about her rehearsal and about the conversation she'd had with her choir teacher, the Ms. Nguyen she admires so greatly. We were all pleased to meet Ms. Nguyen, and I found her an attractive, pleasant young woman. It was also a great relief to have the hymns chosen for Granny's service. I called the hymns in to our bereavement specialist at the funeral home. Then I arranged for Steph and Emily to put in the frozen lasagna Tom had brought home and asked Em if she'd make one of her favorite zucchini pies to go with it. They both seemed happy to help. That's when I turned to Aunt Shirley.

"Buster looks like he could use a walk," I said. "Aunt Shirley, would you like to come with us?"

Melissa gave me a quick look and ushered Jason into the family room. It's tough to get much past that particular daughter.

"Sounds great," Shirley answered.

From the family room, Melissa called, "You two take your time. I'll help the girls with dinner if you're slow getting home."

"Thanks, Mel," I called back, grateful for both her willingness and her insight.

Shirley spent a couple of minutes tying her high-top sneakers, but she was soon ready.

Emily asked, "Do you have any zucchini already picked or shall I get some from the garden?"

"I think you'll need to check the garden," I answered, "but there were some small ones a couple of days ago that should be ready by now."

"Good. I'll get those," Em said.

I turned to Shirley. "Emily's been working on building a catalog of her own recipes," I explained. "It's one of her Personal Progress projects for Young Women."

"That sounds great!" Aunt Shirley said, and Emily warmed to her praise.

I suggested to Emily, "You can work on it while we're gone. We'll toss a salad and help put dinner on when we get back."

"Sounds good," Emily said.

Shirley and I left Emily puttering in the kitchen as we walked away from the house with Buster trotting happily ahead of us on leash.

"As you were saying . . ." I prompted as we rounded the first corner.

"I think we covered the essence of it," Shirley said. "Judith had symptoms that manifested as serious psychological illnesses. They became worse with each pregnancy, and yet because she planned to have a large family, she refused to allow the doctors to treat her." She paused as though that told the whole story.

"When did Rocio come into the picture?"

"When Carrie was a baby, around the time that Judith became pregnant with Mikey or a little after." Shirley turned at the corner, apparently assuming I had intended to. I hadn't planned to turn there—it wasn't the usual route I took with Buster—but I decided it wouldn't hurt us to try something different. I slid around the corner and caught up with Shirley as she continued her story.

"The way I heard it, Tom Sr. came home from the college around dinnertime one day to find Carrie in the front yard playing in a mud puddle all by herself wearing nothing but a soggy diaper. She wasn't even a year and a half old. It was so cold, there was ice at the edge of the puddle, and it was obvious she hadn't been changed in several hours, maybe not all day."

I shivered just thinking about it. "Where was Judith?"

"Inside, asleep in her bed, still wearing the pajamas she'd had on when he left for work that morning. Tom Jr. had gone to Cub Scouts with a neighbor who picked him up at school. There was no dinner started, and the kids didn't seem to know where their mother was." Shirley sat heavily on the bus stop bench. I sat beside her. "Mary and Steve were playing in the basement. The kids in the basement had knocked over a table lamp.

There was broken glass and blood on the floor, along with a pile of papers from plastic bandages Mary had used to try to bind up some minor cuts on Steven's hands. I guess Tom must have been terrified to think of what might have happened to their babies."

"I can imagine," I said, sitting next to her. Why hadn't my husband ever told me these stories? "My Tom must have been about ten then, right?"

Shirley considered that. "Yes, about ten, I think. Mary couldn't have been older than seven, and Steve was probably about four."

"That must have been tough for everyone."

"I would guess so." Shirley sighed and stood. We began walking again. "Tom cleaned up the messes and the kids and loaded them all in the car. He picked up Tommy at the church and took all the kids out for pizza. By the time he got home, Judith was up and frantic. She railed at him for leaving without saying anything and went on and on about how frightened she had been for their children when she woke up and found them gone. She seemed to think it was still early morning. Tom realized then just how serious their situation had become."

I shuddered. It had always been easy to accept my Tom's account of his father's betrayal. Tom Sr. had been the villain, Judith and her children the victims, and the story had been simple. I was seeing a different side of it now, and I couldn't help thinking . . .

"Why didn't Tom—my husband, I mean—ever tell me this side of it?"

"I've wondered that over the years." Shirley turned another corner I hadn't expected her to turn, and I followed. "I think maybe he didn't ever see it."

"What? How—"

"What I mean is, that first awful night that I just told you about? A neighbor had picked him up at school and taken him to Cub Scouts at the church. His father met him there and took him to dinner with his family. When he got home, his mom was up and dressed; there wasn't any mess, and all Tom Jr. heard was an awful fight between his parents. He knew his dad had taken all the kids out to eat but had left his mother home. It was probably easy to see her side of it."

"I guess, but that couldn't have been the only time."

"No, but Tom—the older Tom, my brother—got pretty good at compensating." Shirley turned again, and I realized we had walked to the gate of the cemetery. She gave me a meaningful look, and we turned in, Buster leading the way.

"He found a neighbor who agreed to watch Carrie during the day when he was at the college, and the older kids went to her house when they got home in the afternoons. Then around five thirty or so, the neighbor would take them back to their house along with a dinner she had prepared for them. Tom Sr. would come home to find dinner ready and the kids well cared for, neat and clean, with their homework all finished. By then Judith was usually up and put together too. Maybe that's all Tom Jr. ever saw. I'm not sure how long that went on, but I don't think it was more than three or four months. Then one day when Tom Sr. was at work—"

"He taught chemistry, right?" I interrupted. "At the college?"

"Right. My brother Tom was a chemistry professor. Anyway, he was at the school one afternoon, chatting with some of his graduate students, when his office phone rang. It was his neighbor telling him that her husband had taken a job out of state and her family would be moving. He knew then that he would have to make other arrangements for his kids. One of the grad students read between the lines and guessed he would need a new babysitter-housekeeper. She came to him later and told him her roommate was leaving and she was going to need to make new housing arrangements. She wondered if maybe the two of them couldn't help each other out."

"Rocio," I said. "That's when she came to live with them."

"Rocio Maria Consuelo Hernandez. Her name, Rocio, means Dew."

"Dew," I repeated. It seemed such a gentle, lovely name for "The Other Woman." "So she was a grad student in chemistry?"

"She had finished all of her coursework and most of the research for her thesis. All she had left to do was the writing. That made it easy for her to watch Carrie during the day, work on her thesis while Carrie was sleeping or playing quietly, do some necessary housework and such, and then table her work for another day while she helped the older kids with their homework and got their dinner ready."

"And where was Judith in all this?"

"Sleeping a lot. Watching soap operas upstairs in her bedroom. Making scrapbooks in her basement hobby room. Working on her calligraphy. She seemed to get further and further removed from the family as the days went on. I was visiting frequently then, partly because Mother was so worried about Tom and his family. I came to visit them often, and I have to say things didn't look good for the future of that family even before Mikey was born."

"I had no idea."

"I don't suppose your Tom had much of an idea either. He was only twelve when his father left."

I sighed. "He has told me what that was like for him—coming home from school one day to find the house half empty, his dad and Rocio gone, Carrie and Mikey gone, Mary and Steve hiding in the basement, the kitchen cold, his mother frantic and screaming . . ." I cut off the image. "That afternoon was probably the defining moment of his childhood."

"It must have been awful for everyone," Shirley said, "especially for her." She pointed and I followed her gesture. It shouldn't have surprised me that we were standing in front of Judith's grave.

"For her and for her twelve-year-old son," I said. "For Mary and Steve, who'd lost their baby sister and brother, for all of them."

"Yes, for all of them." Shirley stood before Judith's grave, her hands folded in front of her, her head slightly bowed. She closed her eyes as if in prayer. Buster looked at me and whined. I pulled him closer and patted his head. Then I turned to read Judith's gravestone, the red marble one I had helped my husband pick:

Judith Grace Willis Burnett
Beloved Mother
6 October 1943–18 April 2007

Shirley looked up. "Shall we start for home?"

I turned Buster back the way we had come. Shirley and I began the return walk. After a moment I broke the silence, "She was broken by that. Judith, I mean. She was never the same again after Tom and Rocio and her little ones left."

"If you ask me, she was broken long before that happened." There was a bitter edge to Shirley's voice that I couldn't remember hearing before. "That was before we moved to the Bay Area, so Rob and I were still in the county, and I saw a lot of what was happening. Some days Judith was the sweetest, most gentle woman you could ever picture. Others she was a shrieking fishwife, cursing and throwing things and making unreasonable demands . . ."

Shirley let the sentence trail off in a sigh. "Mary and Steve even created a little code between them. Mary always got home a few minutes before Steve did. If she went into the house and found Nice Mama, she'd get out her homework and sit at the kitchen table. Then Steve would come home and join her. If she came in to find Mean Mama, she'd wait on the front porch for Steven. Then the two of them would go down to the basement together to get their homework done."

"But that was after Tom and Rocio left, right? After Judith really lost it."

Shirley shook her head. "It started well before then. I know because Rocio was in on it. If she saw the kids head down the stairs with their books and such, she'd run interference for them, letting Judith vent at her instead of taking it out on the kids."

"Really!" Certainly none of this fit the few stories I had heard of that time.

"Saw it myself," Shirley answered. "Judith could be pretty scary in those days."

I felt frustration building. "So why didn't Tom see this? My Tom, I mean. He was only twelve when they left, I know, but you'd think that if even Mary and Steve had a code for Nice Mama and Mean Mama, Tom would have seen it too."

"Don't underestimate Oedipus." Shirley's tone was wry. "By then Tom Jr. was already his mother's primary protector and defender. He had learned all kinds of coping skills for keeping Mama happy, and when she was unhappy, it was never her fault. Someone had done something wrong. To him, her anger was always justified."

"I see," I said, and certainly, I was beginning to. One of the therapists we had seen with Tom's mother over the decades had used a stock phrase that came up often during family sessions. He liked to remind us that where there is an emotionally ill person, there is almost always an emotionally ill family: "One person gets sick and the others all develop ways of coping and compensating," he said. "It can make for a whole load of psychological illness."

"I see," I said again, seeing more clearly already. Buster barked at a cat across the street. It bristled and ran, and I pulled Buster in next to me. "Tom's never gotten over any of this, you know."

"Oh, I know!" Shirley paused at the bus stop again. Once again, I sat beside her. "It was one of my mother's great sorrows. She always hoped Tom would open his eyes, that he would just look and see things the way the rest of us saw them."

"She wanted him to turn his anger in the right direction?" I said, pondering.

"If you mean she wanted him to be angry with Judith, then no. I don't think so."

I gave her a quizzical look.

"Mother wasn't angry with Judith—oh, maybe a little, maybe about her refusing to take the medicines that the doctors said could help her stay on an even keel—but overall, no. She wasn't angry, and she didn't want Tommy to be angry."

Shirley stood, and we began walking again. "Mother always recognized that Judith was ill, that—except for that business about the medicine—her illness was out of her control and she didn't want to be that way. I think she just hoped that Tommy would see that his mother *was* ill, that the illness and the refusal to treat it preceded Rocio's arrival and eventually led to everything else that happened."

"I know what you mean. Tom has always told me that his mother's illness began with her broken heart after her husband and her babies left her, after they all ran away with the scarlet woman who poisoned his father's mind and led to his disaffection."

"Rocio was never that way, you know." Shirley's assertion was calm. "The poisoning scarlet woman, I mean. I don't think there was anything other than professional respect between Tom Sr. and Rocio for most of the time they all lived together. The rest seemed to develop . . . later."

I pondered that. It wasn't really my business, but . . . "How much later, do you think?"

"It's hard to say. Rocio moved in a while before Mikey was born, and she probably finished her thesis sometime during that next year and was awarded her degree. Then there was a year or so when everything just sort of seemed to go on hold with everyone going about the patterns they had recently established. Judith even took her medications for a while, and everything started looking up for the family. I think Tom hoped that he and Judith would be able to get over the bad bump they'd encountered and move toward a happier future. Anyway, it still seemed that he was investing in his marriage back then."

"Around that same time, Rocio started going to professional conferences, interviewing for jobs of one sort and another, apparently preparing to leave. What no one in the extended family realized was that somewhere during those weeks, Judith had stopped medicating. Things were getting rough at home again."

"Let me guess," I interrupted. "Tom told Judith she needed to get back on the medication, and she said no, that she wanted to have another baby."

"You've got it," Shirley answered. "Tom said no, absolutely not, that another pregnancy was out of the question, and when she refused to hear him, he must have started interviewing too. That's about the same time he moved a sleeper sofa into the basement and started sleeping down there." She gave me a meaningful look.

"He wanted to make sure there wouldn't be another pregnancy," I concluded.

"That's the way it seems," she answered. "Anyway, much to our surprise, he and Rocio were both interviewing by then. Then, when Rocio was offered a job with a company in Waco, Texas, and Tom found a teaching position at Baylor, they both accepted and started making their plans. It only appeared to the family like a fast break when they left later, but Tom must have signed his teaching contract at least two or three months before that. No one seems to know when Tom and Rocio's, um, *personal* relationship changed." Bless Aunt Shirley, she actually blushed.

"I don't suppose they were broadcasting that," I said. "At the same time, if they were living under the same roof, and Tom had stopped sleeping with his wife—" I had no trouble piecing that scene together.

"As I said, no one knows. All we can say for certain is, once Tom's divorce from Judith was final, he and Rocio were married in Texas and started a family of their own."

"Three more, right? Christina, Amanda, and . . ."

"Marco."

"Marco," I repeated. "That's right. I couldn't remember the boy's name."

"He isn't a boy anymore," Shirley said.

"I guess that's true. He must be about thirty now, right?"

"Mother and I were just looking at family group sheets last month. He'll be thirty-one this year."

"Thirty-one. Wow. It's funny, thinking about all these people who are my close relatives that I've never seen. You know some of them are coming, right?"

"I know Carrie is coming."

"Christina and Amanda are coming too, as well as all their children. Some of hers too."

"That's good. Very good. It will be great to see them, but do you have room?"

"I've spoken with Ruby. She says we can put them up in your mother's house."

"Oh, of course. That will be fine," Shirley answered. "You know, Ruby has agreed to stay a month to help me get Mother's house ready to put on the market. She has a son in Southern California who has invited her to live with his family. He manages a convalescent home, and he thinks he will have paid work for her there, so it looks like she'll be okay."

"I'm glad. She has certainly meant a great deal to Granny these past years, and I think it's been good for Ruby too."

"Yes, I know it has. Mother needed the help and the companionship. Ruby has been a good friend to her." Shirley straightened. "In the meantime, it will be good to see some of Mother's 'Texas family' again."

"Again? I mean, I know Granny Adelaide stayed in touch—"

"Many of us did. Mother went out two or three times a year, and after I lost Bob, I went with her sometimes. Even if there hadn't been occasional visits with her, I saw them all at Tom Sr.'s funeral."

"Ah yes, that funeral. I tried to talk Tom into going out for that. I thought it would be a good way to give some closure to . . . to everything."

"It would have been," Shirley agreed. "We were all disappointed when he refused, but his brothers took it harder than anyone. From their point of view, their oldest brother should have been the one to try to bridge the gap and put the family together—and he should have done it long before their father's death."

I nodded. "I always thought so too, but you know Tom wasn't hearing it from any of us. He always blamed his father for everything that happened—everything: his mother's illness, even her cancer and early death. When his father died of a heart attack some three years later, Tom took it as some kind of divine retribution, a punishment well deserved and a little late in coming. I always thought Tom would be happier if he made some peace with his father and let it all go. I think maybe that's what Adelaide had in mind when she requested this family reunion-style luncheon, a chance for the two halves of the family to meet face-to-face, maybe put the past behind them."

"I think so too; only she knew better than to assign the task to Tommy. She asked you instead because she knew that's how it would get done."

I sighed. "Are we all so predictable?"

"I think to Mother we were. She knew us all very well."

"Yes. She did."

Without consulting each another, we had both stopped walking. We had turned the last corner and could see the house just up the block. Shirley turned to me. "Is there anything else we should cover before we finish our, um, walk?"

I considered that. "One thing," I answered, remembering.

"And that is?"

"Rocio is coming to the funeral."

Shirley sagged. "Oh."

"Oh, indeed. I haven't told Tom yet, but I doubt he'll take it well."

She pursed her lips, her voice flat. "I think we can safely predict a negative response."

I smirked. "Exactly."

Shirley straightened her spine and let out a long sigh. "Well, my dear, there's nothing to be done about it now. Tom has to face his demons someday, and Rocio has to face hers too. My best suggestion is that the two of us do our best to stay out of the way when it happens and then pray for a peaceful outcome."

"I'm with you on that one, Shirley." I patted her shoulder, and she pulled me into a quick hug.

"It's going to be okay," she said as we parted. "I'm not sure how, but it's going to be okay."

"Well," I answered. "It's going to *be,* whether it's okay or not. We'll give it our best shot and pray that it ends without bloodshed."

"I'm with you on that one," Shirley answered with a sigh.

Together we led a tired Buster toward home.

Lentil Salad

2 C. cooked lentils
1 Tbsp. red wine vinegar
1 tsp. salt
½–1 tsp. ground black pepper

3 Tbsp. extra virgin olive oil
¼ C. thinly sliced green onions or
  scallions
3 Tbsp. chopped parsley

Directions

1. Sort and rinse 1 C. lentils. Place them in a saucepan with 2 C. water and 1 tsp. salt. Bring to boil; reduce heat. Cook until tender, about 30 minutes. Drain, reserving ½ C. cooking liquid.
2. Transfer lentils to a large bowl and toss them in vinegar with salt and pepper. Let sit for 5 minutes. Add more vinegar, if needed, to taste.
3. Add olive oil, green onions, and parsley. Toss together. If mixture seems dry, add some of the cooking liquid back in.
4. Chill. Serve cold.

Variations

1. Add ½ C. diced cucumber, or toss in a handful of halved cherry tomatoes. Substitute cilantro for parsley. Consider adding ½ tsp. ground cumin. You can also toss in 1–2 Tbsp. sesame seeds. For a blow-out event, take ¼ C. each diced red and green pepper, grated carrot, and minced celery, and cook until tender (5–7 minutes) in 2 Tbsp. olive oil. Toss these into the finished salad.
2. For a simpler salad, cook lentils, add green onions and parsley, and toss in ½ C. tomato salsa. Add salt and pepper to taste.

CHAPTER 16

Saturday, June 16, Evening

STEPHANIE BURNETT

SATURDAY IS USUALLY MY NIGHT to cook, and Dad had made it much easier by bringing home a frozen casserole. Emily had her zucchini pie prepared and baking with the lasagna when I decided to start a lentil salad. The lentils were cooked and cooling and the other ingredients were ready to add to the salad by the time my dad finally walked in. He didn't usually work on Saturday and hadn't worked any weekends in my recent memory. But except for the little staged scene the night before with the movie and the gourmet popcorn, we'd hardly seen Dad since Granny's death, and his absence was becoming obvious. I wondered if I maybe should say something.

He didn't give me much of an opportunity, just said, "Hi, Steph," and burned through the kitchen on his way to the office, where he shut the door behind him. My mom, who was just a few feet behind me setting the table, watched him pass. Then she took off her apron, set her jaw, and went after him. From the look on her face, I decided it was just as well I hadn't said a thing.

Mom and Dad have always been pretty good at keeping us kids out of their problems. Not that we didn't know when they were unhappy. Tempers flare easily in the Burnett family, and it can be tough to miss it when the flaring starts, but usually they work out their disagreements in private, choosing not to air their problems in front of us.

I guess maybe they thought the closed office door meant they were in private, but it didn't take any eavesdropping to hear everything that went on. Unless I had chosen to leave the dinner half cooked and shut myself in my room upstairs, I could hardly have avoided the distress and raised voices that came next.

It started when Mom opened the door and Dad said, "Oh, hi, Karen. I'm just picking up a few things I'm going to need. I have to go back to the office tonight."

I heard Mom's voice drop a register as she said, "Tom, it's Saturday. You hardly ever work Saturdays and never in the evenings."

"Well, I have to work tonight. It's an unusual situation—"

"It certainly is. It's the night we planned to review the program for your grandmother's funeral, the night we were going to go through her old files to find pictures of her, the night—"

"Don't start this, Karen. I have to work."

"No, you don't! You're *choosing* to work, and I, for one, have had about enough of it."

Dad's voice went up the register Mom's had dropped. "How dare—? What do you know about my work schedule?"

"I know you, Tom, and I know avoidance and denial when I see them."

"Oh, so now you're a psychologist," Dad snarled.

"It doesn't take a psychologist to see what's happening here. You've hardly spent an hour awake in this house since Granny Adelaide died. I'm not the only one who has noticed it either." Boy, could I ever second that!

"I was here all last evening. I brought home a movie, I made popcorn—"

"Yes, you did, and you made a point of pretending everything was just fine. It won't work, Tom. You're going to have to confront the reality—"

"Karen, stop."

"No, Tom. *You* stop. You're being unfair—to the girls, to me, to Granny, but especially to yourself. Granny's death has affected you more than you want to admit." Mom's voice softened. "I know it and you know it too. You need to mourn, and this family needs to mourn with you. *With you*, Tom. Not by ourselves while you come up with excuses to stay at the office, pretending nothing has happened."

"You don't know anything about it!"

"I know a lot more than you think I do."

"You don't understand, Karen!" Then he said it again, more quietly. "You really don't understand."

Mom's voice gentled, and I pictured her touching him. "I understand this is hard for you, honey, maybe harder than anything you've ever done in your adult life. I also understand that if you don't mourn now, with the rest of us, the grief and pain will sneak up on you when you least expect them to, and they'll overcome you, Tom, just like they finally overcame your moth—"

"You leave my mother out of this!" Dad's voice almost echoed, it was so loud.

There was a long moment of shocked silence, then my mother's quiet statement, "Your mother is at the heart of this, and you well know it. You've never really come to terms with her illness or her death, or with your father's . . . troubles."

"Troubles? Is that what they're calling it nowadays? The word is *adultery*, Karen. Basic, ugly adultery. He left his family and ran away with the babysitter—"

"And you have never dealt with it."

There was a loud sound like something heavy hitting the floor and then the slam of a desk drawer. "Well, I certainly don't need to have my wife playing amateur shrink on me in my own home," Dad said. "I'm going back to the office." The office door started to open.

It abruptly closed again. "No, you're not," Mom said. I was surprised how calm her voice sounded.

"What do you mean, I'm not? Karen, get out of my way."

"No, Tom. I'm not moving until you hear me."

There were more sounds, like things shifting around, and then I heard the creak as my dad sat in his desk chair. Mom's voice was deceptively, frighteningly calm as she started to speak. "When you first applied for this job, part of what attracted you was the fact that you wouldn't have to work on Sundays anymore and only rarely on Saturdays. We prayed together, and you promised the Lord that if you were able to get this position, you would faithfully attend your church meetings every Sunday and have home evening with your family every Monday night, that on Saturdays you'd do home projects or activities with the rest of the family. You worked today, but there's nothing at the office that can't wait for you to get back to it; you *do not* have to go in this evening."

"Karen—"

"I'm not finished!"

Dad grew silent and Mom went on. "You've kept that promise for more than ten years, and I'm holding you to it now. *I'm holding you to it,* Tom. You promised, and you're going to keep that promise. You're going to stay home with the family this evening, and you're going to help us work out the final details for Granny's funeral."

There was a longer pause and the sound of more things being moved around. Dad's voice was quieter, almost quiet enough to miss when he finally said, "Okay. I guess this work can be put off until Monday, but I will have to get in early. You're right, though. I did make a promise."

"Yes. Yes, you did." There were more quiet creaking noises, and I could almost see them holding each other.

"So we need to start locating pictures tonight, hm?"

"That's right, and I'm hoping you have the list of pallbearers and honorary pallbearers all put together."

"I have most of it."

"That's good," Mom said. "We can take it from there." Things were quiet again for a moment, and I caught myself smiling. One of the good things about the way tempers flare around our house is the making up afterward. "Now," Mom said after a minute. "Let's go help Steph and Emily get dinner on the table."

"I do have a few calls I have to make for the high priests group," Dad said.

Mom's voice was sweet. "Can you make them after dinner, honey?"

There was a pause, and then Dad said, "Sure. Yeah, sure," and the office door opened. "Do I smell zucchini pie?" Dad asked.

"Yep," I said. "Lentil salad too."

"Sounds great." The door opened, and Mom and Dad came out together to finish setting the table.

* * *

Dinner and cleanup went smoothly—for the most part. If I hadn't overheard that earlier conversation, I might not even have been aware of the constant undercurrent of tension between my parents; although there were a few moments when it practically bubbled out of my dad.

For example, when we were reviewing the line items for the program and Emily shared the hymns she had chosen. Before anyone could respond, Dad snapped, "Why those?" Emily gave her explanation—a good one, I thought—including a mention of Granny's request to avoid the cliché good-bye hymns commonly used at funerals and concluding with the discussion about the gospel and Ms. Nguyen's suggestion to choose hymns of the Restoration.

Dad fairly sneered. "Well, if Ms. *Nguyen* says it, then that's what we'll do."

Emily gasped. She looked as if Dad had struck her—a shocked expression on her face, sudden tears glistening in her eyes. We're all a little tired of hearing Emily's hero worship of her choir instructor, but still . . .

Mom said, "Tom?"

Dad cleared his throat and looked away. "Yeah, yeah, those hymns will be okay, I guess."

Emily excused herself to use the restroom and didn't come back for several minutes. When she did, Dad mumbled a generic apology that she accepted a bit too quickly.

That was the worst of it. Except for that, most of the evening was peaceful and fairly productive in terms of getting the rest of the program organized. The only other touchy moment came when Mom asked Dad for the list of pallbearers, which he quickly produced. He had listed himself, Uncle Steve, Aunt Mary's husband Bill, and Great-Aunt Shirley's two sons, Bruce and Roger.

"That's only five," Mom observed.

"Yes, well . . ."

"Come on, Tom. You can do better than this. You know you'll need at least six, and eight would be better. Maybe we can move some from your list of honorary pallbearers. If you can let us see that?"

Dad looked embarrassed. "Um . . ."

"You don't have a second list?"

"I don't know who is coming!"

I saw Mom set her jaw again and wondered what would come next. Her reply was deceptively sweet. "And why don't you know?"

Dad drummed his fingers on the table. "Well, you were the one who was keeping in touch with everyone."

Again the sweetness: "And why is that?"

"Ah, come on, Karen!"

The sweetness became almost cloying. "Need I remind you that these people are *your* relatives?"

Dad's voice mirrored my mother's. "Well then. You let me know which of *my relatives* will be coming to this shindig, and I'll see they get put on the list."

A twenty-second stare-down followed, everyone else trying to be inconspicuous while Mom's will clashed with Dad's in the middle of the room. Mom broke the silence: "Tom, may I see you in the office?" They both rose stiffly and stalked into the office where one or the other of them slammed the door closed.

This time I tried to eavesdrop, but we were farther away—sitting at the dining room table instead of working in the kitchen—and they were apparently making a greater effort at keeping their voices down, possibly because this time the whole family was there, including Emily and me, Aunt Shirley, Melissa and Jason. I did catch a few words or phrases, but I couldn't hear much. From what little I gathered, they were negotiating.

I heard Dad say, "Wednesday morning. That's all."

Then Mom said, "Unacceptable."

I heard Dad's protest but wasn't sure just what he was protesting, and I heard the calm tone of Mom's voice again, although I couldn't hear the words. About then Aunt Shirley asked if anyone would like some lemonade and went to mix up a batch. I wondered whether she was trying to distract us or just hoping to hear better from the kitchen.

When I could hear again, Mom was speaking somewhat louder, her tone determined. "We have a deal, then," I heard her say. "You will take off Tuesday through Thursday *to spend with the family*, and I will call the other relatives to complete the list of pallbearers."

"Does this deal have to include Thursday?" Dad said, his voice whiny.

"Thursday is necessary," Mom said. Then her voice softened. "I know it's your birthday, Tom. We'll try to make it nice."

"Okay," Dad said, though I could tell he was pouting. Then they opened the office door and came back to the table, again acting as if nothing unusual had happened. I wondered how much of this we were going to have to go through before this awful week finally came to a blessed end.

*   *   *

One more interesting thing happened during the evening. This one came from outside the family and looked back at the sketchier parts of my recent past. It started when three young women knocked on our family's door, and I was the one who answered.

"Hi, Steph," Allie said as I opened the door. "I hope we're not intruding?" She looked fine; she looked well. It was clear that the other two had let her speak on purpose to reassure me she was okay and no longer holding our little incident against me.

"No, no. You're not intruding at all. It's great to see you guys! Come in, come in."

"Actually, we've gotta run," Allie said. "We just came by to see if you're doing okay . . ."

"Yeah. I'm sad, but I'll be all right," I reassured them. I stepped out onto the porch to hug each one in turn and each returned my hug with a tight squeeze. It felt like redemption when they hugged me that way. Of course, in the process of hugging them all, I almost tripped over the big box they had sitting near their feet. "So, what's this?"

"Well, we heard about your great-grandmother—" Megan began.

"We're all so sorry, Steph," Jessica added. "We know how much Granny Adelaide meant to you."

"Thanks," I said, "but she was a century old. No matter how we wanted to, we couldn't keep her here forever."

"No, I guess not," Jessica said, "but still—"

"We wanted to help," Allie continued, "especially since we won't be able to be here for the funeral. We're all going to take some summer time away from classes to go visit our own families."

"Yeah," Megan added. "We'd have left already if Jessica's car hadn't had a meltdown a couple of days ago."

"I hope it's going to be okay?"

"Yeah, looks like it," Jessica said. "I got it out of the car hospital this morning, and it's running okay, so we'll be going first thing tomorrow."

"But we know you'll be having the funeral this week and a lot of people coming from out of the area . . ." Megan said.

She turned to Allie, who pushed the heavy box forward. "Here," Allie said. "We took up a collection in the singles ward. Lots of people wanted to help."

"We hope this will be useful," Jessica added.

"What is it?" I asked.

That's when Megan picked up another box that had been sitting behind her, tucked into Mom's gardenia bush. "It's all inside these two boxes," she said. "Let us help you move them inside, and then you and your family can look at them whenever you have a minute."

"Sure," I said. "Thanks, you guys. You know you didn't have to do any of this."

"We know," Jessica said, giving me a quick hug. "We also know you'd have done it for us."

"We love you, sis," Megan said and leaned forward to hug me too.

"We love you *lots*!" Allie added with her hug. "And we want you to know that, well, that we want you to be okay . . . and to have a good life."

By this time, the tears had started—for all of us. "Thanks," I said again. "Thanks so much."

"You're welcome," Jess said and hugged me again. Then they were gone, the three of them waving as they half ran down the path to Jess's car.

"I love you guys!" I called after them.

"We love you too," Jess and Allie both called back, almost in unison.

"Me too!" Megan shouted as she hopped into the car. I stood there, waving like a crazy woman—which is not a bad comparison, now that I think of it—wiping tears and watching as they disappeared from sight.

"What's this?" Dad asked a minute later, joining me in the entry as I closed the front door.

"Jess and Allie and Megan came by," I answered, still sniffling. "They brought some things they thought we could use this week."

"What's in the boxes?"

"I don't know, Dad. I haven't seen them yet."

"Then let's take them into the dining room, and we can all see," Dad said. He picked up the larger, heavier box, and I hefted the smaller one, which was light enough for me to carry, even though I was grateful when I got to the dining table and was able to set it down.

We opened the larger box first. It contained six two-liter bottles of lemon-lime soda, six tall cans of pineapple juice, and some powdered drink mix, the ingredients for a favorite punch the girls and I had often made for birthday dinners or other special occasions or for Relief Society events in the singles ward. It also had enough tall plastic drinking cups to serve one hundred fifty people.

"Wow!" Em said. "That's really cool, Steph!"

"Yes, it is," my mom added. "That was very thoughtful of your friends."

"What's in the second box?" Aunt Shirley asked.

Dad opened it. "Oh-h-h-h," he said, drawing it out with a tone of true appreciation. He began lifting items from the box.

My friends and former roomies had done themselves proud. They had purchased heavy paper plates—the really quality kind that look like good china—small salad plates, a second set of small plates (some for salad and some for dessert, maybe?) and matching small bowls. It was a full set of disposable "china." Enough for eighty people. They had also included big boxes full of good quality plastic utensils—the kind that look like silverware—as well as big packages of large, linen-look table napkins.

"This is so thoughtful," Mom repeated. "We have all the paper goods, utensils, and punch ingredients for the family funeral lunch."

"Probably double what we'll really need," Aunt Shirley said, thoughtfully eyeing the stacks on our dining table.

"Many people will be a long way from home," Mom said. "I expect we'll need to feed people for more than one meal." She paused, handling and counting the paper goods the girls had brought. "This is wonderful, so thoughtful."

"I have good friends," I said, smiling through tears. I found the girls' effort so touching. It meant so much more than anyone, even my parents, knew. This gift, together with the hugs, had been an act of forgiveness. My roommates were telling me that their proffered love was real, without conditions. One other thing stuck out to me: although my old roommates had made the biggest effort, they weren't the only ones who had helped. The items in these boxes represented a substantial investment of cash as well as time and care. Many people in the singles ward must have contributed to make this possible.

"Yes," my mother said. "Yes, you do have excellent, Christlike friends." She put her arm around me, and I noticed she too was getting a little teary.

"I'll send them a thank-you note next week, after things have settled down."

"Thank you," Mom said. She pulled me close, and I had a momentary impression that I should talk to her, tell her about my roommates and why I had moved home. Before I found myself foolishly blurting out more than I wanted to say, I cut the thought off and stuffed it away to consider carefully at some later date.

"Well, we've finished reviewing the program," Aunt Shirley said. "Once we call in these last lists of names, I think we'll have it all together."

"Sounds good," Dad said without argument. I noticed he was still looking thoughtfully at the boxes from my friends, and I couldn't help wondering if maybe he wasn't beginning to add up facts. The odd, speculative look he gave me just then made me wonder if maybe it was time to talk with both my parents, and that thought was so scary it gave me chills—on the hottest day we'd had all year.

Steph's Red Beans and Rice

A simple meal, good anytime

1 can (14 oz.) chicken broth
1 C. water
2 C. dry white rice
½ C. finely diced onion
(1 medium onion)
1 can (15 oz.) red kidney beans,
rinsed and drained
1 pint homemade chili salsa

5 slices bacon, crisp-cooked and
crumbled
1 Tbsp. fresh chopped cilantro
Grated jack or mild cheddar
cheese, as garnish
Finely chopped green onion, as
garnish

Directions

1. In a large saucepan, bring chicken broth and water to boil. Stir in rice and onion. Cook until most of the liquid is absorbed.
2. Stir in beans, salsa, and bacon. Just before serving, add cilantro, conserving a little for garnish.
3. Serve hot with cheese and green onions on the side.

Variations

Alter this recipe according to individual taste. For a hotter, south-of-the-border flavor, add 1 tsp. red chili powder and 1 tsp. cumin (or more, to taste). You can also add a small can of diced green chilies. Make the whole recipe milder by adding a second can of beans and a can of diced tomatoes. Give it a South American twist by substituting black beans for the red, or a Southwestern twist by using pinto beans. You can also add any leftover cooked meat you happen to have around. It's delicious fresh or reheated.

Chapter 17

Sunday, June 17, 2:34 A.M.

TOM BURNETT

I EMPTIED THE REST OF Steph's red beans and rice into a glass bowl and popped it into the microwave, covering it before closing the door. Then I watched as the bowl went around and around while the dish reheated.

The rest of my family had been asleep for hours. I wanted to sleep, knew I needed sleep, yet somehow it kept eluding me. I felt like that glass bowl, going round and round and round, covering the same territory over and over again. Somehow it always came out the same way.

It was simple, it was obvious, it was painfully clear. So why didn't anyone else get it? First there was Granny with her impossible demands that I set aside a lifetime of grief and pain and anger, expecting me to welcome into my life and home a group of strangers, wanting me to treat them like family. Didn't she realize that some of these people never should have existed? That others had made themselves my enemies almost before I was old enough to know what real enemies were? How could she expect this of me—and so calmly, as if she were asking nothing at all? And now even Karen seemed to have turned against me, demanding that I participate in this sham when all I wanted to do was to be anywhere else. Why didn't she understand—even if no one else did?

I could go over it again, like that bowl making round after round in the microwave, but why? Facts were facts, and no matter how many times I reviewed them, nothing ever changed. My father had brought a stranger into our home—a pretty, young Latina woman he should have regarded with professional distance, one of his own students, for goodness' sake. Then, while the rest of the family ignorantly went about our business, good ol' Dad had plotted to find another teaching position halfway across the country. One day when we older kids were all at school, he had simply packed up and left, taking the two youngest children and many of the household goods with him, abandoning his wife and his three older children while he ran off with the babysitter.

It was adultery. It was a violation of everything our family had ever held sacred. It was anathema to his wedding vows and his temple covenants. It was *wrong*, and no amount of my reviewing it was going to make that change.

It was wrong, and it had left me holding the bag. I was only twelve when I came home from school that day to find my father and Rocio gone, my beloved little sister and baby brother gone, and my mom half crazy with grief and heartbreak. Mom had never been the same again, and I had been thrust into the role of man of the family, taking care of a mentally ill mother and two younger siblings largely by myself, trying to clean up the mess my dad had left. It was simple, it was obvious, it was painfully clear. Why didn't anyone get it?

The timer beeped, and I took my midnight snack out of the microwave, burning my hand on the bowl that had become too hot. "Ow!" I said aloud, then realizing I might have awakened Karen, I mumbled a mild curse. Couldn't anything go right?

I filled a glass with milk, got out a fork, and sat down at the kitchen counter. That's when I heard the bedroom door open and knew Karen was about to catch me red-handed, eating red beans and rice in the middle of the night—a violation of a small promise I'd made to myself to avoid eating between dinner one evening and breakfast the next day. Well, at least I wasn't breaking a promise to anyone else. If my dad's betrayal had done nothing else, it had taught me to keep the important promises, the ones I made to others.

"Hi, honey," Karen said, her voice smoky with sleep.

"Hi, yourself." I lifted my fork defiantly. Just let her say something.

"Couldn't sleep, huh?" she asked. I guessed she must be postponing the inevitable assault on my dignity.

"No. You either?"

"I slept pretty well for a while." She looked at the bowl of hot food, and I knew what was coming next, but my sweetheart surprised me. "I don't suppose you have any more of that?"

"Um, uh, no. No, this is the last."

She sighed. "Pity. I'll find something else then."

I watched as she opened the refrigerator and started looking through its contents. "No comments about eating in the middle of the night?"

She turned and gave me a sweet, sleepy half smile. "Sometimes it's good to break the rules," she said. "Frankly, this seems like a good time for some comfort food, don't you think?"

"Yeah. Yeah, I thought so." I took another bite of the spicy leftovers. Comfort. That was it, exactly. Well, at least Karen understood that part.

"Oh, yeah. This will do it." She came out of the refrigerator with her arms loaded and calmly went about making a sandwich from Friday's meatloaf and two slices of wheat bread, spreading mayonnaise and catsup with abandon. "Yum, this looks great!" she announced as she put the condiments away and started toward the counter to sit beside me.

"You're not obsessing about the calories?"

"Calories, schmalories. We worry about them all day every day. A little letdown under these rather extreme conditions might just help us remember we're still alive and still need a little peace and comfort where we can find it—even in food." She took a big bite from the sandwich. "Ummmm, that's good!"

"Glad you're enjoying it."

We sat for a while, eating side by side in companionable silence. A few minutes later, my bowl was empty and Karen's sandwich gone. I finished the last of my milk and—I couldn't help it—I burped loudly. "Oops! Sorry. I guess the old stomach doesn't necessarily agree with your philosophy about midnight comfort food."

Karen rubbed her own middle. "My old stomach isn't all that happy about it either," she said. "I think I'm going to help myself to some antacid. Shall I get some for you too?"

"Yeah. Thanks."

She brought over a bottle of peppermint-flavored tablets, and we sat quietly chewing. In another minute, even that was gone. A moment of strained silence followed.

"Well? What's next?" I asked her. "Do you think you can go back to sleep now?"

Karen arched one eyebrow. Her voice was smoky again, but not with sleep. "Come with me and I'll help you sleep too," she offered.

She always looked so beautiful when she grinned like that. I couldn't help remembering all the reasons why I loved this difficult, amazing woman. "You've got a deal," I told her.

I put my arm around my sweetheart and led her back to our bed.

Aunt Shirley's Sinfully Delicious French Toast

1 loaf crusty bread (baguette,
French loaf, etc.)
4 whole egg yolks
2 C. half-and-half
1 Tbsp. sugar

Zest of one lemon (about 2–3 tsp.)
1 Tbsp. vanilla
Sifted powdered sugar for serving
(optional)

Directions

1. Cut bread into ½-inch-thick slices. In a dish, mix together egg yolks, half-and-half, sugar, lemon zest, and vanilla. Whisk to combine.
2. Dip bread slices in mixture, coating both sides, then remove from dish and set aside. Repeat until all bread is coated.
3. Heat iron skillet or griddle over medium heat. Sizzle butter in the pan when hot. Cook French toast on both sides until golden brown, being careful not to burn.
4. Dust with powdered sugar.
5. Serve with cream cheese, peanut butter, and various syrups. Recipe for berry syrup follows.

Variations

Alter the flavor to taste by replacing the lemon zest with 1 tsp. cinnamon and ½ tsp. nutmeg. At Christmas time, soak the bread in premade eggnog. You can also dust the finished toast in cinnamon and sugar instead of powdered sugar. For the lactose challenged, replace the half-and-half with almond milk. This recipe is delicious every way!

Elderberry Syrup

4 C. clean berry juice
¼ C. freshly squeezed lemon juice

4 C. white granulated sugar
¼ tsp. butter

Directions

1. Pick and wash the berries. Use a steamer-juicer to extract the juice, about 60–75 minutes or use the standard juice-bag method.
2. Mix in lemon juice and sugar, and cook over medium heat until all sugar is dissolved.

3. Add small pat of butter at the end to reduce frothing and to add flavor.
4. You can bottle this syrup and process in a water bath, just as you would with jelly or fresh juice. Delicious!

Variations

This syrup is excellent made with red raspberries, blackberries, blueberries, or any variety of berries. It can also be made with the juice of grapes, crabapples, plums, or most other fruits, although you may want to experiment with the amounts of juice and sugar. (Sweeter fruits require less sugar.) You may also wish to eliminate the lemon juice for very tart fruits. Try mixing juices for a delightful change.

CHAPTER 18

Sunday, June 17, Morning

KAREN BURNETT

AT 10:35 SUNDAY MORNING I sat outside our stake center, waiting for Carrie and her van full of relatives to arrive. I'd have been nervous that they weren't here already except that Carrie had called a couple of minutes ago to say that one of the little ones had lost her shoes, so the group was running late. While we were on the phone, the shoes had been found and the crowd had started loading into the van, so I knew it wouldn't be much longer now. Granny's house was only five or six minutes away.

Aunt Shirley sat just inside the foyer, waiting for me to give her the signal before she joined us in the heat outside. Emily waited with her. Steph had planned to join us too but had acceded to a last-minute request to run some reports over to the singles ward. I hoped she'd be able to join us before the meeting started. My one regret? My husband was not here to meet these people who were so important in his life.

I had awakened with a sense of urgency as the threads of a nightmare dissipated. I looked around for my husband, but Tom was already up and out. Then I remembered that we were meeting his long-lost relatives before church this morning and the panic subsided. One way or another, some good would come from this day. I hurried through my normal preparations and started down to the kitchen. As soon as I opened my bedroom door, delicious aromas alerted me to someone's presence in the kitchen. I could hear Tom's voice and someone else, maybe Aunt Shirley? I hurried down the stairs.

"What smells so wonderful?" I asked as I entered the kitchen.

"French toast," Shirley said. "We're almost ready."

I looked around to find Steph and Emily setting the table while Tom sat at the counter, watching Shirley cook. It felt both pleasant and disquieting to see the morning moving forward so well without me. "I can warm some berry syrup to go with that," I offered.

"Karen made some great elderberry syrup this year," Tom supplied.

Shirley said, "That sounds great. Please do."

Minutes later Tom offered our morning prayer, and we began a breakfast feast. I felt so grateful for the ease and peace Shirley had brought to our home. Everyone was hungry and conversation was limited as we gratefully consumed the delicious meal. I tried to think of a diplomatic way to raise the topic of meeting Tom's relatives this morning—despite his apparent good humor, I could see that his hands were trembling—and I was just about to bring it up when the phone rang.

I said, "I'll get that," and got up.

It was Brother Hartwell asking for Tom and, just like that, Tom had a perfectly legitimate excuse for postponing the inevitable. Brother Hartwell had been invited as a guest speaker in our stake's Spanish branch and had planned to take his son, recently returned from the Chile Rancagua Mission, as his companion speaker. Then his son had awakened with all the symptoms of strep throat and a fever over 102. Since the Spanish branch met at ten, Brother Hartwell was desperate for a pinch-hitter who could prepare a strong, last-minute talk in Spanish. Tom's recent stint in the presidency of the Spanish branch made him better prepared than anyone for the assignment, and he seemed more than grateful to accept.

What was I supposed to do? Complain at him for fulfilling his church responsibilities? I felt sadly disappointed that we'd be meeting these family members without him, and I knew Carrie would be disappointed too. Still, there was nothing to do but soldier on. I helped Tom prepare by looking up a few references in our Spanish scriptures and marking them for him. A few minutes later Brother Hartwell arrived and Tom was out the door, on his way to serve the good people of the Spanish branch some twenty-five miles away, and it was time for the rest of us to prepare to go to our own church meetings without him.

There was an eager sense of anticipation as Aunt Shirley, Em, and I loaded into the family car and headed for the stake center. When Carrie called to tell me about the shoes, I told her about Tom's assignment in the Spanish branch, hoping to get the disappointment behind us before we met.

The prelude music was playing inside by the time the van pulled into the parking lot, and people began piling out of it like clowns at the circus. I knew it had to be our relatives. Who else arrived at church with so many adults in one twelve-passenger van? I waved to Aunt Shirley and Emily, who came out to join me. We quickly spotted Carrie, who looked much like her older sister and who came up to me with open arms. "Karen, I presume?" she asked.

"And you must be Carrie," I said as we stepped into a tight, sisterly hug. The rest of the crowd came up behind her.

I asked, "Carrie, will you introduce everyone, please?"

They trooped through, a dozen of them, while I did my best to try to put a name to each face, especially among the young people, and then to pass each person along, together with the correct name, to Shirley and Em.

It was easy to tell Christina from Amanda. Though they both had the near-black hair, dark eyes, and deeper coloring inherited from their mother, Tina was taller and very thin while Mandy was somewhat shorter and pleasantly rounded. Looking at them side by side, I thought Rocio must be a striking woman. My husband's half sisters were both lovely.

It was even easier to tell Jeffrey from Teryl. Like his wife, Jeff was beanpole tall and athletically lean, his dark brown hair only beginning to gray at the temples, while Terry was four or five inches shorter and built like a wall—not fat, but square, a stand-out with bright-red hair and wildly rampant freckles.

It was tougher to pin down the kids, although the Juanarena girls, Candi and Sofie, stood out because of their coloring. Then I spotted a little boy—very little, barely a toddler—who was as dark as the girls or maybe even darker. "Who's this?" I asked, stroking his hair as the little one went by.

"That's my boy, Tommy," Mandy said. "He got my mother's coloring, I think."

"He's a beautiful child," I answered, feeling the small knot forming in the back of my throat as I thought of how my Tom would react to this child who bore his same name. "They all are."

We visited, but only briefly. Inside there was a change in the music. I looked at my watch. "We aren't quite late yet, and I've saved us a bench so we'll all be able to sit together—"

"But it's time to go in, isn't it?" Jeff said, and we moved in a clump toward the front doors and into the chapel.

As we trooped through the doors, I offered up a silent prayer that these once cast-off relatives might find a home among us and that we could fulfill Granny's wish to be reunited, to become one family at last.

Indonesian Rice Salad

An excellent choice for vegan or lactose intolerant guests

2 C. short-grain brown rice
⅓ C. peanut oil
3 Tbsp. toasted sesame oil
½ C. orange juice
1 medium clove garlic, crushed
½ tsp. crushed red hot pepper
2 Tbsp. tamari
1 tsp. salt
2 Tbsp. honey
2 Tbsp. cider vinegar
1 C. chopped pineapple
2–3 minced scallions

1 stalk celery, finely minced
½ C. raisins
½ C. chopped roasted peanuts
½ C. toasted cashew pieces
2 Tbsp. sesame seeds
1 C. mixed red and green bell
   pepper, diced
Optional:
1 C. thinly sliced water chestnuts
A handful of fresh, raw snow peas
½ pound fresh mung bean sprouts

Directions

1. Set up to cook short-grain brown rice in 3 C. water.
2. While rice cooks, combine in a large bowl the peanut oil, toasted sesame oil, orange juice, crushed garlic, red hot pepper, tamari, salt, honey, cider vinegar, and chopped pineapple.
3. Add hot rice to dressing, mix well, and add in the scallions, celery, raisins, roasted peanuts, cashew pieces, sesame seeds, and bell peppers.

CHAPTER 19

Sunday, June 17, Late morning

STEPHANIE BURNETT

I SLID INTO MY OLD accustomed place on the third row next to my family—*all* of my family—just minutes before our eleven o'clock sacrament meeting began. I looked down the long row and nodded to family members I hadn't met yet. They smiled in return.

Half a minute later, Ruby Dashov slid in on my right. That was the first time it occurred to me to wonder what Ruby will do now that she no longer has Granny Adelaide. I remember celebrating Ruby's birthday—her sixtieth, I think?—at Granny's just a few months ago. She has lived there since Granny's eyesight first started fading, some ten years ago, if not longer. What will happen to her now?

The bishop was just coming to the stand when Ruby slipped me a three-by-five card with a recipe on it. The title read, "Indonesian Rice Salad."

"This is one of the family recipes Adelaide wanted your mother to have," Ruby whispered.

I read through the recipe and wondered why anyone would combine those ingredients that way. "It doesn't sound very good," I whispered back.

"It's delicious," Ruby said with a twinkle, "much better than it sounds. And Judith used to make it every year for the family reunion."

Judith. That was a name we didn't hear much, but I guessed we'd be hearing it more over the next few days. I knew that Grandma Judith, my dad's mother, had a brother who had served a full-time mission among Indonesians living in the Philippines, so it made sense she'd have a favorite Asian recipe to add to her menu. Maybe this would help Mom with Granny's version of *Mission Impossible*. "Thanks," I whispered back, tucking the card into my purse. "I'll see she gets it."

The bishop began with announcements, starting with plans the ward was making to celebrate the Fourth of July and ending with the sad news of the passing of Sister Adelaide Burnett. There were a few gasps and shocked whispers, but the grapevine had already done its job. Most of the ward members had already been giving our family curious, sad looks even before the announcement. They were probably wondering what we were doing here.

To be truthful, I was kind of wondering myself. Since sacrament meeting is where Burnetts are on Sundays, it never really occurred to any of us to miss, even days after a death in the family. At the same time, I was suddenly finding it a bit tough just keeping myself together in the face of the sad, compassionate looks we were getting from people I'd known all my life.

The opening hymn sounded lovely with various Burnetts singing in parts, almost as if we were our own choir. Although I don't usually get teary over the hymns, I found myself choking up at this one since I couldn't help thinking how much Granny would have loved to hear it and how much she'd have enjoyed singing with us. Even in her older age, she could still sing—not the same high notes she had reached when she was younger, but her voice was generally clear and on key. It didn't seem fair she had left us before sharing this family occasion.

Then again, maybe this was the way she preferred it, with the family getting together to enjoy one another and to remember her all at the same time. I didn't know. What I knew was that I suddenly missed her so much it was hard to get a breath or to try to sing over the tight, hard knot in my throat. My chest felt constricted, and I couldn't hold back the tears. Though I mouthed the words and tried to feel them, I wasn't really singing anymore.

Emily, on my left, gripped my elbow. I saw the tears on her cheek and knew she was having a similar experience. I took her hand. On my right, Ruby had also stopped singing. I reached across and took her hand too. The three of us sat there like a human wall, trying to face off emotion enough to avoid sobbing our way through the opening song. The quiet moments during the sacrament a few minutes later were almost worse.

In fact, much of the meeting went that way. As we sat there through the meeting, holding each other, holding ourselves, I couldn't help noticing the curious looks from my mom and Aunt Shirley. I'm known in the family as Stoic Steph, and they don't always mean it kindly. It's as if they think I don't feel what everyone else does.

What Granny had figured out about me, what I think my mom is just beginning to suspect, is that I feel things just as much as anyone else does—maybe even more—but I try hard to hold myself together in front of people. I'm always afraid that if I let go, even just a little, I won't be able to regain any control at all, so I save the letting go for quiet, alone times, especially since—well, you know. That Sunday morning, I was having more than my usual struggle keeping my feelings to myself.

As soon as we added our amens to the closing prayer, I handed Mom the card Ruby had given me along with her explanation. "I think I need to take Emily home," I added. Em gave me a sharp look, but she seemed to get it, and she wasn't complaining about the reprieve. Neither of us was going to make it much longer without breaking down completely.

"Okay, hun," Mom said. "I need to stay for Relief Society . . ."

"I know. I'll get some lunch started."

"Thanks, Steph. Save the big roast for dinner tonight, and remember, we'll probably have the extended family over."

"Got it," I said. "No problem."

Then Mom took my arm, looking at me with concern. "Are you okay to drive?"

"Who, me? Yeah, sure." If I'd been able to think of one, I might have added a sarcastic comment about Stoic Steph always being okay, but A) I couldn't think of one, and B) Mom would have seen through it, anyway.

She gave me a small, sad smile. "Be safe, then. I'll see you in a couple of hours."

I thought of the resolve that had been growing in me. "Uh, Mom? Do you think maybe we can talk? Later, I mean?"

She gave me a long, searching look. "Sure, honey. Just let me know when you're ready—and we have a quiet minute." She gestured toward the bench full of relatives.

"I will," I promised.

As Em and I started for home, I found myself thinking about what I might say to Mom. Could I really explain to her what had happened and what it had meant to me? It was easier to focus on fixing a simple lunch. I was grateful for the task.

Orzo-Spinach Salad

1 package (16 oz.) uncooked orzo pasta
1 package (10 oz.) baby spinach leaves, finely chopped
½ pound crumbled feta cheese
½ red onion, finely chopped
¾ C. pine nuts
½ tsp. dried basil
¼ tsp. ground white pepper
½ C. olive oil
½ C. balsamic vinegar or lemon juice

Directions

1. Bring a large pot of lightly salted water to a boil. Add orzo and cook for 8–10 minutes or until al dente; drain and rinse with cold water.
2. Transfer to a large bowl and stir in spinach, feta, onion, pine nuts, basil, and white pepper. Toss with olive oil and balsamic vinegar. Refrigerate and serve cold.

Variations

For lactose intolerant guests, make the salad without the cheese and serve the feta or Parmesan separately, to be added at the table. You can make this same salad with other pasta varieties or even using quinoa instead of pasta. Mangia!

CHAPTER 20

Sunday, June 17, Midday

KAREN BURNETT

As always, Sister Tanis gave a wonderful Relief Society lesson. It invoked the Spirit, accomplished the goals in the manual, and helped the sisters to feel the powerful bond of sisterhood I have often associated with Relief Society. Warm and peaceful feelings were so strong in the room that, for a time, I almost forgot the burdens I had carried with me to church that morning. So strong that I even forgot—momentarily, anyway—the sign-up sheet Larissa was passing around with the roll.

I had to hand it to Larissa. She had been plain enough in explaining the situation, beginning with a reminder of Adelaide's passing and then telling the sisters that, at Granny's request, we would be providing a very special combination reunion dinner and family lunch following Wednesday's funeral service. She explained the dishes we served would be old Burnett family favorites and that anyone who signed up would receive the necessary recipes within the next couple of days. She also suggested that helping with this dinner might be a final gift to Adelaide. Then with a small flourish, she put her own name at the top of the list and handed off the clipboard to the front row.

I watched as that clipboard passed from one sister to another, never sure whether the sisters were just signing the roll or actually looking at the other pages circulating with it. I still felt torn, not wanting to be a burden to anyone else's family but hoping to get the help I would need in order to spend important time with my own. It was after the practice hymn that I realized I had actually been chewing my lip. Then Sister

Tanis began her lesson, and for a little while, I was able to let go of it all, focusing instead on the blessings of the gospel and the good news of the Lord's Atonement. It was that long ago, much-anticipated miracle of the Savior's Atonement and Resurrection that took the sting out of Adelaide's death, out of all the sad or lonely or disappointing experiences of our lives. The gratitude I felt at that moment almost overwhelmed me.

The truly overwhelming moment came at the end of the lesson when Larissa showed me the sign-up sheet. She smiled and said, "Are you ready for this?" handing me the paper. She had asked for names and phone numbers and had made spaces down the left side—only five since I hadn't let her put more. Yet those first five slots must have filled up on the first row. Beneath them, the whole first page was filled, and the names and numbers spilled onto the back of the page as well. Some sisters had written notes in the margin ("Please call me!" "I can do two recipes." "Don't do this without me!"), and one, Sister Dana Richards, had listed herself twice, once with her home phone and a second complete entry for her cell. The list, front and back, included almost every person in the room. I could hardly have been more touched.

I was sitting there, holding that page in my hand and trying not to cry, when the John Williams Olympic fanfare began playing. "O my gosh, my cell phone!" I rummaged in my purse, embarrassed that I hadn't thought to turn off my phone or leave it in the car the way I usually did during church meetings. "That could have gone off during the sacrament," I mumbled to myself. "I can't believe I—" I looked at the screen. "It's a text message," I said to no one in particular, then to Larissa, "Steve, my husband's brother."

"Go ahead and read it," Larissa said. She began folding the tablecloth and putting away the flower arrangement.

During my round of phone calls the day before, I had called Tom's brother Steve to ask if he remembered any favorite family recipes. When no one answered, I'd left a message to that effect, and now he was answering. His text read, "I remember Mom used to make a kind of pasta salad that was almost like a rice dish. Don't know where you'd find the recipe, but it was good stuff. Good luck digging up all the old favorites!"

"Ummm," I murmured to myself. "That doesn't help much."

"What doesn't help?"

"Oh, sorry. Tom's brother just sent me a text about a recipe, only he doesn't have the recipe—Well, here. Look." I showed her the screen.

Larissa looked thoughtful. "Maybe I can help." She began digging in her purse.

"Don't tell me you just happen to have this recipe sitting in your wallet?"

"Actually, I might. Well, sort of . . ."

I cocked one eyebrow in response and then lifted them both when she came out with her smart phone.

"A couple of years ago I saw a recipe for an orzo salad that really sounded great. It was made with feta cheese and lots of other good stuff, and I thought I'd give it a try." She flipped through messages on her screen as she talked. "I got it from that obnoxious chef that always does the cooking shows. What's his name? You know the guy I mean."

"I don't remember his name either," I said, "but I know the guy you mean. I guess you liked the salad?"

"Yes and no." Larissa was still digging. "My family doesn't like the feta cheese. We use mozzarella instead."

"Normally I like feta," I told her, "but I'm not sure how I'd feel about it in my pasta salad."

"That's the way my family felt too," Larissa clarified. "Anyway, when my sister-in-law ate the salad at our place, she asked me for the recipe, so I sent it to her by e-mail, and . . . Yeah, I've got it! Here it is." She showed me the screen.

"This looks simple enough," I said, reaching for a notepad and pen. "In fact, it looks great." I started to write on the back of an envelope.

"Oh, don't bother writing it down," Larissa said, taking her smart phone back. "Here, I'll just forward it to your e-mail." A couple of strokes later, her cell phone made a metallic cuckoo sound. "There. You should have it when you get home."

I shook my head. "The joys of modern technology!"

"Well, it has its downside," she answered, "which just makes it that much sweeter when it can come through for you in a pinch."

"No kidding!" I said. Then, "Thank you, Larissa. Thanks so much."

"No worries. Hey, tell you what. I'm on the sign-up sheet to help with the family luncheon. Let me make the orzo salad. I'll do a triple batch so there'll be plenty to go around . . . Of course, I can make something else too, if you need more help—"

"No, no, that will be fine. Really, Larissa, I don't feel great about this, anyway—"

"Remember, Karen, we're doing this for Adelaide because we *all* loved her." She laid her hand on my arm.

I laid my hand on hers. "For Adelaide," I answered. "Thanks."

The recipe was there in my e-mail when I got home, and it looked even better when I had a chance to go over it again. Then, after having a little while to think about it, I was glad Larissa was planning to prep this dish for us. That would probably guarantee a better product, given everything else I had going, and would give me one less detail to worry about. I suddenly felt another wave of gratitude toward Shirley and Larissa and all the wonderful sisters who were coming through on the promise to "bear one another's burdens." Their help would allow me to focus on the emotion of the day, not the cooking.

I watched Emily and Steph working together in the kitchen, getting ready for the extended family, who had gone back to Granny's to change clothes and should be joining us any minute. I wondered what Steph wanted to discuss and felt grateful once again that my sisters were giving me the opportunity to focus on emotions. There seemed to be plenty of emotions to absorb all the focus we could give them.

Dinner Rocks

Meat and veggie pockets

One batch sourdough bread
   dough (included earlier)
2 pounds hamburger
1 head cabbage

1 medium-sized yellow onion
1 tsp. salt
½ tsp. black pepper
1 tsp. cumin

Directions

1. Preheat oven to 350.
2. Brown hamburger and onion, seasoning to taste.
3. Boil head of cabbage until soft, not mushy. Drain cabbage, stir in meat mixture. Add pepper and cumin until spicy to taste.
4. Break off chunks of bread dough; roll out and cut into approximately 5 x 5 squares.
5. Spoon meat mixture into center of squares. Fold corners up and seal to make a pouch.
6. Bake for 25–30 minutes or until golden brown.

Variations

You can vary this recipe according to taste. Add some chopped, cooked carrots, or replace the cumin with ground red chili. You can replace the cabbage with potatoes if you prefer. Serve with catsup, mustard, or chili salsa.

CHAPTER 21

Sunday, June 17, Early afternoon

STEPHANIE BURNETT

A BIG DOUBLE BATCH OF dinner rocks was baking and the counter was set up buffet style before Mom and Aunt Shirley got home from church. Mom told me to expect the relatives any minute, but then Carrie called to say Candi had misplaced her shoes again and they'd be a little late.

Emily had made a huge green salad, and she was chilling some applesauce we'd helped Mom can last fall. I also put out some flavored crackers and a simple spread made of sour cream and dry onion soup mix, so I thought we'd have enough food for everyone, but just in case, I made a quick berry cobbler and put it in to bake with our main dish.

"It smells delicious," Mom said as she entered from the garage.

Then Shirley said, "It smells familiar too. Is that Mother's cobbler recipe?"

I paused, remembering where I'd learned to make the basic berry cobbler. "Yes, it is," I told her. "Granny Adelaide showed me how to make it using the berries she grew at her house. I think I was just little when we . . ." I stopped when I saw the stricken look on Aunt Shirley's face.

Mom laid her hand over Shirley's. "It's tough, I know. I'm sorry."

I almost choked on emotion. "I'm so sorry, Aunt Shirley. I didn't think—"

"Don't be sorry, darling," Shirley said, patting my hand. "We have to be able to remember her." She brightened as if by an act of sheer will. "In fact, I was thinking this afternoon about the time she decided to build a greenhouse."

"A greenhouse?" Emily asked as she joined us. "You mean, like where you start little plants and stuff?"

"Exactly," said Shirley. "She told Dad she wanted a place where she could keep an orchid growing or start tomatoes in January or sit under a bower of something fragrant she grew herself while she read a book and sipped a cup of peppermint tea."

"I don't think I know this story," Mom said. "It must have been before I joined the family."

"Oh yes," Shirley agreed, "probably a long time before. I think I was in my mid to late teens when this happened."

"A *long* time before," Em said, and Shirley smiled indulgently.

"Tell us about it," I encouraged.

"Well, she was quite a gardener even up into her nineties, but when I was little, she grew much of our family's food. Flowers too. Mother *loved* flowers." Shirley paused and gave herself a gentle shake. "Anyway, one day she told Dad she'd wanted a greenhouse for a long time. He said he'd be happy to buy her one—as soon as she won her big jackpot in Vegas. Since neither of them gambled, and Mother had never even been to Vegas, his meaning was clear enough. Mother just said she didn't see any reason why they had to be all that expensive."

"I can almost hear what your father would have said to that," Mom interjected, "something like, 'Well, I don't guess they hafta be, but they sure as shootin' are.'" She dropped her voice, trying to mimic my great-grandfather. I don't know whether she was close or not since he died when I was tiny, but Shirley chuckled.

"Yes, Dad's answer was something very much like that. Mother just said she thought it was time she had a greenhouse, and she didn't think she'd need to spend a fortune to get it. Dad answered that if she could find one that didn't cost anyone any appendages, he'd be happy to help her buy it." Shirley paused, smiling.

"So did she buy one?" Em asked.

"No," Shirley said, "she *built* one."

"Built it?" I said. "Like with her own hands? Did she order a kit or something?"

"Nope, and there wasn't an Internet to turn to in those days either. She just figured out what she wanted and sketched it on paper. Some few weeks later, she was driving to a part of town she didn't visit often, going out to take Lenore to a dental appointment, I think, when she saw some men delivering a backhoe to a job site. They were getting ready to tear down an old house. She stopped and asked them if she could salvage materials. They told her the place had already been stripped by a professional salvage company and everything of value had been removed. It was probably their way of getting her out of their hair. Mother just said, 'Then you won't mind *what* I take, seeing it has no value.'" Shirley chuckled at the memory.

"She was tough when she needed to be," Mom said, her tone full of admiration.

"Indeed she was," Shirley answered.

"So I guess she ended up stripping the salvage piles," I prompted.

"Uh-huh. That first evening, with the supervisor's reluctant permission, she carefully removed all the windows in the building so she could save the glass. It would all have been broken once the backhoe started in on the walls."

"And the man let her onto the site?" Mom asked.

"*Let* isn't really the right word," Shirley said, "but he did suggest that if the windows happened to be gone before they got there the next day, it would save him from having to clean up a lot of broken glass. Mother got Lenore to her dental appointment and back, put on dinner for the family, then headed out the door with Dad's truck and leather work gloves. I think she took a claw hammer too. By the time it got dark outside she was home again with a stack of windows that she positioned against the back fence."

"How did she talk your father into that?" Mom asked. "I can't imagine him approving her taking off like that."

"She didn't ask," Shirley answered. "Dad was going home teaching that evening and, since his families were all in our neighborhood, he planned to walk. He ate a quick dinner and put on a white shirt, then he and my brother Bob went out to do visits. As soon as they were gone, Mom grabbed Dad's gloves and the keys to his truck and took off. When Dad got home, he wondered where Mom was, but she was home again with the truck and the windows before he got any answers. I think he gave her some kind of talking to while he helped her unload the windows, and I remember him asking lots of questions about what she was going to do with all that 'junk,' but he helped her line the old windows up against the fence.

"Over the next few days, she went back to that job site several times, and she always came home with items that fit her plans. She even salvaged old nails or boards with nails in them—although in the end, she spent a couple dollars on new nails. Turns out that's all she had to buy, except for some paint to pretty it up at the end."

"Wow," Em said, admiring. "She got everything she needed?"

"Everything," Shirley answered. "She wanted her greenhouse to have water piped into it, so she salvaged pipes and fittings and an old laundry sink and set it up to connect it to a garden hose from the outside house faucet. She wanted it to be solid, not easily moved by a stiff wind, so she brought home timbers from walls and roof trusses. She saved every bit of glass she could get her hands on so the greenhouse could have glass walls, and she saved the hinges from the old windows too, so some windows could open when she wanted the breeze to blow through.

"From the fireplace and hearth of the old house, she saved enough brick to lay a floor in her greenhouse. There was even a little garden bench in the back of the old place that nobody had bothered to take. Before she was done, she hauled that home to put under that 'fragrant bower' she planned to grow. In the end, she also rescued the house's front door, which became her greenhouse door.

"Then the building started. When Dad came home and saw her nailing boards together, he declared she had no idea what she was doing and the place would never stand. She had to work around her regular chores, of course, so it took her a couple of weeks, but in the end, she had a greenhouse—and she'd built it all herself."

"Wow," Em said.

Shirley agreed. "Wow, indeed. One day Dad came home from work and found her sitting on the bench. There hadn't been time for her to grow anything fragrant, of course, but she was sitting on her bench, in the place where she intended her fragrant bower to grow, reading a book and sipping a cup of peppermint tea inside a pretty, painted greenhouse she had built all by herself. It was a bit lopsided and the corners weren't all square and the door didn't hang quite evenly—she had to sort of pick it up on one side in order to latch it. But she had her greenhouse— complete with running water and a sink, windows that opened and closed, glass on all four sides and parts of the ceiling, and even a brick floor. Dad had to admit she'd done a fine job."

Mom's brow furrowed in concentration. "I think I remember that greenhouse."

"You probably do. It stood for decades," Shirley answered. "I don't think it ever would have come down on its own, but she finally let the family take it down when they decided to add the big enclosed porch on the back of the house. By then she didn't have much family at home anymore, and she wasn't doing as much gardening."

"But she had her greenhouse when she wanted it," Mom added, finishing the story.

"Yes, she did," Shirley answered, misty again. "There were few things my mother really wanted that she didn't figure out how to get for herself—or for her family."

"Like violin lessons for you," Mom said.

"Yes," Shirley looked up with tears in her eyes. "Or ballet lessons for Lenore, grad school for Tom . . ." She swallowed hard, letting the thought drift away.

"She was quite a woman," Mom said.

Shirley agreed. "Yes, she was."

Em piped up, "Did I ever tell you about the snake?" We all stared at her.

"No," my mother said, "I don't think you did."

"I was little," Em began, "probably about three. Granny's eyesight was beginning to go, but she could still get around, and Ruby hadn't come to live with her yet—"

"Yes, you were probably about three then," Mom confirmed.

"I know the other kids were in school, but Mom had a doctor appointment or something and she had arranged to leave me with Granny Adelaide, at her house, just for an hour or two.

"I was playing in the backyard, and I came around the corner of the little porch hearing a funny noise. I thought the neighbors' automatic sprinklers must have gone on. Then I looked up to see a snake coiled and hissing, its tail in the air, ready to strike."

I shuddered. "You must have been terrified."

"I ran in the house screaming for Granny, yelling that a rattlesnake was trying to get me. Granny put on her tall gardening boots and got a sharp hoe from the garage, then she followed me. I stopped at the corner of the house and told her the snake was around there. She positioned the hoe in front of her and went prepared for a fight. I saw her step around, and I heard the snake hissing that same awful loud noise, and then Granny stepped back smiling."

"Smiling?" Now it was Mom who had the shudders.

"She said it wasn't a rattlesnake, just a little gopher snake and that it protected itself by acting like a rattler so predators would leave it alone.

She told me it was useful because it caught gophers that would eat her garden, and then she brought me around the corner, holding me up high so I wouldn't be afraid, and she showed me that it had no rattles at the end of its tail. I said I was still afraid of it and I didn't want to play in the yard if it was there."

"Can't blame you for that," I said. "I'd have felt the same way."

Em smiled. "Granny said I didn't need to be afraid, but if it bothered me, that was no problem. She took me up onto the porch and put me on a chair where I could see the snake through the screen. Then she went back outside and picked it up by its tail."

"She didn't!" Mom said, as astonished as I felt.

"She did," Em assured us. "She picked it up and when it tried to lift its head up toward her, she just gently shook it down. Then she carried it to the fence and carefully put it over the other side. After that, she came back to the porch and got me. She said it would be safe to play in the backyard now if I wanted to, and I think I stayed out there until Mom came to get me."

"Wow," Mom said. "You'd think I'd have a memory of something like that."

"Maybe I didn't tell you," Em answered. "By the time you got there, I had probably moved on to other things. But I remembered it yesterday when I was thinking about Granny. I always thought Granny Adelaide could do anything, that she was—I don't know—indestructible or something, like some kind of superhero."

There was a moment of silent reverie at the table, and then Aunt Shirley said, "She was always something of a superhero to me."

"She certainly impressed me," Mom said, "right from the first time I met her."

"Me too," I added.

We sat there, the four of us, indulging in our own private memories of a great lady. The spell was broken when Mom said, "Thank you all for your help with the lunch."

"No problem," I said. I found I was looking forward to Granny's service and to learning more about her remarkable life.

All through the rest of the day I thought about Granny building her own greenhouse or picking up a snake by its tail. I felt proud that Granny's genes were a part of me. That's a pretty strong contrast to what I can recall about Grandma Judith. I remember what she was like in the last years of her life, and it wasn't pretty.

For some time now, years maybe, I've known that I could be like that—self-absorbed, demanding, and occasionally completely off my rocker, a helpless and hopeless victim who makes everyone around her feel miserable. I knew Judith didn't want to be like that and, in a way, that made it worse. I mean, if I have the same genes, couldn't I end up exactly the same way? Not wanting to make unreasonable demands on people but unable to help myself? Not wanting to hurt my roommate but not even being able to remember how it happened when I had?

I had wanted to talk about it even before the whole dark incident with Allie, but then I tried to picture myself sitting down with my dad to say, "Hi, Daddy. What do you think the odds are that I could end up a total, off-the-wall nutball like Grandma?" That sort of took the energy out of the whole idea.

Silently I had feared for years that one day I would suffer a major blow, something equivalent to having my husband and half my children leave me, and then—genetically predisposed as I was—I'd lose it as completely as Judith had. It was almost enough to make me fear getting close to people. I'd been hesitant to date even when I was a teenager, and then, after the weird thing with my roommates . . . well . . .

Now a new thought was occurring to me, and I found it comforting. Yes, I had Grandma Judith's genes, but I had Granny Adelaide's too. Maybe there was no predisposition in Granny, or maybe she just had a stronger will than Grandma Judith. Who knew? What I did know was Granny had suffered through some terrible losses, and yet she had remained encouraging and cheerful, a beacon of strength and hope to others around her, right up until the end.

She'd passed that on to Great-Aunt Shirley too. I had some of the same genetics that made her such a dynamo—even at her age. She had to be approaching seventy, and yet here she was, taking care of all of us.

Then there is my mother, whom I maybe don't appreciate as much as I should. I remember how she coped with Grandma Judith's illness and still seemed to have energy left for everyone and how she has always seemed like such a strong, centered person, whether visiting the county's mental health offices or helping a neighbor family or guiding one of her teenagers through some typical moment of angst. I have her genes too. In fact, half my genes come from her.

With a mix like that—with Granny Adelaide and Mom and my stalwart dad all mixed in—maybe there was no reason to succumb to Grandma Judith's side of my genetics. Even though I may have the same predispositions, there wasn't any reason I couldn't take better care of myself and end up doing better than she did. Was there?

As that thought came to me, I felt an almost overwhelming rush of love and gratitude toward Granny. She hadn't had an easy life, yet she had done well. She hadn't just coped, she had thrived and had made a beautiful life possible for many of us because of all she had done.

It suddenly struck me as ironic that, in accepting Granny's death, I was finally giving some rest to the ghost of my Grandma Judith and the way her illness and death had haunted me. There was a nice kind of symmetry in that, and I realized then that, despite the pain I still felt at losing Granny, I was looking forward to my own future with greater eagerness and joy than I had in some time.

I closed my eyes and silently thanked Granny. Then I thanked my Heavenly Father that He had made me of strong stuff, inherited from such strong people. I knew I must have that talk with my mom, but I felt encouraged. With a little help, I hoped I would never need to be so fearful of my future again.

Fresh Corn Casserole

8 ears fresh whole corn
⅔ C. whole cream
1 tsp. salt

⅔ tsp. fresh ground pepper
2 Tbsp. finely minced red pepper
3 Tbsp. butter

Directions

1. Scrape the corn from the cobs into a deep bowl. Continue scraping the cob until you have extracted all the "milk" as well.
2. Add cream and salt. Grind in pepper.
3. Stir in fresh red pepper and butter.
4. Pour into buttered baking dish.
5. Bake at 350 for roughly 30–35 minutes (may take longer in some ovens) but just until warmed through. Don't overcook.
6. Serve while still warm with barbeque, other meat courses, or a completely vegetarian menu.

Variations

You may add roasted, bottled red pimiento instead of the fresh red pepper or garnish the dish with fresh chopped Italian parsley. Some folks also enjoy a stalk of diced fresh celery added to the recipe.

CHAPTER 22

Sunday, June 17, Early afternoon

KAREN BURNETT

THE RECIPE MARY GAVE ME for fresh corn casserole was not exactly like her mother's, yet Mary thought I should include it at the luncheon. As she reminded me when she called just after church, she was only nine years old when her father left and after that, her mother didn't cook much, ever. Apparently it had been just a few years ago when a friend gave Mary this recipe for corn casserole, and when she tried it, it reminded her of a similar dish her mother had made years before. Although she had experimented to try to get it to taste more like her mother's—even adding celery—her family had always preferred the version she was giving me.

I had dutifully taken it down just as she read it to me, and now I was entering it into the computer while we waited for the relatives to arrive, getting ready to pass it off to one of the generous sisters who had agreed to help with my strange and rather burdensome requests. I reminded myself they were doing this for Adelaide. Whenever I thought of it that way, I realized I'd have done the same thing. That didn't keep me from feeling remarkably grateful to everyone who had signed up. By the time I finally put this meal together, I was going to need help from almost every one of them.

I finished entering the recipe into my computer, clicked Save, and reviewed what I had collected. It definitely wasn't enough. We had more deciding to do—and soon. Our main dish would be the "Some-Like-It-Hot Tacos." With a wide variety of salads on the side . . . ? It still wasn't enough. I needed to come up with more.

I sighed and went back to helping the girls in the kitchen.

*   *   *

MELISSA BURNETT KINGSLEY

Jason was driving us to my parents' home to meet the many relatives from Texas who had come for Granny's funeral. We were coming straight from the meeting block in our own ward across town, and I couldn't help wishing we had stopped at the house to get something to eat. My belly was growling like a starved thing.

"We should have stopped by the house," I grumbled, giving the growler a good rub. "I need to get something in my stomach."

"You know it won't be long now, babe," he said, his voice taking on that patronizing quality I was learning to dislike.

"And you know I can't afford to let my stomach get empty," I snapped. I saw him grimace and immediately felt sorry. "Sorry, babe," I said in a gentler tone. "I'm just not feeling well today."

"I know," he said. His expression of concern seemed genuine enough. "I'll try to see that you get something to nibble on right away—especially if it's going to be a little while before the meal."

"Thanks, hon."

"You're welcome. We're in this together, you know." He grinned and patted my knee. I grinned back, squelching the thought that I'd happily give him half the exhaustion and nausea.

We were quiet for a moment, Jason humming tunelessly with the elevator music on the radio. He usually preferred a louder, more metal sound, but he had been softening it lately in deference to me. The sweetie.

"I've been wondering: do you think maybe we should just tell everybody? Mom's been giving me funny looks. I think she suspects. It would also help with gatherings like this. People would understand if I needed to eat before the meal was ready, or—"

Jason looked surprised. "I thought we weren't going to say anything until you were showing."

"I know that's what I said, but, well . . ." I felt myself getting teary. "I wasn't counting on this, you know? Granny dying and all the relatives coming from Texas and . . . and everything."

"You okay?" Jason asked.

I nodded, then I realized he couldn't see me while he was driving. "Yeah," I croaked. "Just sad, I guess. I just thought our news might lift everybody's spirits. You know, life going on and all that? And we're past three months now. I'm nearly through the first trimester, and it won't be long before I start to show . . ."

My husband gave me a sweet, sad smile and gripped my hand. "I'll leave it up to you, babe. If you want to tell people, we'll go with it."

"Okay," I said, then I found myself shaking my head. "No, I have a better idea. I'm really not myself just now, what with . . . everything. If you see the right opening, right place, right time, *you* say something. I'll chime in."

He raised an eyebrow. "Sure you want to do it that way?"

"Yeah. Why not? You're more likely to be able to sense the current in the room. I've been pretty . . . um, self-absorbed lately."

"Baby-absorbed," he corrected me with a grin.

"Just now the two are pretty much the same," I said, "but thank you for that. It just proves I married a gentleman."

"So long as you find me a gentle man," he answered.

We rounded the corner that led to my parents' home.

* * *

TOM BURNETT

I got out of Brother Hartwell's car and leaned in to speak to him. "Thanks, Jim. I'll just get my things—"

"No, thank *you*, Tom. I always know I can count on you when I need a pinch hitter to speak in Spanish. Your talk on why we take the sacrament was one of the strongest I've ever heard, in any language."

The undeserved praise was unsettling. "You know I took most of it from Elder Oaks and other conference talks," I answered.

"Well, it was great anyway. Thanks again for coming."

"Thanks again for asking." I closed the front door and opened the back, lifted out a box, said thanks again, and watched as Jim Hartwell disappeared around the corner.

So here it was Sunday afternoon. We had made it this far. I took a quick look around, gratefully noting the lack of strange cars; Karen had warned me the Texas relatives should be arriving today. Like I wanted to spend the next four days weeping and grieving and indulging the fantasies of a lot of strangers who pretended to be family now, after all this time. None of them had shown the least bit of interest in the past thirty-five years. They'd left us. They all had. And no one seemed to understand—or care—how I felt about it.

Granny Adelaide, who had been like a mother to me after my own mother was crushed by my father's betrayal, had arranged this punishing scenario, and all the other relatives seemed to be buying into it. Even Karen—the woman who claimed to love me, who had lived with me for nearly twenty-five years and borne my children—seemed to think I should buck up and take this punishment like a man. Well, not if I had anything to say about it. She'd been able to trick me into avoiding my downtown office for a good chunk of the next few days, but she couldn't make me sit around and be part of the family charade.

I hefted the box and started for the kitchen door. I had the perfect excuse. The guys at the funeral home wanted a pretty portrait of Adelaide for the cover of the program, and Karen had asked me to dredge up some nice pictures to set on the table in the foyer where the funeral "guest book" would be. *Yeah, right. As if a dead woman can entertain guests.* I snorted at the thought. Maybe I'd indulge my dream of becoming an author one day by writing a book called *American Funerals: Inhumane Punishment for the Living.* If I could market it only to men, it would probably be a bestseller.

I juggled the box while I opened the door. I pushed through, arms full of box, to discover a kitchen full of women. *Figures.* "Hi, everyone. I'm home."

"Glad you're here," Karen said, walking toward me.

Nope. I was not getting drawn in to whatever she had in mind. "Well, good to see you all," I said, shouldering through. "I got Jim to take me by our storage unit, where I picked up this box of photos, so I'm just gonna go into the office to dig through them. I'd appreciate it if nobody bothers me for a while. See you all later."

I made the announcement as I pushed through the kitchen and into the office, finally closing the door behind me. Out of the corner of my eye, I saw my wife and daughters exchange quick looks. Then Steph whispered to Emily, "It's like I told you. He really hasn't come to grips yet," and Em responded, "I hope he'll get there soon." What did they expect of me, anyway?

In the office, I put down the box, stretched my aching back, drew in a breath, and huffed it out in a rush. Well, I'd faced down the first challenge. Probably only two or three hundred left over the next four days. I couldn't help wondering if I was up to this.

* * *

TOM BURNETT

I could smell the cabbage, hamburger, onions, and yeasty sourdough. The girls were making dinner rocks, and given the strength of the aroma, lunch was just about ready. It had been some time since breakfast. The scent seemed to grow stronger by the minute, exciting my appetite while feeding my imagination—and memory. My mother had baked her own brand of dinner rocks when I was just a child, back before . . .

The familiar ache hit me hard in the center of my chest, only this time it came with a kind of sick dread. If everything went as scheduled, it was only a matter of time before Carrie—the adult, grown and married Carrie, not the child I remembered—would be here in my living room. Although I'd come up with excuses designed to put off the inevitable, I couldn't avoid facing her forever. Soon I'd have to deal with it all—all the memories, all the betrayal, all the pain.

The thought came, *She's still your little sister*, but she wasn't—not really. So much had changed . . .

I uttered a mild expletive, too stressed to feel bad about it. I felt prompted to pray, but hadn't I been trying to pray about this for years? I could never make the thoughts and the anguish turn into words. The best I'd ever been able to manage was to *feel* that pain toward heaven, hoping the Lord understood. Hadn't the Savior been abandoned by those He loved the most? Somehow that fact alone gave me validation, comfort, hope. Somewhere there was One who knew, who truly understood how difficult this was.

I tried to focus on the box of pictures, despite the growling of my stomach and the pounding of my heart. The effort failed. I pushed my chair back and grimaced at my own cowardice, feeling twice as bad when I heard Melissa and Jason arrive and I realized I'd trapped myself in the office, unable to greet part of the family without facing the rest.

"Dang," I said aloud, and then I thought of something else, something I should have told Jim Hartwell—a message delivered at the meeting with the Spanish branch that I should have passed on before I left Jim's car. How could I have forgotten? I looked at the clock and realized Jim was probably in the middle of a late lunch with his family. Still, I knew he would want this information as quickly as possible. Best to call now, even if it meant leaving a message on his voice mail.

I reached for the phone and found it missing from its cradle. As much as I hated to admit it, Karen had been right about the portable phones;

they too frequently walked away. I looked around the office only to realize the handset wasn't anywhere nearby. To complicate matters, I'd left my cell charging in the bedroom upstairs. If I was going to leave that message for Jim, I was going to have to leave my sanctuary.

It took only seconds for me to realize I'd better go find a phone. The closest was in the family room—assuming it hadn't also walked away. I could slip out of the office, make a dash down the hall, pick up that handset, and hightail it back in a matter of fifteen or twenty seconds. I opened the door and dashed out.

I almost got away with it too. I was just rounding the corner on my way back into the office when the doorbell rang, catching me a few feet from the front door. Through its glass I could see the shape of a woman silhouetted against the setting sun—someone about Karen's size.

Carrie.

I looked at the office door and considered making a run for it. Behind me in the kitchen I could hear the voices: "Who can get that?" "My hands are covered in goo." "Well, so are mine!" "Where's Aunt Shirley?" I saw the woman reach up to ring the bell again, and I decided.

"Time to face the music," I murmured aloud. I pasted on a phony smile, hoping it didn't look too much like a grimace. Then I stepped forward and opened the door.

For a second, neither of us spoke. I couldn't help staring, taking in the face I almost knew, the hair the color of our mother's, the plaintive look on her face. Behind her I could see a large van full of people—men, women, kids—all waiting with expressions that were half anticipation, half worry. I swallowed hard, and then I spoke. "Carrie?" It squeaked out of me. I'd heard the same sound come from mice caught in kill traps.

Then the woman did something totally unexpected. "Tommy!" she cried and threw both arms around me.

I stood in the doorway with this strange-familiar woman wrapped around me, wondering what to do with my hands. Then slowly I let them settle around her, finding their own way to her back, her hair, stroking and soothing her as she sobbed in my arms. And I felt the tightness in my chest begin to ease.

I felt more than heard Karen as she came up behind me and slowly the scene around me changed. Someone—Karen, I thought—spoke, introducing the other people who materialized around us. Someone else— maybe Stephanie?—invited the people in the van to come in and they all started bailing out like a scene from the circus. Someone said something about dinner and whether people were hungry, and I thought I heard someone else answer yes. Words and actions swirled around us as if caught in a slow-motion kaleidoscope.

"I . . . I'm sorry," I heard himself saying, "but I have a phone call I have to finish." I extricated myself from the embrace of my grown-up sister and stumbled back into the office. Then I was sitting at my desk with the phone in my hands, the call to Jim forgotten as silent tears soaked the blotter. I wasn't ready for any of this—and I knew it.

* * *

I sat in the office, unable to focus on the box in front of me, delaying the inevitable with a game of computer solitaire. I was just pondering how I might sneak out to grab one of the girls' dinner rocks when the office door opened and a tiny, dark-haired cherub floated in. His black hair and Latin features made it clear whose grandson he was, but he was also uniquely, beautifully himself. He walked up to me, held both arms above his head, and said, "Up?" How could I resist that? I lifted the child into my lap.

He reached into my shirt pocket for the pens I always carried, and I parried the move by handing him a pen, the one with a tight cap firmly affixed, while pushing the others to the back of the desk. The boy reached for the stapler, and I handed him a tightly closed box of paper clips, a kind of makeshift rattle. He rattled it once, grew bored immediately, and set it down. Then he reached for the telephone.

We played that game a while—the boy checking out interesting items in my workspace while I redirected his attention to less interesting things that would cause less trouble. Then he looked at the photograph that was up on my computer screen and said, "Gwanny." My breath caught in my throat. Rather than trusting myself to answer, I simply nodded. This toddler, barely out of babyhood, recognized my grandmother's picture?

I must have misheard. I clicked the mouse, bringing up a different picture. The child pointed. "Gwanny." Swallowing over the lump in my throat, I tried it a third time. The boy said, "Gwanny." Then, apparently bored with the new game, he slid out of my lap, his tiny shoes hitting the floor with a thud.

That was when the door opened again. A lovely young woman with darker coloring but with features much like Carrie's looked in and said, "Tommy? What are you doing in here?"

I started to speak, to tell her I wasn't called Tommy anymore, but the boy ran to her, lifted his arms, and said, "Up." She lifted him.

"I'm sorry," she said. "I didn't realize Tommy was in here bothering you—"

"Your son's name is Tommy?"

"Yes, after my father. After *our* father, I think." The woman stepped forward, tentatively holding out a hand. "You're Tom, aren't you?"

I nodded. Then, remembering some manners, I stood and took the hand she offered.

"I'm your sister Amanda."

I heard the words *half sister!* pop into my mind, but instead of speaking at all, I nodded, slowly shaking the hand I still held. "Amanda," I said finally.

She said, "Mandy, if you prefer. That's what most of the family calls me."

"Mandy," I said, though my voice was barely more than a whisper.

"Man-dy!" A woman's voice called from the other room.

"Oops! Looks like I'm needed," Mandy said. "We're getting ready to serve lunch. We can all go in together if you like."

Well, why not? It was time. I let go of Amanda's hand and followed her from the office.

*   *   *

Evening

EMILY BURNETT

It was something of a madhouse—the four of us who live here plus Aunt Shirley, Mel and Jason, and twelve of the Texas relatives, all having lunch together. People and paper plates were spread from the kitchen through the dining area, family room, and living room, and some brave souls even braved the heat to eat on the back porch patio furniture. Thank goodness Steph and I had made a huge batch of dinner rocks. There was tons of salad and lots of applesauce too. I think everybody had enough to eat.

What with Candi misplacing her shoes again and Dad straggling in late and everything else that happened, it was well after three before we had lunch, so Mom forgot all about putting the roast in the oven. When people got hungry again around seven, we just got out leftovers from lunch and some sandwich-makings. The whole time Dad was kind of weird. He's usually the social one, outgoing, but he walked around one time, shaking everyone's hand and repeating names. After that he just sat in a corner and watched.

Sometime around eight, the little ones started yawning, and Aunt Carrie said she thought they needed to go back to Granny's house.

My mother said, "Thank you so much for coming. It's wonderful to see this next generation of family coming up. The babies are all so beautiful. I just wish Granny could have seen—" She choked up, and there was a sniffly moment when everyone was quiet.

Then Aunt Mandy said, "She did see them. The last time she came out was less than two years ago."

Dad's eyes went very wide.

"I knew Ruby said she was taking Granny on a little vacation," Mom said, "but I didn't realize they went all the way to Texas. I assume they flew?"

"Yes. It was tough on Granny, but she said that seeing the babies was the only reason she had for still being with us," Aunt Tina answered. "She sat and rocked them, one at a time."

"Everyone who'd sit still to be rocked," Mandy said, and the other Texas family all chuckled at that. Apparently some of the children had refused to be held. "But they all let her tell them stories," Mandy assured us. They seemed to know Granny well, which surprised all of us. We had no idea Granny had been such an intricate part of their lives.

"Granny loved the little ones," Carrie said again, her voice soft.

That's when Jason stood up and spoke up—pretty loudly, actually. "Speaking of little ones, Melissa and I have an announcement." Then everyone spoke at once.

Mom said, "I thought so!"

Aunt Shirley said, "Fabulous, Melissa! When are you due?"

Dad said, "What? Already?"

Jason said, "I haven't even made my announcement yet!"

Mel laughed and stood up next to him. "Yes, honey. You have," she said. Then she looked out at everybody. "We're having a little one of our own around the middle of December."

It took her putting it that plainly before I realized what everybody was talking about. I guess they'd all been expecting it, but I hadn't really thought about it until then. I said, "I'm going to be an auntie?"

I guess I looked as surprised as I felt because Dad grinned as he said, "It happens sometimes, when young people get married."

One of the little girls said, "Will it be a boy or a girl?"

Mel said, "Uh-huh," and everyone laughed. Then there was another round of questions and excitement, all the women checking in with Mel to see how she was feeling and if she was getting good prenatal care and all the men patting Jason on the back as if it was all about him—which I thought was sort of silly, really.

After a few minutes, one of the little kids started crying, and everyone remembered that the Texas family had been gearing up to leave when the big announcement happened. I helped the aunts load the little ones into the van and waved while they drove away. Long after they were all gone, I lay on my bed thinking about Granny and Melissa and a whole family of relatives I'd never known before and wondering what it would be like to be an auntie.

I thought of how sad it was that Granny couldn't see all these people who loved her so much, and then suddenly, I knew. I knew that somehow Granny *was* with us and that seeing us all together made her very happy. I smiled toward heaven through my tears. Knowing that made me happy too.

Italian Bruschetta

Pronounced bru-sketta, this is a national dish of Italy.

1 ½ pounds ripe plum tomatoes (about 6–8)
2 cloves minced garlic
1 tsp. balsamic vinegar
1 Tbsp. extra virgin olive oil

6–8 fresh basil leaves, finely chopped
Salt and freshly ground black pepper to taste
1 baguette sourdough bread
¼ C. olive oil

Directions

1. Parboil tomatoes for 1 minute in boiling water that has been removed from the burner. Drain. Peel. Cut them in halves or quarters, remove the seeds and juice from their centers. Also cut out and discard stems.
2. Place the top rack in your oven, and preheat to 450.
3. While the oven is heating, chop the tomatoes finely. Put tomatoes, garlic, vinegar, and 1 Tbsp. extra virgin olive oil in a bowl, and mix. Add the chopped basil. Add salt and pepper to taste.
4. Slice the baguette on a diagonal, in about ½-inch thick slices. Using a pastry brush, coat one side of each slice with olive oil. Place on a cooking sheet, oil side down.
5. Once the oven has reached 450, place a tray of bread slices on the top rack. Toast for 5–6 minutes, until the bread just begins to turn golden brown.
6. For the more traditional method, you can toast the bread without coating it in olive oil first. Toast on a griddle for 1 minute on each side. Take a sharp knife and score each slice 3 times. Rub some garlic in the slices and drizzle half a teaspoon of olive oil on each slice.
7. Align the bread on a serving platter, olive oil side up. Spoon some topping on each slice of bread and serve immediately so the bread doesn't get soggy.

Serves 6–10 as an appetizer, or 3–4 for lunch. It's also delicious served with cottage cheese or mozzarella slices on the side.

Variations

Consider adding some oregano and black or green olives to the tomato mixture, or toss in some feta cheese. Alternatively, top the bruschetta with shredded mozzarella and give them another 30 seconds under the broiler. You can also forgo the traditional tomato-basil mix and top toasted slices with an artichoke-garlic spread available in many grocery stores.

For a simple luncheon, make two sets of bruschetta, one topped in tomato-basil and the other spread with artichoke-garlic. Serve with green salad (Italian dressing), cheese slices, and fresh fruit.

CHAPTER 23

Monday, June 18, Late morning

KAREN BURNETT

IT HAD BEEN A BEAUTIFUL, cool morning, and I was up early, tending the garden and gathering tomatoes and basil for bruschetta, one of my daughters' favorite summer lunches. Then I put Shirley to work, making Italian-style sourdough baguettes. As I kneaded, I couldn't help thinking of the women who had preceded me, good women who had practiced gardening and bread making and cooking over the eons, passing their wisdom down, making these tasks so much easier for those of us who came after.

That thought led me back to the office, to my computer, and to the menu for Granny's funeral luncheon, and that led me back to worry. No matter how many times I reviewed the menu, there simply wasn't enough food. There wasn't enough variety. There just wasn't *enough*.

Mary had called again with another recipe she recalled, this one for fresh-from-the-garden green beans flavored with garlic and ginger. I'd had my doubts about it, but now as I read over the recipe again, it was making my mouth water, so I added the green bean dish to the menu and entered the recipe into the computer. Now if we could just come up with a few more side dishes . . .

"Hey, everybody!" Emily's voice called from the front hallway. "Aunt Lenore is here!"

"Lenore? Already?" I heard Shirley coming from the kitchen.

I set aside menu questions for later and went to greet Aunt Lenore.

If Lenore Burnett weren't such a gracious lady, I think I would forever feel like a Holstein in her presence. A retired professional ballerina and ballet instructor, Lenore is still a tiny, delicate pixie of a woman, not over five foot three until she appears in four-inch heels or toe shoes, and about as big around as your average third grader's pencil—all of it slim, toned muscle. She wears her silver hair like a crown, and I never see her without thinking of Titania, Shakespeare's fairy queen. The personality can fit sometimes too, but she's typically a sweetheart.

I arrived in our entryway just in time to see Lenore glide in through the front door, embracing each of the women in the family, one at a time. I hadn't seen her since Granny's one hundredth birthday party, but she looked as elegant as ever.

"Lenore, great to see you!" I said, closing the office door behind me as I went to take my place in the hugging. "I'm just so sorry for the circumstances."

"Oh, me too," Lenore said, hugging me as if she planned to squeeze all the air from my lungs. "Me too." She held on for a moment, and I could feel her tears on my neck. Then she turned to her sister.

"So how are things developing here?" she asked, and I realized she was referring to much more than funeral plans. Both of my late father-in-law's sisters had worried about his divided family for decades.

"I guess about as well as can be expected," Shirley said. And then she threw both arms around her sister. "Oh, Lee! It's so good to see you!" The two stood holding each other.

Lee. I knew Lenore had used that name professionally. For decades she had appeared as Lee Burns, first as a principal dancer with the San Francisco Ballet and later in guest choreography stints in various locations, most notably with the American Ballet Theatre in New York. Yet within the family, she was always Aunt Lenore. For a moment I wondered how different her life must be when she was away from us.

"Did you get any rest?" Shirley asked as she picked up one of Lenore's bags. Then, to the rest of us, "Lee was in London when I called her."

"London?" Em asked. "What were you doing over there?"

"I went with some friends to see the ballet," Lenore answered Em, then to no one in particular she added, "Jet lag seems to hit me harder the older I get."

"Let's get your things upstairs," Shirley said. Melissa and Emily helped, and the group moved upstairs together while I went back into the office to work more on the menu.

For a moment I just thought about the two sisters. They seemed about as different as two women could be—Lenore petite and dainty, sophisticated and refined, a celebrity in a large and glittering world. Shirley was both taller and heavier, a solid Mormon mom little known outside her own small circle of family and friends. Each of them could have plenty of reason to be jealous of the other: Lenore had achieved remarkable and enviable successes, even being introduced to most of the world's remaining royalty. Yet it was Shirley who had borne and raised the family that Lenore had always wanted. In fact, she'd once confided to me, early in my acceptance into the family, that she'd give up the world of ballet in a moment if she could meet the right man and have a baby. It had never happened for her, despite her having so much to offer.

So the two of them could have been enemies, consumed by envy of one another. Instead, they were the primary support for each other and obviously dear friends. I reflected they had much to teach the rest of us, and I hoped the pieced-together Burnett clan could benefit from the calm strength I felt in their bond, their mutual support.

Lenore had seemed so weary when she came through the door that I was surprised when she came back down a few minutes later with the rest of the group. "I thought you were going to rest awhile," I said as I stepped back out of the office.

"I will," Lenore answered. "I need to, but first I have some things in the car that need to be taken care of. The girls said they'll help me get them, but I want you to see this, Karen." I agreed and was there waiting when the girls came back in, each of them carrying a large canvas tote.

"I hope you don't mind," Lenore said, "but I stopped at the store on my drive in from the airport. Shirley had told me about Mother's plans to have an old-style reunion dinner following her service, and I want to help."

"You didn't need to do that—" I began, and then I saw what the girls were lifting out of the bags—melons, loads of them. Watermelons, honeydew, cantaloupe, Persian melons, and even a few I didn't recognize. "Oh, Lenore. Thank you! I had figured out most of the menu, but I was stuck for side dishes. Now everyone can fill up on melon, I think we're set. Thank you!" I hugged her.

"I gather it's good then," Lenore said drily.

"Good? You are an answer to prayer."

Lenore smiled gently. "Glad I can help."

We had borrowed a second fridge that Tom set up on the back porch, and I turned it on now, setting the melons inside to chill. Now that we had the basics, I could add some salads and make a complete meal. This was the perfect answer, exactly what I had needed to round out our feast. The girls helped me finish the bruschetta and we ate our simple lunch, then Lenore went upstairs to catch a nap and I settled down to finish the dinner menu and assignments. It felt like a full and useful morning.

* * *

Late afternoon

Lenore was still napping, and Shirley had gone out to do some quick shopping for our evening meal. Stephanie had gone to the university to meet with a professor who wanted to discuss her final paper before assigning a grade. She was nervous when she left, and I said a little prayer for her. Then I went back to the office to put the finishing touches on arrangements for the family lunch. I was still working down my list of phone calls and e-mails when Emily knocked on the office door.

"Come in. Oh, what's up, Em?"

"The family from Texas are supposed to be here later this afternoon, right?"

"That's what they said. I haven't heard anything today. Carrie said they had some errands they wanted to take care of this morning, but I'm guessing they'll be here well before dinnertime."

"I was thinking it might be fun to bake some cookies. I mean, we have the pumpkin bread Aunt Shirley brought, and we'll be putting the roast in soon so there'll be plenty of dinner, but—"

"You don't need to explain, Em. Cookies are a great idea."

"Oh. Good. What do you think of Snickers-doodles?"

"Excellent choice," I answered, giving her a smile. "Why don't you call Aunt Shirley's cell phone and ask her to pick up a couple of candy bars while she's at the store?"

"Okay. Good idea," Em said and got Shirley's number before she went back to the kitchen.

Snickers-doodles are an old tradition in the Burnett family. The idea was new to me when I married in, but I think the Burnetts must have been making them since there were Snickers bars. Certainly they had been a big memory for Tom, who was eager to share them with his new wife some twenty-five years ago. If he remembered them with that kind of fondness, maybe others of the family would too. It was a great idea, and I felt grateful to Em for thinking of it. "Oh, Em!" I called after her.

"Yes, Mom?"

"Make a double or triple batch, okay?"

"Sure thing!" Emily disappeared around the corner with a huge smile on her face, and I felt better too.

Shirley, Lenore, and I had decided to slice the melons ourselves. We'd get them sliced and arranged on trays then deliver them to the stake center kitchen before we went to the family prayer meeting. Charis, my second counselor, had promised to oversee the kitchen. She was willing to toss the green salad as well. Larissa was bringing the orzo salad. As I reviewed my list, I found I had three sisters with slow cookers who were preparing the chili beef, two more working on the spicy slaw, and three more bringing rolls and butter. One of those, dear Dana Richards, had volunteered to bring her own homemade pomegranate jelly and apple butter as well.

Three more sisters had eagerly accepted the recipe and the responsibility for fresh corn casserole, and two more were making ginger-garlic green beans. Charis, Larissa, and Kerry, all of whom were attending the funeral, would set up our luncheon in the Scout room while the family went to the cemetery. By the time we got back to the stake center, they would have a family reunion dinner—perhaps even one reminiscent of the old-time Burnett family dinners—all ready to go. Everything was assigned except the desserts, and I thought I'd probably just call four or five of the women on my sign-up sheet to ask if they'd bring cakes.

I was in the kitchen some thirty minutes later, helping Aunt Shirley put away the prepared foods she'd purchased at the nearby deli and helping Emily cut up Snickers bars, when I voiced that idea—the four or five cakes, I mean.

Shirley and Em exchanged a look. "Isn't that what you'd do for a regular funeral?" Shirley asked.

"Well, yes, but—"

"This isn't a regular funeral, Mom." Em sounded positively scandalized. "This is for *Granny*."

"Yes, I know, Em, but—"

"I think we can come up with some old Burnett family favorites," Shirley said, "or maybe some new ones. What about that coconut pie you made last Christmas, Karen?"

"That's my recipe," I answered, "one I created myself, and it's brand new. The old-time Burnetts would never have heard of it."

"Well, it's delicious anyway. I think we ought to have that—unless you'd prefer not to share it . . ."

I think I blushed. "Oh no, that's not a problem. I was just trying to make it easy on people—"

"Let's make it *nice*," Shirley offered. "People won't mind doing this the right way, especially if they get your recipe for that great coconut pie in the process."

"Okay," I said, smiling at the way Shirley had managed to critique and change my plans while complimenting me at the same time. "You know, Aunt Shirley, you really could have had a diplomatic career."

"I did," she answered with a twinkle. "I grew up a Burnett."

She had her mother's genes for resourcefulness, for certain. Within the next hour, she had dug up Judith's recipe for Pavlova—a special baked meringue dish, the national dessert of Australia—that my late mother-in-law had made only for special occasions, including the annual family reunion. As with some of the other recipes, Judith had shared it with Adelaide, who had kept it in her recipe file for decades. Shirley had remembered a discussion with her mother about it and had gone to Ruby to pinpoint which recipe it was. By the time another hour had passed, I had asked two more sisters to make huge triple batches of Pavlova, had found four more to bake coconut pies, and had asked two others to bring whipped topping for the pies.

It was Monday afternoon, plenty late enough in the game, but I was glad to have the plans finally made for the whole dinner, and I felt good about them too. I thought this meal might be a positive occasion, and maybe even an opportunity for some of the Burnetts to enjoy a few happy memories from their shared past. I was beginning to think I could pull this off after all—with a lot of help from my friends.

Snickers-doodles

½ C. butter, softened
1 C. sugar
¼ tsp. baking soda
¼ tsp. cream of tartar
1 egg

½ tsp. vanilla
1 ½ C. all-purpose flour
2 Tbsp. sugar
1 tsp. ground cinnamon

Directions

1. Beat butter with an electric mixer for 30 seconds. Add sugar, baking soda, and cream of tartar. Beat until combined, scraping sides to include all ingredients. Add egg and vanilla and as much of the flour as you can with the mixer. Stir in remaining flour. Cover and chill dough about 1 hour or until it is easy to handle.
2. Cut a Snickers or other candy bar into 10–12 equal pieces, each about ½-inch square.
3. Preheat oven to 375. Place one small piece of candy into the middle of each 1-inch ball of dough.
4. Mix cinnamon and sugar, and roll balls in the mixture until fully coated. Place 2 inches apart on an ungreased cookie sheet. Bake 10–11 minutes or until edges are golden. Transfer to a wire rack; cool.

CHAPTER 24

Monday, June 18, Late afternoon

KAREN BURNETT

WE WERE IN THE KITCHEN making cinnamon-sugar and preheating the oven when the door to the garage opened and Stephanie came in. I asked, "Well, Steph? You were gone a long time. Is everything all right?"

"Yeah, better than all right. Mom, Professor Morgan says my research could be 'significant.' She wants to help me get it published!"

"Published? As in 'published in a professional journal'?" Steph nodded, and I threw my arms around her. "Oh, Steph! That's wonderful! Published as an undergrad. Oh, honey, I'm so proud of you!" Emily and the two great-aunts crowded in as everyone offered hugs and congratulations.

"It will be a lot of work to get the article into top condition, but I think it will be worth it," Steph said. "And there are still several weeks before fall classes start. My job in the college office is only half time until then, so I'll have some concentrated time to work on my research. Dr. Morgan has some good ideas. She'll be available for most of the summer, and she says she'll help me all she can, looking at drafts and offering ideas. If I include her as a secondary author, she has friends at some of the top journals who will almost certainly take it seriously. I think this could be really good for me."

"It sounds like a wonderful opportunity for you, darling," Lenore said.

I said, "It's great, honey. I'm so excited for you!"

Steph looked toward the office. "Is Dad home? I'd like to tell him too."

"He's home," I told her, "but it might be good for you to wait until dinnertime."

Steph groaned. "He's having another rough day, huh?"

Shirley spoke. "He came home from work with a box of pictures from Mother's house and said he didn't want to be bothered while he looks through them."

"He might make an exception for good news though," Lenore added.

Steph considered it and then said, "No. I think I'll let him stew by himself for a while." She looked at the dough. "So what's this? Snickers-doodles?"

"Right," Emily answered.

"Delicious," Steph said. "Let me help."

"You just want to eat the dough," Emily teased.

"You know it, li'l sis." Steph picked off a chunk and popped it into her mouth, savoring the flavors. "Mmmm."

Emily put the back of her hand to her forehead in a dramatic gesture. "One less cookie already. How can I go on? Oh, what shall I do?"

"Give me another one?" Steph suggested to her sister's delighted giggle. The two settled down to their baking.

* * *

STEPHANIE BURNETT

The first batch of cookies was in, and Emily was busy on the second when Shirley invited Lenore up to the room they were sharing to look at the pictures of their mother she had chosen to display. "I'd just like a second opinion," she said as they left the room together. "You ladies don't mind, do you?"

We all assured her that we didn't, and the great-aunts left together.

"Hey, Em," I said then. "Would it be okay with you if I took Mom away for a minute?"

"More dough for me," Emily teased.

"Don't overdose," I kidded her back. Then I said to Mom, "Does now seem like a good time?"

She gave me a long, assessing look. "Now seems like a very good time." Then to my sister, "Excuse us, Em. We'll be upstairs if you need us."

"Cool," Emily said. She was humming as she worked, and I thought the cookies were as much therapy for her as they were preparation for our guests.

Mom led the way to her bedroom. When we got inside, she said, "What's this about, Steph? Is it serious?"

"I just really need to talk about something," I said. "But Mom, it's kind of tough. Just let me say what I have to say, okay? After that, I can answer questions if you have any. That all right with you?"

Mom's brow furrowed, and I thought she seemed paler than usual, even over these past few days. "All right," she said. She sank to the edge of her bed and motioned me toward the chair. I sat facing her.

Over the next few minutes, I told her the whole story. I talked about what I remembered of Grandma Judith, told her about the way the darkness sometimes closed in on me, and unloaded all I could remember of the incident that had left scars on both my arm and my psyche.

"You said you'd cut yourself on a broken bowl," she said as she sat forward, fingering my scars.

"I did."

"But it wasn't the way you said—or at least, not the way you made us think. Honey, why didn't you tell us any of this?"

"Please, Mom? You said you'd let me finish."

"Okay. Sorry." But she didn't look happy as she settled back, letting me talk again.

I told her about my meeting with Jess and how I'd gotten recipes for Indian foods, all of which we could use during the next few days if she wanted to. Then, just as she was starting to look impatient, I told her about my resolve never to date anyone more than twice, about my plans not ever to marry, and about how I'd been questioning those ideas since I'd realized what a powerhouse of genetic material I had in her and Granny. "I've been thinking maybe I'm made of stronger stuff than I thought, Mom. I've been thinking maybe I can have a real life, but I'm afraid. I've shown myself that I can be like Grandma Judith was, and I don't ever want to do to a family what she did to hers."

"Oh, sweetheart," Mom said. She was crying when she stood and lifted me into her arms, hugging me long and hard. We cried together for a minute or two, and then she let me settle down again into the chair, but she kept my hand in hers while she talked.

"In a way, I can't help wishing you'd brought this up long ago," she said as she began. "In another way, this is the perfect time. As it happens, I've just recently learned some interesting facts about your grandmother's illness."

She unraveled it all then—the schizophrenia, the medications that could straighten Grandma Judith out completely when she bothered to take them, the way she stopped taking them every time she thought it was time to have another baby. She even told me about how my dad's dad had solved that problem by moving out of his wife's bed. She talked about the way Dad had missed or misconstrued most of the clues the other family members had seen and told me about how Mary and Steve had created the Nice Mama/Mean Mama standard to help them cope with the problems my dad had never understood.

When she had unreeled it all, she said, "Steph, sweetheart, I can't promise you that you'll never have the experiences your grandmother had. You're obviously prone to depression, but it helps that you're wise enough to understand it. You've already begun fighting it in some very healthy ways—"

"But, Mom—"

"Shhh, darling. Now it's my turn."

I quieted.

"Honey, we can get you medical help."

"But shouldn't I just be stronger? Just handle it on my own?"

"It isn't a question of being strong, baby." Mom was gently stroking the scars on my arm. She looked like her heart was breaking, and I couldn't help wishing I'd never felt the need to say any of these things. "You're plenty strong," she said. "Just look at you!" Despite the tears on her face, there was pride in her eyes, and I was grateful. I had feared my mother's shame.

"Mental illness is *illness*, sweetheart. True, some people have behavioral problems that can look a lot the same, but real schizophrenia isn't caused by a lack of discipline. Your grandmother couldn't help being ill. Depression isn't a choice either—at least, not for most people. Why would anyone want to feel like that?"

"Mom, I—"

"Hush," she said again, so gently. "Listen, baby, you've read about chemical imbalances, right?"

"Not really."

"Then do so, whenever you find a minute. Go to some credible websites and read up on depression. That will help you understand some of the reasons why you occasionally feel very dark. Another thing that may help is reading the differences between depression and schizophrenia.

Just because you have one problem doesn't mean you're in line for the other."

"I know they come across differently, but don't they all have the same cause?"

"By 'they,' I assume you mean mental illnesses?"

"Right. Craziness of one sort and another."

Mom sighed. "You don't have to use that term, Steph. Mentally ill people aren't necessarily crazy at all." She sighed again; this time it sounded like frustration. "People aren't always sure what causes schizophrenia, Steph, but one thing doctors are fairly certain of. It's different from garden-variety depression, which is often due to a lack of serotonin in your brain chemistry."

"Sarah-what?"

Mom smiled. "Never mind. You don't need the vocabulary yet." She stood, taking in a deep breath. "The first thing you need to know is your dad and I are with you. Whatever you need to help you feel well and have a healthy life, we'll do it."

"Thanks." I patted her arm.

"When Granny's funeral is over and life gets back to what passes for normal around here, let's make a medical appointment for you. Dr. Russell can run some simple chemistry panels to let us know whether he thinks you need some kind of chemical intervention."

I felt my face wrinkle up. "Pills? Do you think that's really necessary?"

She took me by the shoulders. "If the doctor thinks so, yes. Definitely. If only to let you know that things aren't necessarily as dark as you're painting them."

"But what if I have to take regular meds? What if I'm more like Grandma Judith than either of us knows right now?"

"What if you are?" Mom said, and she looked me straight in the eye. "Don't you think you can learn from her experience? Take your meds when you need them? Even limit your family if you must to be healthy?"

I wondered if she'd heard everything I'd said before. "I wasn't really planning on having a family."

I watched as Mom took another deep breath. "That will have to be up to you, of course, but I think it would be a very sad thing for you to deny yourself the blessings of marriage and children just because of a fear that may turn out to be nothing."

"And if it turned out to be something after all?"

"Then you and the man who loves you can figure it out as you go along. You'd have to do that if it turned out you'd inherited my great-grandfather's poor eyesight or your great-great-grandmother's diabetes, right?"

"Yeah. Right," I answered, and I think I smiled a little.

"Have I helped you at all?" she asked.

"Yeah," I said. "A lot."

She drew me close to her and gave me another hug. "Then I guess we'd better get back to helping Emily," she said. We started for the hallway. "You know, you kind of scared me when we first came up here."

"Yeah. I kind of got that impression."

"But there's really nothing to be afraid of, is there?" She looked at me with such love in her eyes.

"No, Mom," I answered. "I guess there's not." Maybe I was even starting to believe it.

*   *   *

Late afternoon

EMILY BURNETT

When Mom and Steph left to go upstairs together, I collapsed into a chair, relaxing a little. Steph hadn't said what was bothering her, but it was pretty obvious something was . . . a lot. I mean, we were all in mourning, grieving for Granny Adelaide, but there was something more going on with my sister. I only had to be around her a little to get that. I was glad she had finally decided to talk to Mom.

Maybe two minutes later I was rolling cookies in cinnamon-sugar, trying to load up the cookie sheet for the next batch, when the phone rang. I took it in the kitchen and was surprised to hear Ms. Nguyen's voice.

"Hello? Is this Emily?"

"Hi, Ms. Nguyen. What's up?"

"It's . . . I feel foolish. Maybe I shouldn't have called." There was a long pause.

"Is there something I can help you with? Did you have a question or something?"

"Maybe. Sort of." She took a deep breath. "I was just working through these hymns you asked me to play, and I started reading the lyrics." She paused again. "These words—'I am a child of God and He has sent me here.' This is a metaphor, right?"

I paused. "I guess I don't understand what you're asking."

She cleared her throat. "Well, most people think we are God's creations, like the planets and the birds and animals and so forth. In that sense, we are all children of the Great Creator. I guess that's what you mean by this, right?"

"No, not really," I said and took another deep breath, thinking a quick prayer in my heart. "We believe that God is our Heavenly Father. He's the father of my spirit the same way Tom Burnett is the father of my body."

"Really?"

"Yes, ma'am. All of us lived with Him as spirits before we were born on the earth. He knew us and planned for us there."

"Oh, okay. I see now." Her voice suddenly sounded hurried, and I realized she just wanted to get me off the phone. I wanted to find something to say to make her feel better, but I didn't know what.

"Ms. Nguyen—"

"Well, thank you, Emily. Sorry to bother you. I'll have the music ready for tomorrow. See you then."

"Ms. Nguyen, I—"

"Bye, Emily. See you tomorrow." She hung up.

There were tears in my eyes when I put down the phone. I didn't want Ms. Nguyen to think badly of me, or of our Church, but I didn't know what more I could have said. I was glad she was willing to play for Granny's funeral, and I hoped she wouldn't feel bad about being there tomorrow.

I closed my eyes and said another short prayer for her. It seemed like all I could do.

* * *

Early evening

KAREN BURNETT

"We're having last night's dinner tonight," I said as I greeted the relatives at the door. "Let me get out some paper plates and we'll be ready to go."

"Ooh, do I smell cookies?" Jeff asked, rubbing his hands together.

Carrie stepped into the kitchen. "Snickers-doodles! Oh, it's been so long . . ." She was tearing up again.

"Ladies, you can put your purses on our bed if you like." I began moving among the relatives, trying to greet everyone. I wondered when Tom would emerge from his lair and whether it was worth it to consider bothering him. For the moment, I decided to give him some space.

Emily had taken a phone call just as Steph and I went upstairs, and the cookies hadn't made much progress since I'd last seen them. "Girls," I said to my daughters. "we need the kitchen to serve everyone's dinner. Why don't you put away the candy and the rest of the dough? You can get it out again after dinner."

"Maybe we can help, then," Carrie said, her voice a little unsteady. "I used to make Snickers-doodles, years ago."

"Sounds good," I answered and went about organizing the troops. Confrontations and calamities and thinking about all Steph had told me could wait until later. Right now there were people to feed, and feeding hungry people was something I clearly understood.

Ginger-Garlic Green Beans

1 pound fresh green beans
2 tsp. vegetable oil
8 cloves garlic, minced

2 Tbsp. fresh ginger, peeled and
  minced
⅓ C. low sodium chicken stock

Directions

1. Wash the beans, trim the ends, and cut into 2-inch pieces. Arrange beans over vegetable steamer and place over boiling water. Cover and steam 5 minutes, until the beans are tender-crisp. Drain beans and set aside.
2. Heat vegetable oil over low heat. Add garlic and ginger, and sauté 3 minutes, or until tender. Add chicken stock and stir. Add beans and cook 4 more minutes, stirring occasionally. Serve immediately.

Serves 4–6.

Variations

You can tinker with the amounts of ginger and garlic. Also try using peanut oil instead of plain vegetable oil or water instead of chicken stock. For an Italian-style side dish, cut the ginger and finish the beans in a mixture of ¼ C. tomato juice and ¼ C. chicken stock; add 2 tsp. flaked Italian herbs. This is a savory approach to a plain dish and beats, by far, the canned soup casseroles found on many a holiday table.

CHAPTER 25

Monday, June 18, Evening

EMILY BURNETT

IT's COOL DAD HAS SO many relatives. They sure filled up our place when we settled in to have dinner. I was glad we had that huge roast. Then Great-Aunt Shirley bought two dozen ears of corn, premade potato salad, and lots of fresh fruit so it was easy to feed everybody. Of course, Mom insisted on trying her new green bean recipe before she had other people serve it to us, and that made the kitchen fill up with the yummy scents of garlic and ginger. But that was almost the only cooking she did besides the roast, so I knew cleanup would be easy.

I was also glad Mom had plenty of paper plates and stuff in the boxes Steph's friends brought over since Monday is one of my days to wash the dishes. I guess that's a selfish thought, but by the time Melissa and Jason showed up and Great-Aunt Shirley brought Ruby over, we had twenty people at dinner and that's a mess of dirty dishes for anybody. Anyway, it made me grateful for paper plates.

Meeting everybody yesterday was weird; they all sort of blurred together in my memory, and I had trouble recalling who was related to who and how—except for Uncle Terry. Nobody I know is that color of red. Him I can remember! Meeting them all again for our family home evening dinner has helped me sort out the blur a little, especially when Dad came out and spoke to Aunt Carrie.

One other person stuck out to me too—little Sofie. She came back to the buffet line for seconds about the same time I did, so it was just the two of us. I said, "Hi. Which cousin are you?" She didn't seem to get that, so I said, "What's your name, cutie?"

"Sofie." She ducked her head and had to take one finger out of her mouth when she said it. She was kind of swinging back and forth, and she had the biggest, blackest eyes I've ever seen.

"How old are you, Sofie?"

She held up four fingers.

"Can I get you something?"

She nodded and pointed to the fruit salad.

I looked around. "Where's your plate, sweetie?"

She pointed back toward the dining area, so I got her a new paper plate and put some salad on it. "There, is that it?"

She shook her head and said, "Agua, por favor."

This time I was grateful to Señora Morales-Soto from Spanish III. I poured some water in a paper cup and said, "Can you say, 'Water, please'?"

Sofie nodded but didn't say anything. I laughed and helped her carry her plate and cup back to her chair, which is where I learned that Sofie is the youngest daughter of my Aunt Carrie, my dad's sister. Someone had left the seat on the other side of Sofie, so I sat by her awhile. By the time we were cleaning up after dinner, Sofie and I had become best friends, and she wanted to go everywhere with me. She was letting go of some of her shyness and even starting to talk—in English. I guess she'd figured out by then that she was playing to an English-speaking crowd.

We were kind of underfoot in the kitchen, so with Aunt Carrie's permission, I took Sofie outside to meet Buster, and she loved Brian's dog. He went crazy trying to jump up on her and lick her all over her face. That usually scares little kids away, but Sofie giggled, obviously loving it. Before long, I was sweating in the June heat and wanting to go back inside, but it was tough to separate Sofie from Buster. She fussed about going in (I had to promise her I'd bring her out to see Buster again), and he whined at the door for several minutes after we left. I couldn't blame him for being crazy about her. Sofie is adorable.

Most of the mess was cleaned up when we got back to the kitchen. Every last green bean had been eaten; that made Mom feel good about the recipe she'd chosen, and I think she felt even better when Aunt Carrie asked for the recipe. When the dishes were picked up and the food was all put away, I told everybody I'd wash up the green bean pot and the few dishes we had used for serving. "After that, I'll get the dough out and make some more cookies," I said.

"May I stay and help?" It was Aunt Carrie.

I guess I gave her a funny look because she said, "I used to make these cookies with your dad. I'd like to stay and maybe talk with him some more."

I said sure, that would be all right with me, and then I asked, "If you're going to stay awhile, can Sofie stay too?"

Carrie looked at Sofie and asked her if she'd like to stay and bake cookies. She nodded yes and took my hand. Aunt Carrie smiled. "I just need to see if your mom can give us a lift back to Granny's place later on—"

That's when Mom walked back into the kitchen and said, "Of course, Carrie. Stay as long as you like. I'll be going over to Granny's with the crowd, but I'll drive my own car so I'll be back soon." There was something more going on between them, something under the surface. Mrs. Dorset, my English teacher, calls it a subtext, and I could see a whole lot of it in the way they looked at each other and the tone of their voices. I knew they were thinking of Dad and the way he's been lately. Dad doesn't know how many prayers are being said for him. Some of them are mine.

Within the next few minutes, the other Texas relatives all loaded up to head over to Granny's. They said they'd get breakfast on their own, and Mom and the other women worked out a plan for a big lunch at our place on Tuesday. Then Mom got in her own car and followed the van over to Granny's to make sure Ruby got home and to check out some pictures of Granny that were still at her place. The great-aunts went with her. Steph left at about the same time for her regular meeting for the Young Single Adults, wishing me good luck with the cookies on her way out. It was only after we waved good-bye to them all that Carrie, Sofie, and I went back into the kitchen, just the three of us, and I got out the candy and cookie dough again.

That was when Dad wandered into the kitchen. "Are there any leftov— Oh, hello Carrie. I thought . . ."

"You thought I was gone already," Carrie said.

Dad gave her a long look and said, "Well, yeah, but I think I'm glad you're here."

Carrie looked back at him, and for a few seconds, they just looked at each other. I wondered what it had been like for them to find each other again after so many years. They'd been apart most of their lifetimes. How weird would that be?

Then Carrie said, "We're making Snickers-doodles. What say you and I jump in and take over?" She gave me a look and I got the hint.

"I promised Sofie I'd take her to see Buster again," I said. "Come on, Sofie." She let me lift her down off her barstool and I led her out of the room.

As we left, I heard Aunt Carrie say, "Sit down, Tommy. I'll roll the dough into balls and hand them to you. You can roll them in the cinnamon-sugar and put them on the cookie sheet. Okay?"

"Okay," he responded, then he said, "It's Tom now. I'm not Tommy anymore." That's when we got out of hearing range.

We did see Buster, but it was still pretty miserable outside, so I let him into the mud porch and we played with him there for a few minutes. Then I fed him—my job since Brian left—and put him back out. By then Sofie was rubbing her eyes, so I took her into the family room, close to the kitchen, and got out one of my old storybooks. I started reading but hadn't gotten through more than a couple of pages before Sofie was lying on the couch with her head in my lap, fast asleep. I sat there stroking her hair and thinking. That's when I realized that without the four-year-old noises, I could hear most of what was happening in the kitchen, so I tuned my hearing to eavesdrop.

". . . same recipe we used to make when we were kids?" Carrie asked.

"Yeah, I think so," Dad said. "It tastes the same, anyway."

"That can't be bad!" There was silence for a moment except for some banging of pans and utensils. It sounded like they were just getting started.

Dad asked, "We made these cookies the day before you left, remember?"

"I remember," Carrie said. "Michael and I ate those cookies with our lunch in the car the next day. Mama Rocio said—"

"Don't call her that."

"Huh? Don't call who what?"

"Don't call that woman Mama. You had a mother, a real mother who—"

"Oh, stop it, Tom." Her voice sounded tired. "I know this has all been tough for you, but Rocio is the only mother I've ever known. She's the one who raised me."

"That's bull! You had a mother, Carrie. You were four when you left. Surely you must have some memories of our real mother—"

"Oh yes, I have memories of our mother, all right." Carrie's voice had suddenly changed. "I remember the way Rocio used to go up and get her out of bed around two o'clock every afternoon. She'd make her wash her hands and face, then she'd put some clothes on her and bring her downstairs. Usually Mom would zone out in front of the TV—that's if we were lucky. If we weren't, she'd start screaming at us, giving us orders, and calling us ugly names. When she was like that, not even Rocio could handle her."

"Oh, cut the crap, Carrie! That's all wrong," Dad said. "You were a little kid. You don't really remember at all. Mom was never like that until after you guys left us."

There was a sharp sound to Aunt Carrie's voice as she said, "So which is it, Tom? Am I old enough to remember our very ill, schizophrenic mother, or am I too young to recall what it was like? You can't have it both ways."

"Well, you must have been too young to remember if you think it was like that!"

"No, you're the one who doesn't remember."

"Oh, come on, Carrie. I was—"

"No, seriously, Tom. You were always gone—at school, or at Cub Scouts, or at soccer or T-ball, or shooting hoops at Billy Gilstrap's house . . . By the time you got home, Rocio had dinner on the table and Dad had Mom under control again and everything looked just like a normal, happy family. Maybe you never saw the rest of it, but I did and I remember it very well. Billy Gilstrap, Tom. You see? I do remember."

"No, you don't! You couldn't, because Mom wasn't that bad even after you left. For a few days, she was in shock. I guess we all were. I mean, half our family had run out on us. Who wouldn't be?"

There was silence for a moment, and then Dad said, "She stayed in bed, or when she got up, she cried all the time, but that wasn't surprising because we were all crying. Something terrible had just been done to us, and Granny had to come over to take care of us while we got through that initial shock. But then Mom pulled it together and began the business of taking care of the family on her own. She was really pretty put together— for a while, anyway."

Aunt Carrie seemed thoughtful. "Granny always said she did better when she was on her meds. Maybe she started them again when she realized she had to get her head in gear."

"Is that the lie Dad fed you? Because it's wrong too. Our mom was never on any meds until a year or so after Dad betrayed her with Rocio. Then she realized she was in trouble and went to see a doctor. That was when the medications started."

"She was in trouble long before that. Dad told me she first started medicating for her condition sometime before I was born. Then she'd quit the meds every time she wanted to have another baby. She quit before me and she quit again before Michael and she was off them again when Dad finally gave up and left her. If she'd just been willing to take the medications the doctors prescribed for her—"

"If that were all true, you would never have been born!"

There was silence for a moment, and then Carrie said, "No, I don't suppose I would have. And in that respect, I suppose I'll have to be grateful for how things went, but it was Mom's stubbornness to accept treatment that finally drove our dad away. It was convenient that Rocio was there when he decided to leave, but I think he would have left Mom anyway. He was done with fighting it by then."

"That's bu—that's nonsense. There was *nothing* wrong with our mother before Dad betrayed her, and it was Rocio who drove our dad away. There was nothing wrong with Mom before that, Carrie. Nothing! I suppose Dad had to justify his actions to you, and I realize you feel you have to defend your actions now, but—"

"*My* actions? What actions would those be?" By this time she was furious. I could hear it clearly in her voice.

"You left us, Carrie. You and Mikey and Dad—"

"I was *four*, Tom. Four years old, the same age as Sofie. Michael—not Mikey, anymore—wasn't even two. What were we supposed to do? Hide under beds to keep Dad from finding us?" Her voice softened. "Surely you can't blame us for leaving? We were *babies,* Tom, just babies. For all we knew, we were going on an adventure with Dad and Mama Rocio. It was days before either of us thought to ask where you and Mary and Steve were. We thought it was just a vacation or something. By then we were in Texas. Did you really expect us to start walking for California?"

"I . . . I don't know what . . ." Dad's voice trailed off.

"Seriously, Tom. Have you really spent all these years blaming Michael and me for leaving you? How sensible is that?"

"It's not that. It's just . . ." Dad's voice broke. "It was so lonely here, and . . . so hard. I missed you all so much."

There was a long pause. I heard their feet moving, and there was some sniffling. I could almost see them holding each other, the way they were holding each other when I first saw my Aunt Carrie. I knew they were both crying. The tears were running down my face too. After a while,

Carrie said, "Tom, I know you were damaged by what happened. We all were. It was difficult for every—"

"Don't start with that!" Something hit the counter, hard. "I don't want to hear how tough it was for poor Rocio, who had to wait for the guy she wanted to leave his wife before she could have him all to herself. I don't want to hear how difficult it was for our father to run off with the babysitter and leave his wife and three of his children without support. I don't care to know—"

"That's it exactly! For thirty-five years you haven't cared to know!" By now Carrie was practically shrieking. There was so much pain in her voice. I sat there crying too, feeling guilty for eavesdropping and wishing I didn't have to hear anymore, but Sofie was sleeping on my lap so I couldn't easily leave, and their voices were so loud I couldn't help overhearing them. Carrie's voice was angry when she asked, "Do you know how much Michael resents you?"

"Resents *me*? What did I do?"

"Nothing, Tom. Exactly nothing! We sent you invitations when we graduated from junior high, high school, college, when I was married in the Dallas temple, even for little things like birthdays. Mama Rocio tried to help us keep in touch. We had no response for years, then when we did start getting responses, they were always cards signed "Karen and Tom" in your wife's handwriting. When I was married, she also sent a gift card . . . Did you ever even *see* the invitations? Did you look at them?"

Dad's voice went nasty. "Now who's lying, Carrie? There were no invitations, no communication at all—not for years. I think the first thing I ever saw was when you were married."

Aunt Carrie's voice dropped in a way that made me shiver. "I'm not lying, Tom. I *do not lie*. We sent them, from very early on."

"So what did you do? Tell *that woman* you wanted them sent and expect her to follow through?"

"Will you cut it out? *That woman* was my mother! She was the only one who ever cared at all about me, and yes, she mailed the invitations. She used to take us with her to the post office and make a big deal of it. We saw every one of them go into the mail slot. Did you ever see them at all?"

"Well, yeah. Like I said, I saw your wedding invitation, with the picture—"

"And you just couldn't be bothered with the blood of your blood who had 'left you,' could you, big brother?"

"It wasn't like that!"

"It was *exactly* like that. Even when our father died, you couldn't be bothered. The least you could have done was to help us bury our dad, get some closure . . ."

"I didn't want to see him! Not after what he did. It was wrong, Carrie. It was adultery! How could you—"

"Oh, for heaven's sake, Tom. Grow up! It's been thirty-five years, and no matter what he did, he was still your father. Don't you think it's time you made peace with that?"

Dad's voice went soft. "Some injuries just never, never . . ." A pan clattered against the counter, and his voice changed again. "What would you know about it anyway?"

"Apparently more than you do. At least I'm trying."

There was a long pause. I could only imagine what was going on in there. Finally I heard Carrie speak. "I get it, Tom. I get it now. You aren't mad at Dad for taking us away. You're mad because he left *you*, because when he and Rocio went to Texas, you're the one who had to deal with our crazy mother."

"How dare—"

My dad started to interrupt, but Carrie spoke right over him. "You're furious because he didn't take you too!"

"Stop it! Just stop it! I don't have to listen to this kind of garbage in my own home!" Dad stormed out of the kitchen and into his office, slamming the door behind him. I could hear Carrie sniffing in the kitchen, along with the sound of bowls and pans being moved around a little harder than usual.

After a few minutes, I eased Sofie down onto the couch and wandered back into the kitchen, pretending to know nothing of what I'd heard. "Hi," I said as I entered. "Sofie's sleeping on the couch. Can I help you finish the cookies?"

Carrie sniffed and wiped a hand across her cheek, but her voice was pretty normal when she said, "The last batch is in the oven now. I was just starting to clean up."

"Here, let me do that." I stepped up to the sink and starting filling it with hot, sudsy water to get the grease off the cookie sheets. Then I decided to start a new conversation. "Your little Sofie is adorable."

"She is a cutie, isn't she? I'd like to have you meet my whole family. Maybe sometime you can come out to Texas—"

"I'd love to!" I said, hoping Dad hadn't heard that suggestion. "Maybe I could come out next summer?"

"Great idea!" Aunt Carrie said. "Seguin is on a major road in Texas, and we have lots of hungry travelers passing through in the summer. We always hire extra help, so . . . we'd pay you if you wanted to work . . ."

"Of course, I'd have to ask my mom and dad," I said, looking toward the door where my dad had just slammed out of the room.

"I hear you," Aunt Carrie said. "Well, let's see how the next few days go anyway. And it's still a year away. Maybe we can work something out by then."

I shrugged. "Worth a try."

We worked quietly for a few minutes. The bowls and cookie sheets were washed, dried, and almost put away when Mom and the great-aunts got home. Aunt Shirley and Aunt Lenore headed upstairs, then Mom said, "Are you ready to go yet, Carrie?"

She looked at me and nodded. "You have a good kitchen assistant here, Karen. We could use her help at the restaurant next summer if you could part with her for a few weeks."

"That's an idea worth considering," Mom said. "Where's Sofie?"

"Sleeping on the couch in the family room," I said.

Carrie nodded toward me again. "She's a good babysitter too."

Mom smiled. "Good to hear. I know we appreciate her." She winked at me and I smiled.

A few minutes later, Carrie had picked up Sofie, who was sleeping in her arms, and Mom had taken off for Granny's house with both of them in the car. I wandered back into the kitchen to find one of the Snickerdoodles we'd made. It was while I was sitting at the counter, munching on a cookie with a glass of milk, that Dad finally made another appearance. He looked like a cartoon the way he stuck his head out the door and looked in both directions before stepping toward the kitchen.

"It's okay," I said. "The coast is clear."

He ignored my comment. "Any cookies left?"

"In the cookie jar." I held up the gallon of milk. "If you get your own glass, I'll share."

"Sounds good." Dad got a glass and a plate, helped himself to a handful of cookies, and came over to the counter. He sat down beside me and poured a glass.

"Interesting evening, huh?" I watched to see his reaction.

"Yeah. Interesting." He mumbled it over a mouthful of cookie. For a little while we just sat there, dipping and munching, but we both looked up when my great-aunts came down the staircase, obviously in the middle of something.

"Well, do you remember where we put it?" Aunt Lenore was saying.

"I thought we gave it to Judith," Aunt Shirley answered.

"Then you'd think it would be here, right?"

"Not necessarily. It might have gone to Mary or Steve—"

"What's up?" Dad asked as they reached the bottom of the staircase.

Aunt Lenore answered. "There was a beautiful portrait of Mother that we wanted to have out at her service, maybe even include on the printed program. We'd like to get copies of it made for ourselves and anyone else in the family who'd like one, but we don't know where it is now. We thought we gave it to your mother and that it likely would have come to you, but when we asked Karen about it—"

"Asked me about what?" Mom said as she came in from the garage. Lenore repeated it all.

"Ooh, right. I remember seeing that portrait up in Judith's home . . . Tom, you probably remember it too. It showed Granny as a young woman, probably not yet thirty. She had her hair up, and she was wearing a polka-dotted dress with a delicate lace collar and a string of pearls. The frame—"

"I remember," Dad said. "The frame was black—wrought iron, I think—with a little bit of something silver wrapped into it, like a vine. It stood on Mom's mantle for years."

"That's the one!" Lenore said, looking triumphant. "Do you know where it is now?"

Dad shook his head. "Sorry. I looked at everything in the box I got from storage, and I've almost dug to the bottom of the box I got from Ruby, but I haven't seen anything like that yet. I'll keep looking though. I need to get the one for the program to the funeral home by tomorrow morning, latest." He dunked his last cookie.

"There is one other possibility . . ." my mom said.

Dad said, "Yeah? What?"

Mom put her car keys down on the counter. "When Mary and Cathy and I were cleaning out the last of the small things from your mother's house, we came across a couple of boxes she had tucked in the corner of her bedroom, actually, under her bed. We were moving fast, trying to get out of there before the Realtors came, and we just packed them up without even opening them. Then we packed a couple more with odds and ends that we hadn't found better places for. Brian helped us move all of those boxes here, probably four or five altogether. We put them in the empty space above the garage."

Dad said, "Oh. I didn't even realize we still had more of her things to sort out."

Mom said, "Well, there weren't many, but there were some papers and a few small items, mostly knickknacks and such, plus a few old files. It's possible that the portrait you want is in there."

Lenore looked toward the garage. "Maybe Shirley and I can—"

"Oh no! No way," Dad said. "I know what's up there!" He almost smiled, then he picked up his dishes and said, "Tell you what. We don't need any aunties falling through the ceiling of the garage or felled by black widow spider bites. I'll do a bit more searching through that big box in the office tonight. That way I'll either find what we're looking for or I can go up into the rafters tomorrow in the daylight, when I can at least see the spiders coming. Trust me, it's better that way." He grinned at his aunts and started to pass by them with his plate and glass, headed for the dishwasher.

As he passed, Aunt Lenore caught him by his shirt-sleeve and took his right hand. "Is that the same CTR ring you got before you left on your mission? The one your dad sent just before your farewell?"

I watched Dad's face harden. It went from relaxed to tense in about zero-point-two-hundredths of a second. "The answer to that would be yes and no," he growled. "Yes, this is the same CTR ring I wore all through my mission, and no, I didn't get it from my father. My dad never sent me anything, not a single thing."

"No, I'm sure that's the same ring," Aunt Lenore said, examining it more closely. "Your dad and Rocio showed it to me when they came to see the ballet in New York. That was just before you left. I remember the ring because of that unique silver filigree. It's a little like the silver on the frame around Mother's portrait—the one we were just talking about."

Dad's face was reddening. He seemed to be struggling to control his voice. "Yes, the ring has a silver vine pattern, and yes, I got it before I left on my mission, but my *mother* gave it to me. I repeat, my dad never sent us *anything*. In fact, he never sent a single red penny for the upkeep of the family he left behind—not unless it was twisted out of him. He'd have let us *starve* if Texas hadn't had good laws against deadbeat dads." By that point, he was shouting. He dropped his things into the sink and the glass shattered explosively.

"What is this, anyway?" he said, turning on us all. "Where is everybody coming up with this stuff? Is this Revisionist Family History Day or something?" His face was so red it was almost purple. I don't think I've ever seen him like that.

Mom reached toward him, "Tom—"

"I've got work to do!" he shouted and stomped into his office. The slamming door shook the whole house.

There was a long pause while we all took a breath. Then Aunt Lenore said, "That went well." It took about three seconds before the four of us burst into hysterical laughter, tears pouring down our cheeks.

Confetti Salad

1 can (about 1 ⅓ C.) crushed
   pineapple
2 Tbsp. olive oil
1 Tbsp. granulated sugar

1 head purple cabbage (4–5 C.),
   finely shredded or grated
2 carrots (about 1 ½ C.), grated
1 sweet apple, grated
1 C. sweetened shredded coconut

Directions

1. Open the can of pineapple. Drain 1–2 Tbsp. of the juice, but retain the remainder, leaving the pineapple soupy. Pour into a bowl.
2. Stir the olive oil and sugar into the pineapple.
3. Toss together the cabbage, carrots, apple, and coconut.
4. Add the "dressed" pineapple and toss thoroughly.
5. Chill.

Serves 6–8 as a side dish.

Variations

Add ½–1 C. regular green cabbage, grated. Stir in ½ C. celery cut in very thin slices. You can also add ½ C. golden raisins. This is a spicy-sweet, very colorful salad.

CHAPTER 26

Tuesday, June 19, Morning

KAREN BURNETT

TOM WAS IN THE OFFICE when I went to sleep Monday night and in the office when I got up Tuesday. If it hadn't been for the rumpled covers beside me, I might have thought he'd spent the night holed up in his office, treed like a hunted cat. He was certainly acting the role. I had thought we were making headway after he joined us at dinner twice in a row, but I could tell both from Carrie's subdued manner and from Tom's reversion to temper that something had happened between them, something that had brought all the family's past differences back into the foreground.

I sighed and turned to my morning prayer. Again I asked the Lord to bless Tom with wisdom and clarity, to help him understand and cope with the truth, whatever it was. I wanted to feel optimistic, yet I couldn't help fearing there was more grief to come before anything got better.

During the family dinner the night before, I'd heard enough quiet talk among the Texas relatives to know Aunt Lenore was probably right about Tom's CTR ring coming from his father. Shirley said she suspected that much of what Tom's father had sent to his children in California had never been credited to him. She couldn't guess whether Judith had done that deliberately or whether her illness had hidden the reality even from herself. Either way, I couldn't help wishing Granny could be here now to make some sense of all this for my husband. Tom had always listened to Granny Adelaide, and I never missed her more than I did as I looked at that closed office door, wondering who or what might get through to this quirky, difficult, wounded but wonderful man I married.

I debated going in to speak with him but decided I had nothing new to offer and went into the kitchen to get some breakfast started instead. I looked once more at the closed office door, wondering what it would take to trigger the long-delayed healing process for Tom. I have always known that he bore deep wounds. Until Granny's death I had never realized how deep they were, nor had I known that many of them, perhaps most, were barely scabbed over and not at all healed.

I walked up to the door, put my hand on the knob, and changed my mind again. *Not yet*, I thought. *Give him a little longer*, yet I knew this couldn't go on indefinitely. Mandy would be picking her mother up at the airport anytime now, and Rocio would be here when the family came for lunch in less than three hours. I knew I should speak to Tom before then, but—

The ringing telephone gave me an out, but when caller ID showed the bishop's name, I felt a cold chill of foreboding run down my spine. Was this about tomorrow's service? Or was something else happening? As I clicked to talk, I wondered how much more I could load on an already over-filled plate.

"Sister Burnett? It's Bishop Rawson calling. I'm sorry to bother you at a time like this, but . . ." He hesitated.

I felt it in my bones. "There's a problem, isn't there? Something serious."

"It's Anna Campbell. I know you're already in over your head, and I wouldn't bother you with this except . . ." Again he paused.

"What's happened?"

"She's had a heart attack—a serious one. The doctors are saying it's only a matter of time, maybe just hours. Anna's asking to see you, if you're able to come."

Guiltily I remembered my promise to call and of how, with every-thing else going on, I had forgotten that promise completely. "Tell her I'll be right there." I got the room number from the bishop and took just long enough to find Stephanie to let her know what was happening. I paused briefly, asking if she was doing okay and giving her an extra hug, wondering when I'd have time to give some serious attention to this dear daughter who seemed to be hurting as much as any of us. Then I sprinted for the garage and headed for the hospital, praying I would arrive in time.

*   *   *

STEPHANIE BURNETT

The Texas family was due to arrive at eleven thirty. A little after eleven, I started setting up the buffet. I thought about bringing Em in to help out, but when I checked her room, she had gone to sleep while writing in her journal. I decided to let her rest. Certainly none of us had been resting very well lately.

I felt another wave of gratitude as I got out the paper plates and cups provided by my former roomies and my other friends in the singles ward. Last night's dinner, today's lunch, and the big lunch following the funeral tomorrow could all be accommodated easily from the supplies they had brought. Their kindness wasn't just about convenience though. They couldn't know how much this gesture had meant to me.

I went to work setting up the buffet table and getting out leftovers from yesterday's roast, plus lettuce and pickles, red onion and fresh tomatoes. I couldn't help thinking of the talk I'd had with Mom.

Poor Mom. It didn't even occur to me until after the talk why she'd been so scared. I wonder what she thought I was going to confess anyway. But despite the way I'd scared her, she had been there for me, and when I had told her the worst I had to tell, she seemed relieved that it wasn't worse still. In a way, that was a great relief for me. I had been so afraid that Mom would be ashamed of me. I knew Grandma Judith had given Dad and Mom some very worrisome times. Maybe if she saw me becoming like my Grandma Judith, she wouldn't want anything more to do with me.

Mom's reaction had made me feel so hopeful. She didn't think I had Grandma's problems at all, and I couldn't help remembering what she'd said, that even if I did develop Grandma's illness, I didn't have to become like her. The thing that stuck with me most was the way Mom had said she wouldn't want me to miss the blessings of marriage and family. Maybe that was something I really needed to think about, and I was thinking about it—a lot.

As I worked I couldn't help noticing the closed office door. Dad had been locked up in there since the relatives had left us the night before, almost like some kind of hibernating bear—and just about as cheerful. I wondered if he knew the Texas relatives were due to arrive again in a few minutes. If he didn't, he was going to have to find out from somebody else. Some may consider that avoidance; I think of it as self-preservation. I got out some of Mom's good trays and started organizing sandwich makings.

* * *

TOM BURNETT

I reached the bottom of the box I'd picked up from Ruby without finding any of the pictures of Granny I had expected or hoped to find. The people at the funeral home had been patient but had finally explained that if I wanted a picture of Adelaide on the cover of the funeral program, I would have to get it there right away, so late yesterday I took them the picture Karen and I had kept for years on the mantel. It wasn't the one the aunts wanted to find, and it wasn't my favorite picture of Granny either, but it was a flattering photo that would allow people who attended the service to see how Granny had looked a couple of decades ago. It would do for the program cover.

I scanned in the rest of the pictures I had collected of Granny Adelaide, knowing that other relatives would want copies. I would need to climb into the unfinished space above the garage to see what I could turn up for the foyer display. I didn't really want to do it, but it looked like it couldn't be helped.

I looked at my watch. I hadn't checked my e-mail yet. The climb into the rafters could wait until after lunch, couldn't it? I paused. Lunch. Karen had said something about today's lunch, something that had unsettled me at the time. What was it? I had the troubling feeling I'd remember soon enough. Ah well. Whatever it was, it could wait until then. I opened my e-mail server and began to check my messages.

* * *

KAREN BURNETT

I hummed a comforting hymn as I made my way through the parking lot and found my car. My visit with Anna Campbell had been way too similar to my final visit with Granny. Just two doors down from where we'd last met with Granny, I had entered Anna's room to find a half-dozen relatives gathered while the patient herself lay quietly, gray with the pallor of approaching death. Yet even in these extremes, Anna was brave, warmly generous, and thinking of others. Although I was suffering a fit of psychic self-torture over forgetting her, Anna was having none of it.

"Dear, dear, Karen," she said taking my hand. "I've been waiting for you."

"I'm so sorry, Anna," I said. "I didn't mean to forget—"

"Shhh, dear." Her smile was gentle. "I know how your week has been. And now, well, I'm afraid I'm adding to your troubles." She sighed and shifted a little in the bed. "I asked the bishop to call you; I know it's a bad time, but—"

"I want to be here for you, Anna," I assured her.

"I just want to thank you for all you've done for me over the years. Even before you were my Relief Society president, you've always been so kind. I wouldn't want to leave without saying good-bye—"

"Don't say that, Gramma!" A small young woman spoke from the corner of the bed, her face streaked with tears. "You're going to get better. Isn't she, doctor?"

Anna reached up with her free hand and twined the young woman's fingers in her own. "Oh, darling," she said. "Don't put the poor doctor on the spot like that. An old bird like me can't last forever, you know. It's time for me to let you young ones take over." I winced, remembering Granny's voice saying almost the same words, but I noticed the doctor looked relieved that he hadn't had to say it.

We visited for a few minutes, and Anna kept the conversation turning back to gospel topics. At one point, she said, "You know, Adelaide and I were visiting teaching companions for years. Do you think she needs a companion now?" I assured her Adelaide would be there to welcome her if it was in any way possible. A few more minutes passed while Anna talked of looking up loved ones on the other side, and then suddenly her breathing became labored and she moaned in obvious pain.

The doctor asked us to step away from the bed while he listened to her heart. He looked up over Anna's head, directing his gaze toward the relatives, and solemnly shook his head. The way Anna was positioned, I know she didn't see the doctor's expression or his signal to the family, but she didn't have to see to know what was happening.

She reached for the bishop's hand. "Bishop," she whispered, her voice raspy. "Will you please give me a blessing . . . and my . . . release?"

The girl in the corner began to sob. The man beside her, presumably her husband, put her head against his chest and let her cry. Bishop Rawson answered, "Of course, Anna," and asked her son to assist him. Dr. Doyle, a member of the second ward, stepped back, and I stood near the door, blocking unwelcome interruptions.

The men took their positions on either side of her, and the bishop asked, "Are you ready, Anna?"

Anna took the question quite literally. She said, "Good-bye, my dear ones. I love you all." Then she nodded to the bishop. I stood at the door while two honorable priesthood bearers performed a final service for a faithful sister both had loved. As they spoke, her breathing eased. By the time they closed the blessing, she could no longer speak but merely nodded her thanks. Within minutes she had lapsed into unconsciousness, but her breathing was easy and I knew her passing would be as well.

The doctor checked her pulse. "It won't be long now," he said.

The family drew in visibly around her, and the bishop stepped out of their circle to speak to me. "Thank you for coming, Karen," he said.

"I couldn't miss seeing her."

He nodded. "I understand." Then he gestured toward the door. "I'll do whatever needs to be taken care of here," he said. "You'd better get home to your own family. Is everything set for tomorrow?"

"As far as I can tell," I assured him. If he hadn't been preparing for another vigil, I might have confided what was happening with Tom, but this was clearly the wrong time, place, and situation. I decided to let it go for now.

"Thank you," I said. "See you tomorrow," and I headed for the parking lot thinking what a week it had been. It was only when I started my car and saw it was already 11:35 that I remembered Rocio was coming with the Texas relatives today—and I had said nothing about it to Tom.

My stomach dropped, and I gunned the engine, hurrying just a little bit faster than usual in my rush to get home.

* * *

STEPHANIE BURNETT

Dad's relatives were nothing if not prompt. It was 11:29 by our kitchen clock when the front doorbell rang. Mom wasn't home yet, and the grizzly had not emerged from his den, so I went to the door to greet everyone. There sure were a bunch of them! I couldn't help thinking of our last talk with Granny and how she had kept in touch with these relatives over the decades, claiming she didn't have enough grandchildren to let any of them slide. Well, I suppose "enough" is variable. The van was full to bursting, and this morning there was a second car as well. I opened the door and welcomed them all inside.

One new addition stood out right away: I'd been warned the infamous Rocio was going to be joining our family lunch, but the slightly overweight Latina in the simple polyester pantsuit didn't look much like my image of the Wicked Witch. My first thought was, "Why is everyone so afraid of you?" but I managed to greet her warmly.

To all appearances, Rocio seemed a kindly, gentle woman, and the way the grandchildren greeted her, crowding in for hugs and kisses, told me she was loved. Family lore suggested I should treat her with cool suspicion; I thought I'd prefer to sit near her, watching the way she held the children. Instead of doing either, I invited her and the rest of the family to come in and have a seat.

We stepped into the family dining area, where I had started organizing the lunch buffet, and the women started setting out their salads and side dishes, including a brightly colored dish Carrie called confetti salad. We were almost ready for lunch. I wondered if Mom would get home soon. I wondered if I should invite Dad to come out of the office. Instead I just waited, hoping whatever happened was good.

* * *

KAREN BURNETT

I pulled up to the house to find the driveway filled with cars. I wasn't going to be able to pull my car into the garage until some of the family moved their vehicles later. I parked across the street and half jogged up the front walk, getting out my key to the front door. I stepped into the front hall just as the gentle older woman who could only be Rocio stepped in from the dining area. There was Tom, positioned between us, half turned, in profile. I could see the tension in the back of his neck, the hard set of his jaw. Behind Rocio, the relatives I had already met were moving into the hallway, their faces bright with greeting. That was when Rocio stepped forward. "Hello, Tom," she said. "It's been a long time."

Tom glared at her. "Not long enough," he said.

All around I heard the sharp intake of breath while expressions dropped and unexpressed pain filled the room. In the center of the storm, Tom dropped his chin, squared his shoulders, and stalked through the house, long strides taking him through the kitchen and out the side door. I could hear the creak of the wooden ladder as he climbed into the attic space above the garage.

"I'm sorry," I began, "I—"

But Rocio stopped me. "I knew it wouldn't be easy," she said. Then, perhaps a bit too brightly, she asked, "Is everyone ready for lunch?"

Following her cue, we went into the dining area. I called on Jeff to offer a blessing and the family began to eat.

I served food, acted the role of hostess, and pretended nothing was wrong, but I promised myself that as soon as I could do so without drawing the attention of the rest of the family, I was going to climb that ladder myself. Tom's selfish, childish, boorish behavior was way out of proportion to anything these good people had ever done to hurt him, and I, for one, had had more than enough of it.

As soon as lunch was safely over, I planned to give my dear husband a very large piece of my mind.

Maui Onion Straws

2 C. canola oil
1 large egg
½ C. milk
2 C. all-purpose flour
1 tsp. cayenne pepper
1 tsp. paprika

1 tsp. garlic powder
Kosher or sea salt and freshly
   ground pepper
1 sweet onion (Maui, Vidalia, or
   Walla Walla)

Directions

1. In a medium sauce pot, heat the oil to 350.
2. Whisk the egg and milk in a medium bowl. Mix the flour, cayenne pepper, paprika, garlic powder, 1 Tbsp. salt, and 1 tsp. freshly ground pepper in another medium bowl.
3. Cut the onion in half; slice into 1-inch-thick half rings; separate into short straw-like pieces. Add to the milk mixture to soak.
4. Once the oil is hot, remove the onions from the milk mixture, shake off excess and dredge in the flour mixture, 4 or 5 pieces at a time.
5. Add to the pot and fry until golden brown; drain on paper towels.
6. Serve with ketchup or fry sauce.

Splendiforous Fry Sauce

1/3 C. real egg mayonnaise
1/3 C. ketchup
2/3 C. Thousand Island dressing

2 Tbsp. sliced or chopped olives
½–1 tsp. red chili powder

Directions

Mix all ingredients together in a small bowl. Chill before serving.

CHAPTER 27

Tuesday, June 19, Afternoon

TOM BURNETT

IT TOOK SEVERAL MINUTES TO locate the correct pile of boxes. The delay was partly due to the vicious red haze that had blinded me from the moment I saw Rocio's face. That woman—in *my* home? And no one had even thought to mention it! Fury was a mild description for what I was feeling. It drove me across the house and up the ladder, heedless of the threat of poisonous spiders. *Black widows. Right.* At least the spiders were honest about their murderous intentions toward the males they targeted.

I clicked on the overhead light and began pawing through the attic space, barely mindful to step carefully lest I fall through the flimsy wallboard of the ceiling. Clearly the rage was only a small part of the explanation for my lack of direction. Until this minute, I hadn't realized how much—how very much—junk had been pushed into the rafters, stacked on make-do plywood floors. Just sorting through and organizing these old items could take days. I shrugged. That would have to wait. So where were my mother's boxes?

When I finally found them, I was surprised I hadn't seen them sooner. Unlike most of the other boxes in the attic—gathered from all sorts of places and reclaimed from all kinds of original purposes, stacked and piled among pieces of old furniture and bags of used clothing—the five boxes from my mother's home were identically sized and shaped, commercially made of double-strength cardboard with tightly fitted lids and carefully labeled with felt-tip marker—some in my mother's handwriting, some in my wife's.

For years I'd known these kinds of organizational efforts were my mother's way of trying to codify the mess in her wildly erratic mind. She had begun the process with the first two boxes Karen had found under the corner of her bed, and Karen had followed through in dealing with the last of my mother's scattered things.

I laid a small piece of unused plywood across the rafters next to where I sat on an abandoned barstool. Then I began moving the boxes so I could go through them one at a time. Remembering what my aunts had said about the picture with the silver vine in its frame, I started with the boxes Karen had packed.

I was surprised to see the wide array of stuff that had accumulated in Mother's home over the years, junk that had finally ended up here, stuffed into boxes and pushed into a corner of the attic, out of both sight and mind. Recognizing that much of it should be thrown away, I grabbed a bag half filled with clothing, added the clothes to the top of another half-empty bag, and laid the empty one beside me on the plywood, preparing to fill it from the box as I went along.

Putting the bag to good use, I worked my way through receipts for utility bills due—and I hoped paid—five and six years before. Then I moved into the boxes from the previous decade. I examined and tossed stacks of folders my mother had carefully labeled and then filled with random bits of junk mail, saved for who-knew-what purpose. I marveled at how disorganized and whimsical her mind had become in those last years. In the midst of one mess, I found old doctor bills and lab reports, all kinds of stuff that should have been disposed of long ago. And then I spotted something that stopped me cold, something I had to examine twice to make sure I had seen it correctly.

It was a prescription for psychotropic drugs, the typical anti-psychotics we had come to know well during the last years of my mother's life. Yet this prescription was clearly different. It hadn't ever been filled but had been placed instead in a folder labeled "Bills" in my mother's hand. It had been written by a family doctor my mother had stopped seeing years ago—so many years I barely remembered the doctor's name. And it had been written the year before Carrie was born.

I looked at it, dismissed it as a stupid but explainable error, and dropped it into the garbage bag, then I took it out and studied it again. It seemed to be genuine, and it seemed to be just as old and just as real as Carrie had suggested. But it couldn't be. Could it?

I dropped the old prescription back into the garbage bag and kept digging through the files. It was when I found a second unused prescription for the same drugs, written by the same doctor during the years between Carrie's and Mikey's births that I went back into the garbage bag to find the first one and set the two side by side. By the time I got to the bottom of the first box, I had found seven such unfilled prescriptions, all written by the family doctor Mom had stopped taking us to see when I was still in grade school. Was it possible that some of what Carrie had said was true? These scraps of paper certainly seemed to suggest that.

I closed my eyes against a sudden wave of nausea. It passed but left me feeling weak and shaky, as if the foundation beneath me had suddenly shifted. I placed the old prescriptions on top of a broken-legged coffee table and opened the second box.

This one was filled with knick-knacks and pictures my mother had kept on her mantel. I quickly found the portrait my aunts had been looking for and set it atop the old coffee table. Then I picked out a couple of pretty things I thought my daughters might enjoy and added them to the collection of items I meant to keep. I selected three more pictures from the bottom reaches of the box, loaded the rest back in, and put the top back on, preparing to open the third box.

It also contained mostly family pictures, old doilies, plus some small handmade objects my siblings and I had created in school over the years and brought home as gifts for our mom. I went through it quickly, found a few more pictures I wanted to keep, and set the third box aside.

It was with some trepidation that I opened the fourth box, one Karen had found hidden under my mother's bed. If unfilled prescriptions dating back forty years could be found in a folder labeled "Bills," what would I find in boxes she had deliberately kept hidden?

I took a steadying breath, then a second, and a third. It was time I knew the whole truth—even if I didn't like it at all, even if it didn't sit well, even if it showed me to be as big a fool as I was beginning to think I surely was. The past may not have been exactly as I remembered it, but however it really was, it was time I knew. I took another deep breath and opened the fourth box.

To my immediate relief, it looked much like the first—filled with files and junk mail, bills paid long ago or long overdue, and other paperwork that made even less sense. There were more unfilled prescriptions as well, two more from the same doctor who had written the others, and three from a doctor whose name I didn't recognize. With twelve unfilled prescriptions lined up on the broken table, I knew that at least that part of Carrie's story was true.

It was shocking—mind-blowing, really. I'd always known for a fact that my mother's illness had been caused by my father's betrayal. Now I was faced with the certainty that this "knowledge" wasn't real. How much more of what I remembered might be equally false?

With a prayer wringing my heart, I opened the next file and found a large manila envelope labeled at the top with two dates, a little more than five years apart. I would have been between thirteen and eighteen then. Curious to see what my mother had saved from that part of my life, I opened the envelope.

It contained photocopies of checks, front and back, one each month for more than five years. They came from the joint account my father had shared with Rocio in Waco, Texas. The front of each check showed the dates; the back showed my mother's endorsement. The handwriting was not my father's, so it must be Rocio's. A note attached by paper clip to the front of the stack was written in the same hand:

Judith,

Please note the checks are all here, each written at least ten days before the required due date. Tom has never failed to send child support as ordered by the court and has often sent more than the court requires. You may summon us to court yet again, but you cannot win on these grounds since this evidence proves that your claims of nonsupport are false.

Please also note that the most recent check includes an extra $150. Please see that Tommy gets the bicycle he wants for his eighteenth birthday, a gift from his father and me.

Rocio Burnett

I remembered that bike—a shiny red three-speed with coaster brakes. I could see it in my mind, could almost feel the handlebar grips under my palms and the pedals under my feet. I had ridden it through my first year of college before receiving my mission call and had left it for Steve when I headed for Mexico. I had always assumed—no, I had always *known*—that bike had been a gift from my mother.

Just like the CTR ring, I heard myself thinking. "Oh, dear Lord," I said aloud, dropping my head into my hands and silently begging forgiveness.

I wanted to turn my fury on my mother, who had fed me so many lies. Yet I knew what Carrie had said was true: our mother could not be judged by her illness. Who knew how much of her behavior she truly understood?

"How much else was a lie?" I asked aloud, looking heavenward. "How much else of all I knew was just plain wrong?" I pulled the last two boxes down next to me and began rooting through them, seeking answers. It was time. I was finally ready to know it all.

* * *

KAREN BURNETT

The mantel clock rang out the Winchester chimes followed by three deep bongs. I had to look at it a second time to be certain I'd heard it correctly. It was tough to believe I'd been visiting with Tom's long-lost family for more than three hours. The conversation had been so pleasant and peaceful, the people so cooperative with all the plans we'd made. I wasn't sure what I'd been imagining when I'd heard they planned to join us at the funeral, but it wasn't this lovely, relaxed family time. Already I was coming to know Tom's sisters well, as if I'd known them my entire life.

At one point while my daughters were helping me clean up, Stephanie had whispered, "Rocio isn't at all like I pictured her."

I whispered back, "Were you picturing a green complexion and large warts?"

Steph giggled. "Something like that, yes."

"Don't forget the pointy black hat," Emily whispered.

I nodded. "I thought the same thing, but she's sweet, isn't she?"

"Tina and Mandy look a lot like her," Steph said and went back to cleaning plates and saving the meat scraps for Buster.

Nearly three full hours had passed since then, and I had been steadily more impressed by the kind woman who had married Tom's father and by the daughters she had raised. All three of them, Carrie included, were strong, beautiful, poised, and elegant women; faithful sisters, daughters, and mothers; dedicated Latter-day Saints; kind and thoughtful people. The two brothers-in-law who were here, Jeff and Terry, were good men, and I knew from the way everyone spoke of him that Carlos must be a fine, faithful man as well. These were wonderful people whom anyone should be pleased and proud to claim as family, and yet my husband—

I cut off the thought. I had to if I was going to think of anything other than how disappointed I had been with Tom today. I had spent my whole married life hearing Tom's side of things and believing it to be the truth, yet recent events had taught me that very little of what Tom remembered had happened as he recalled it. His behavior toward Rocio this morning had been disgraceful and embarrassing, beyond rude and totally uncalled for. If I hadn't been certain it would have caused an even bigger scene, I'd have followed him up that ladder into the rafters. I'd have . . .

"I'm sorry," I said, blushing as I realized that I had once again allowed my distress at Tom's behavior to distract me from the immediate conversation. "I was thinking of something else, Jeff. Could you repeat the question, please?"

Tom's aunts and I had covered the funeral program with the Texas family, and they had been completely supportive of everything we'd done. They seemed especially pleased with Emily's choices of music, which had thrilled Em. They had also chimed in with some small additions and suggestions that would make the funeral service even more poignant and touching for Granny's closest family and friends. Now Jeff was asking about the luncheon afterward.

I began explaining what Granny had asked me to do. Since I still had her envelope in my purse, I was able to show them the lists Granny Adelaide had prepared for me. Then I started reviewing the menu.

"We're going to have the tacos as a main course," I said. "We have sisters from our ward preparing the salads and beans, and we're starting to organize some desserts—"

"And onion straws," a deep voice said, "with fry sauce." We all looked up as Tom walked in from the garage. He had a plastic bag under one arm and a framed picture in the other.

"Excuse me?" I said, standing as he entered. I could feel the heat creeping into my face, but I didn't know whether I was feeling defensive toward him because of his most recent scene or defensive of him because of how awful he looked. His face was splotchy, and it was clear he'd been crying. That frightened me since I couldn't remember the last time I'd seen my husband cry. Even since Granny's death, he'd teared up a few times, but that wasn't the kind of weeping that left a man looking like this.

"Mom used to make a special onion dish for holiday meals or reunions," my husband said, his voice subdued. "I just found her recipe among some of her old things. Oh! And I have the picture you ladies were looking for too." He showed the portrait of Granny to Aunt Lenore and Aunt Shirley, who aahed and reached for it.

"Tom—" I began, ready to invite him to step into the office.

"I need to talk to Rocio, if you don't mind," he said.

"Tom—" I said, speaking louder.

"Actually, what I need to do is *apologize* to Rocio," he said, "and to you, Karen, and to all the rest of you. But I really need to apologize to Rocio first, if the rest of you can excuse us for a few minutes?"

He looked around the room. One by one the relatives began to move. "I need to check on Tommy anyway," Mandy said. "He doesn't usually nap this long." She started down the hall.

"I think my girls are in the backyard playing with the dog," Tina said. "I know Em's with them, but it won't hurt to see how they're doing." She drifted toward the enclosed back porch.

"I'll just see if she needs any help," Jeff said. Then Terry blushed crimson, said, "Me too," and dashed after Jeff. The aunts headed to the kitchen, where Steph and Emily were already busily working on dessert for the evening's dinner.

Soon Tom and I were alone with Rocio. He gave me a meaningful look. "I think I'll stay," I said. He gave me a longer, speaking look. I stared back at him. Our unspoken conversation ended when he gave me a quick nod.

"All right," he said, and then he turned to the kindly woman he had never called his stepmother. "I owe you a great apology," he began, "not just for the ugly way I treated you this morning, but for decades of misunderstanding and . . . *belligerence* is probably a good word."

Rocio just nodded, waiting to hear what Tom had to say.

"I've been laboring under some false impressions," Tom began, "and some of them have lasted a very long time. I just now found evidence that tells an entirely different story." He set the bag down on the table between them and started pulling out papers.

His "evidence" was all there and all real. Over the next several minutes, Tom produced the paperwork to prove everything the relatives had been telling me. The unfilled prescriptions went back decades, showing that Judith's illness had begun long before the problems in her marriage, even before Tom's father had met Rocio. The checks his mother had endorsed and cashed proved that his father had provided well for his

California family. Perhaps most shocking to Tom were court documents which showed the many times Tom Sr. had attempted to win visitation rights, albeit unsuccessfully.

There were notes too, some from Tom Sr. and many from Rocio, that showed the efforts the Texas family had made to try to stay in touch with the children they had left behind. Finally, Tom produced a series of unopened envelopes addressed mostly to him, although some bore Mary's or Steve's names. Three dozen or more letters and cards sent to them from Texas that their mother had hidden without ever opening or acknowledging.

"I'll give these to Mary and Steve after the luncheon tomorrow," he said, setting the smaller stack on the table. He lifted the second stack and then slipped them inside his jacket pocket. "These are letters to me, written by the father I thought had abandoned me, over a period of years. I'll read them later, when I have more time to think about them." He turned to Rocio and then to me. "I have a lot of old pain to deal with," he said, "and I think I'll be easier to live with if I deal with it alone—at least to begin with."

I recognized that as a plea for my understanding, and I nodded with what I hoped was grace. The Tom I was seeing now was reminding me of why I loved him.

"Rocio," Tom said with a sigh. "I've been difficult, childish, and mean. Can you ever forgive me?"

As he looked toward her, I felt new tears spring to my eyes. I recognized how difficult this must be for the man who had been so gruff only a few short hours ago. As angry and disappointed as I had felt only moments ago, I now felt equally pleased and proud. I wondered if Rocio felt the same way.

She stood. She crossed the few feet that separated her from my husband and gently touched his face. "Your father loved you, Tom," she said. "He never forgot you for a moment. Even at the end of his life, he asked for you."

"I'm sorry," Tom said. "I didn't know—"

"Shhh, *mijo*," Rocio said, her voice even more gentle. "I'm not asking for your apology. You don't owe me anything, but I'm hoping you can forgive your father. He would want that. He did want that—very much."

"I . . ." Tom stopped. I thought he had been about to say that he did forgive his father, but instead he said, "Rocio, can I ask you something?"

She sat on the edge of the table. "Of course, Tom. Anything."

"Why did you do what you did?" A cloud of confusion crossed her face, and he spoke quickly to clarify. "I don't mean leaving and going to Texas. I'm beginning to understand that—better than I ever wanted to. What I mean is, why did you take the two little ones? And why did you leave the rest of us?"

Rocio dropped her head and looked away. She hesitated for several moments before she spoke, and when she finally did speak, her voice was trembling and filled with pain. "It wasn't an easy choice," she finally said. "It was one of the few times Tom and I ever really argued. We knew how ill your mother was, and your father didn't dare leave the little ones in her care. He knew his mother would come to help, but he wasn't sure what might go wrong with Carrie and Michael before Adelaide got there."

Rocio sighed and turned back toward Tom, looking him fully in the face, her eyes level with his and less than a yard away. "He also took the little ones because I wouldn't let him leave them. I had learned to love them like my own." She swallowed hard. "I had been caring for your sister since she was tiny and for Michael since before he was born."

She cleared her throat and went on. "Your father had made up his mind to leave because he didn't believe your mother would ever embrace the gravity of her condition. But in his own way, he still loved her. I was jealous of that at first. Once I had made my own commitment to him, I wanted his full attention, and yet . . . and yet I knew he would not be the man I had come to love if he could abandon the mother of his children without a trace of hope."

Her voice thickened and she paused to clear her throat. When she spoke again, there was a note of resignation in it. "He knew you and Mary and Steve had each other, and because you were all gone during the day, what with school and church activities and so on, he thought you'd be all right, but he worried that your mother would lose what little hold she had on sanity if all her children were taken away from her." She paused, folding her hands into her lap.

"You're telling me that he left us behind as a kindness?"

She nodded. "Yes and because he believed you could handle it. He was proud of you, Tom, proud of the way you stepped up and became the man of the family. Even after he made up his mind to leave—in fact, even after we left—it took him a while to realize just how ill your mother really had become. He never meant to leave you with so much responsibility.

He talked about it often. He just hadn't realized how bad it really had become."

She paused, lifting the paperwork from the court. "You can tell something from the way he kept trying to get visitation rights. He never for a moment believed that he wouldn't see you or Steve or Mary again. He always thought that once everyone had recovered from the initial shock of the split-up, he and your mother could work out a settlement that would allow him to spend time with all of you. He never realized what kinds of claims she would take before the court, or that the court would believe . . ."

She stopped, closing her eyes, recovering her composure. "I'm talking too much. I don't mean to say anything bad about your mother, Tom. I never really knew her when she was healthy, of course, but Tom— that is, your father—often told me of good things she did when they were younger and she was stronger. He always thought she had been an excellent mother—before she became so ill, anyway. He believed that even if the two of them couldn't live together Judith would want her children to spend time with the rest of their family. We had both underestimated how . . . ill she really was." Rocio stopped again, waiting for Tom's response.

"I see," he said. Rocio and I both waited. "It's going to take me some time to digest all of this," he said slowly.

"I understand." Rocio stood.

Tom caught her hands in both of his and drew her back to her seat on the edge of the table. "Please," he said. "Please let me finish."

Rocio settled beside him, holding his hands in hers.

"It's going to take me time to work through it all," Tom said again, "but I already know that I've been wrong. I misunderstood the whole situation from the beginning, and I've misjudged you badly. Both you and my father. I misjudged you, and I'm sorry. Can you forgive me?"

Rocio slowly leaned forward and kissed Tom's forehead as if he were a little child again. "Of course I forgive you, *mijo*," she said. "And can you forgive a woman who was young and brash and made many serious mistakes?" She paused. "You need to understand, Tom. I was not a member of the Church then. I didn't fully grasp the meaning of all my actions. Your father did, and I made it more difficult for him. He spent the rest of his life trying to find ways to make right the things he had done to wrong you."

"You've joined the Church now?" I asked, then I suddenly wished I hadn't since my question seemed such an obvious intrusion.

"Oh yes, years ago," Rocio answered, turning toward me. "At first I'll admit I was resentful. I couldn't understand why the man I loved wanted to share all the intimate details of our lives with a stranger, a man he called his bishop, although he wasn't even a priest. In fact, he was an engineer!" She smiled. "Then, over the years, I watched. I watched my husband attending the services, even though he was unable to partake of the sacrament or participate actively in the meetings. I watched him making certain his children attended, and slowly I came to understand what it meant to him and what he had given up—at least partially because of me."

I saw Tom open his mouth to speak and then think better of it. I thought how much he'd changed in the past few hours.

"I was baptized with Christina," Rocio said, concluding her answer. "I wanted the children I had with Tom to be raised in the gospel too." She turned back to my husband. "Now you understand me better, do you think you can forgive me?"

For a moment, he just looked at her. The two of them sat there, staring into one another's eyes, and I had the impression they were seeing more deeply than either of them had planned. Then Tom slowly began to nod his head. His voice was heavy with emotion when he said, "Yes, I can. I do."

He stood. She followed his lead. As I watched, the two embraced and stood there, holding each other.

Lenore stepped in from the kitchen to find Tom and Rocio rocking slowly in one another's arms. She gasped. "Has the temperature just dropped dramatically?" she asked. "Because I think the nether regions have frozen over."

Tom chuckled and let go of his stepmother. "I think perhaps you're right," he said. "Yep. I think you're right."

He reached for his folder and handed Aunt Lenore a piece of paper. "Do you think we can have some onion straws for tomorrow?"

"Onions?" she asked. Then she shrugged. "Sure. Why not? If Hades can freeze solid, I'm sure we can have onions." She went back into the kitchen mumbling to herself while the rest of us chuckled, wiping tears.

Dolma: Stuffed Grape Leaves

2 C. uncooked long-grain white
   rice
1 large onion, chopped
½ C. chopped fresh dill
½ C. chopped fresh mint leaves
2 quarts chicken broth

¾ C. fresh lemon juice, divided
60 grape leaves, drained and
   rinsed*
hot water as needed
1 C. olive oil

Directions

1. In a large saucepan over medium-high heat, sauté the rice, onion, dill, and mint for about 5 minutes, or until onion is soft. Pour in 1 quart of broth, reduce heat to low, and simmer for another 10–15 minutes, or until rice is almost cooked. Stir in half of lemon juice and remove from heat.
2. Take one leaf, shiny side down, and place 1 tsp. of the rice mixture at the bottom (stem) end of the leaf. Fold both sides of the leaf toward the center, roll up from the broad bottom to the top, and place into a 4-quart pot. Repeat with all leaves, leaving no gaps as leaves are placed in pot (to prevent from opening while cooking). Sprinkle with remaining lemon juice and with olive oil.
3. Pour chicken broth over all to cover grape leaves. Cover pot and simmer for about 1 hour (do not boil, because this will make the stuffing burst out of the leaves). Remove from heat; remove cover and let cool for 30 minutes. Transfer to serving dish and serve.

*Note: If using fresh grape leaves, plunge into a deep container of very hot water for about 10 seconds to soften (don't let the leaves lose their fresh green color).

Variations

Add ½ C. pine nuts and up to ½ C. golden raisins. Delicious!

CHAPTER 28

Wednesday, June 20, Early morning

EMILY BURNETT

IT WAS LIGHT OUTSIDE WHEN I woke up. Downstairs in the kitchen I could hear the sounds of pans being moved around and the murmur of voices, so I knew Mom and the great-aunts were already working and I should probably jump up and volunteer to help. Still, for a little while, I just wanted to think about the changes since a week ago when my biggest worry was the choir concert. I knew I felt different in only a week, and I guessed a lot of the rest of the family did too—especially after last night.

When about half the adults in the family all showed up in the backyard at the same time, all "checking on the kids," who were playing with Buster and me, I knew something weird was going on. Then when Dad called us all in for some big speech or something, I didn't know what to think. Once I saw him, I was kind of freaked out.

I've never seen my dad look like that, all splotchy and red with his eyes swollen up. Even last week when Granny died, he didn't look like that, and he didn't cry like that. It was spooky. Then he started talking, and I thought that old line from the Saturday afternoon horror movies—you know, where the character says to the alien, "Who are you, and what have you done with my dad?" He was all about apologizing to everybody and how he'd discovered "evidence" that people had been telling him the truth, and I felt like I'd walked into the end scenes of a movie without seeing the beginning. I mean, the truth about *what*?

When he started in about Grandma Judith and how she'd been sick, I thought, *Duh, Dad.* It's true I hadn't known Grandma when she was young, but for as long as I could remember, she'd been pretty weirded-out and a little scary. I had never liked being alone with her because I never knew what was going to happen. She'd do the weirdest things—like the time she got scared of the light switches and wouldn't let any of us turn the lights on—and then she'd act as if everything was perfectly normal. Anyway, it didn't surprise me when Dad said she was sick. I wondered what had taken him so long.

What was even weirder was when he started bringing out letters that had been written sometime in the Dark Ages and had been mailed but never opened. Some had never even been mailed. Like there was one he found in a folder and gave to Aunt Carrie. It was this really old birthday card. Apparently he had bought it himself, out of his paper route money, when he was even younger than I am. I guess he gave it to his mother to mail, but here it was, dug up from some file somewhere. Dad was seeing it for the first time in years, and Carrie had never seen it before. When she opened it, there was a ten-dollar bill inside. Then she and Dad did some more hugging and crying.

It was another warm family moment. Then, just when we reached the point that I thought we were all going to join hands and start singing camp songs or something, one of the sisters—Mandy, I think—said something about Michael and Marco, and everybody got miserable again.

I raised my hand. "Excuse me? Who?"

Aunt Carrie, pointing between herself and Dad, said, "Michael is our youngest brother."

Then Tina said, "And Marco is *our* youngest brother," pointing to herself and Mandy.

Rocio said, "They said they weren't coming to Adelaide's service, but I told them staying away was not an option. I just got a text from Michael. They're in town and have checked in to their hotel."

"They didn't need to do that," my mom said. I didn't argue, but I wondered where she planned to put them. We're kind of topping out on space to put relatives.

Then Tina said, "They refused to stay with family—either here or at Granny Adelaide's. They rented a car at the airport, and they have a room in town."

"But they're coming tomorrow?" my mother asked.

Rocio shrugged. "I think so. I told them they have to. That's why they're here."

Then Dad said, "Maybe I'd better go talk to—"

Three people spoke at the same time. Rocio said, "I wouldn't recommend it."

Mom said, "Tom, don't try it."

Mandy said, "That's not a good idea."

Dad looked from one to the next and said, "Apparently you ladies disagree."

There were some uneasy sounds, and then Carrie said, "Michael is pretty unhappy, Tom."

"But if he knew what we know now—"

"No," Mandy said. "Knowing that will help, but Carrie and Tina and I should probably be the ones who tell him." She looked a little embarrassed when she added, "He trusts us."

Dad nodded slowly. "I see. How about Marco? Where does he stand in all this?"

Rocio answered, "With Michael. Marco has always followed Michael's lead."

Tina nodded. "They're pretty much a unit."

"Well, okay then," Dad said. "There are things here—cards and letters especially—that I'd like to keep, but you can borrow whatever you want to take over when you talk with them." He gave his sisters a hopeful look. "Maybe tonight?"

"I'm thinking after the service tomorrow would be better," Mandy said.

Rocio quickly agreed. "Right now that's all they've agreed to—just the service. Let's let them get through the funeral before we hit them with anything else."

Mom had been pretty quiet through the discussion, but this was when she spoke up. "After the funeral we can invite them to eat with us. They will have to eat, after all." People mumbled and nodded, and I thought she'd made her point. Then she added, "After lunch maybe there will be a chance for more talk."

Dad seemed disappointed, but he nodded. "Sounds good."

Right about then was when my dad's cousin Scott showed up with his wife and his daughter, Alexis, who is pretty close to my age. The deep discussion and heavy topics all broke up while we got busy finding them places to sleep. Alexis (she said, "Call me Alex") seemed like a fun girl and I invited her to stay in my room, but she said she'd already staked out the easy chair in the family room. That was cool with me.

This morning I was glad that I had my space to myself. It's given me some time to think about everything that happened yesterday, and when I think about it, I like the family I have now even better than the one I had a week ago. That alone makes this last awful week start to seem almost worth it.

* * *

KAREN BURNETT

We were almost ready. It seemed that Granny's impossible request hadn't been so impossible after all. Tom's aunts had gone out very early this morning to pick grape leaves from our vines, using the last of the cooked rice, preparing large batches of dolma for everyone. They were simmering now while the aunts went upstairs to change. All the other food was assigned and the kitchen crew assembled. It looked like everything was coming together—and not just the dinner either. My husband's fractured family was coming together as well, just as Adelaide surely must have hoped it would. The scenes I had witnessed here just last evening had been nothing less than miraculous.

Yes, there were still some miracles still left to work for Tom's younger brothers, but we had made such strides already that even bringing those two around had begun to seem possible.

I looked at the kitchen clock. Soon it would be time for me to change for the funeral, but before I went upstairs, I decided to stop at the office to see how Tom was doing. I found him reading his scriptures.

"Hi," I said a bit tentatively.

"Hello, gorgeous." He reached out to me, the sullen Tom of the past week gone. I went into his arms, and he hugged me tightly. "If I haven't said it sooner, then let me say it now: You've been wonderful through all of this. I owe you, big time."

I grinned and ruffled his hair. "You bet you do, buddy."

He pulled me down into his lap—the office chair not quite big enough for both of us—and kissed me, long and sweet. When he finally pulled away, he said, "Consider that a down payment."

"Just so long as there's more where that came from," I purred, stroking the back of his neck.

"Count on it," he promised and helped me get back to my feet.

"You were reading scriptures when I came in," I prompted. "Getting ready for your talk at the family prayer meeting?"

He shook his head. "Actually, I was reading ahead for the next lesson I'm supposed to teach the high priests group. It refers to the parable of the prodigal son, so I read through it again."

"Does it still end the same way?"

Tom smiled. "You know, it's not the end that I've been thinking about—not so much, anyway."

I waited.

"I've been thinking a lot about that older brother, the one who was faithful and stayed at home handling the family responsibilities. Does that ring any bells for you?"

I hesitated. "It does sound vaguely familiar . . ."

He sighed. "Karen, I've been wrong. I've been haughty and self-centered and unforgiving. Now I have a younger brother I barely remember and a half brother I've never met, both of them furious with me. Both of them need me to step up and set a good example. I need to behave better than the older brother in the Bible story, better than I've been doing. In fact, I don't know if I can do what has to be done here."

"You were doing pretty well last night," I said, stroking his arm. "I've never been more proud of you, Tom."

"Thanks, love. I just don't know how to do that again for these brothers of mine. I mean, how do I kill the fatted calf?"

I tried joking. "I hoped tacos would do."

He barely smiled. "You know what I mean. How do I reach out to them to let them know they're welcome home?"

I sighed and pulled up a chair. "It isn't going to be easy," I admitted. "Lenore and Shirley and I were just chatting about them in the kitchen. Neither has had a great life."

"Really? What can you tell me about them?"

"Just what your aunts could tell me. Michael's had two failed marriages. The good news is there were no children involved. Apparently the second wife was pregnant when she left and insisted on child support, but Michael insisted on DNA testing and, well . . . No children involved." I shrugged.

My husband winced. "Ouch. That must have been bad."

"Um, yeah, I'd say so. It's only been a few months since that was resolved."

"What about Marco?"

"Thirty-one. Never married. A series of girlfriends, but none of the relationships seem to get very serious or last very long. He can't seem to keep a job either."

"Yet they both respected Rocio enough that when she told them they had to come to Granny's funeral, they came."

"After your Aunt Lenore sent them the plane tickets," I added.

Another wince. "Ugh. I didn't know about that part."

"I don't think Lenore intended for us to know," I answered. "Aunt Shirley let it slip while Lenore was putting lemon juice on her stuffed grape leaves."

"Ouch," he said, thinking about how Lenore must have reacted. "I don't suppose either Michael or Marco is active in the Church?"

I shook my head. "Rocio told the aunts this will be the first time either of them has set foot inside an LDS building since your father's funeral."

"Great." Tom sighed. "It doesn't get any easier, does it?"

"Yes, it does," I reassured him. "Things are so much better now than they were this time yesterday—thanks to you."

He pursed his lips but slowly nodded his head. "You're right—but it's no thanks to me. Then again, a lot has changed for all of us."

I smiled sweetly and kissed my husband's fingers. "Except Michael and Marco," I said. "They don't know about the things you found, do they?"

Tom grinned. "You're right," he said. "They don't. Not yet." He took both my hands in his. "How is this happening, Karen? I know everyone loved Granny, but so many huge changes, so fast? It feels like something more is at work here."

"Yes," I agreed. "Yes, it does."

"Do you think Granny arranged all this? With Heavenly Father, I mean?"

"It's possible," I answered. "It sort of sounds like her."

"It really does," my husband agreed.

We stood together, holding one another for the briefest of moments. Then Tom said, "We need to get ready. We're supposed to leave in half an hour."

"We're both quick-change artists," I told him, tugging on his hand. "Come on. You'll see."

"You go ahead," he said. "I'll be along in a minute."

"Guess I'd better get a head start," I said, turning toward the open door.

Tom caught my hand. "One more minute," he said, pulling me to him. Then his voice became rougher. "Thank you, Karen. Thank you for everything." He leaned toward me, and I rose up to meet his kiss. "I love you," he said as we separated.

I put my cheek against his chest and answered, "I love you too."

* * *

Late morning

STEPHANIE BURNETT

I sniffled and lifted a tissue to my eyes. I bought several small packages of them last week knowing I would cry at Granny's funeral. Still, I hadn't expected to be in tears before we even finished the family prayer meeting. It was Dad's brief talk that did it. I've never heard him give a finer speech—maybe because it wasn't intended as some kind of powerful sermon. It was simple, honest, spoken from the heart, and it had us all in tears within minutes.

He talked about Granny Adelaide and how she had loved us all. He shared the story of the prodigal son and told us how difficult it had been for him to acknowledge that he had played the role of the stiff-necked, unforgiving brother. He testified that Adelaide had wanted only what our Savior wanted for us all—to bring us all together again, to guide us safely home. By the time he closed, I was practically sobbing, and there wasn't a dry eye near me. I was glad I had extra tissues to give away.

Of course, we still hadn't seen a glimpse of either of the mysterious *M* uncles. As curious as I was about them, I was glad they hadn't made an appearance yet. If they were as hostile as everyone seemed to think, all that negative energy would have been a serious damper to the warm, loving bond we were feeling.

I'd been feeling that bond since we arrived at the building to find Steve and Cathy, Mary and Bill all waiting for us. They helped us carry food into the kitchen. After all the emphasis we'd had on food since Granny's passing, it seemed fitting that we were all standing in the kitchen when Dad reintroduced Mary and Steve to their sister, Carrie, and their two half sisters as well. We visited briefly in the kitchen before moving into the Relief Society room for the family prayer meeting and our last good-byes to Granny.

We had come to that point. Family members clasped hands as my dad offered the prayer. Then one by one we filed past the casket, touching or kissing Granny's hands or face, saying our individual farewells. With my parents' permission, I placed a handkerchief beneath her folded hands—a beautiful, white, lace-edged hanky embroidered with the Sacramento temple that Granny Adelaide had given me as a gift before the temple dedication. It seemed right that it should be hers now.

When the last of us had passed by her, Aunt Lenore and Aunt Shirley came to the head of the casket and made adjustments to Granny's hair and veil. Then my dad, assisted by two men from the funeral home, lowered the top of the casket and fastened the locks. We lined up behind the casket and prepared to file into the chapel.

How many people come to your average weekday funeral? Thirty? Fifty? I had never seen the chapel so full except during special programs. People had opened the chapel overflow and put out chairs for another hundred or so. They opened the second overflow as we entered and put out still more chairs. It warmed me to see how many others had known and loved our Granny. They were here to celebrate her long and full life, several hundred of them, many from our ward and stake and many others I didn't recognize.

As we entered the room, I saw the uncles. They were sitting near the aisle toward the back of the chapel, but it had to be them. They were uncle bookends: the younger a Latino version of the older, both with features similar to my dad's. Rocio, in line a few people ahead of me, leaned toward them as she neared, speaking in a low voice, and they fell into place in front of her in the family procession and then ended up sitting between Aunt Shirley and Rocio on the bench behind us.

It was then that I noticed the organist, Em's adored music teacher, Ms. Nguyen. She was an Asian princess in a simple black skirt and white blouse, but she handled the stake center's precious pipe organ as if she'd been born to it, and she was playing lovely classical melodies I recognized, although I couldn't have told you their names or composers. She seemed right at home at our organ, and I had the odd sensation that she belonged here with us.

As soon as our family was in place, Bishop Rawson stepped to the podium and the congregation sat. We began with Ms. Nguyen playing the organ while Emily led everyone in singing, "The Spirit of God." It may have been unusual funeral music, but the building rang with it. Except for special arrangements by the Tabernacle Choir, I've never heard it sung more beautifully or with greater enthusiasm. Uncle Jeff gave the opening prayer, and then Jason got up to give the history.

I think Granny would have been pleased with the service. Who knows? I know it came out just the way she wanted it with upbeat, happy music and short, meaningful talks. I heard some great stories about Granny Adelaide that I'd never heard before, and there was frequent laughter. Funerals are often called "celebrations of life" even when they're really somber, sorrowful gatherings of mourners. But this *was* a celebration, a joyful commemoration of a life well lived.

And the music was marvelous! I've got to hand it to my sister: Emily's voice is nothing short of amazing. She has the range of a piano keyboard with high notes only dogs and dolphins can hear, the control and finesse of a lark, and the power of a foghorn, all rolled together in one tidy package. The solo she sang had us all sniffling again, and the madrigal she did with her friends was both lovely and astonishing in its complexity.

One of the most tender moments came when all the little ones—from eight-year-old Candelaria down to little Tommy—got up to sing "I Am a Child of God." It was one of those not-a-dry-eye experiences when the power of music and the innocence of children came together to testify to the truth of the message. Wow. I think even Ms. Nguyen was crying, although she never missed a note on the organ.

We sang "Come, Come Ye Saints" as our closing hymn just under an hour from the time we started—another of Granny's requests, that the service be short—and I couldn't help thinking as we followed her casket from the room that she must surely be well pleased with the send-off we were giving her. I hoped when my time came, I could do even half as well.

Karen's Coco-Nutty Pie

3 eggs, slightly beaten
1 C. Karo light corn syrup
½ C. white sugar
⅓ C. brown sugar
1 Tbsp. butter, melted
1 tsp. vanilla
1 ½ tsp. cinnamon

¼ tsp. nutmeg
⅛ tsp. salt

1 ½ C. unsweetened coconut
⅓ C. slivered almonds
1 9-inch unbaked pie shell

Directions

1. In large bowl, stir first nine ingredients (eggs through salt) until well blended.
2. Spread coconut into unbaked pie shell and top evenly with slivered almonds.
3. Pour the filling into the pie shell, making sure to dampen all the coconut and to keep the nuts spaced more or less evenly.
4. Bake at 350 for 50–55 minutes or until toothpick inserted halfway between center and edge comes out clean.
5. Cool. Top with whipped cream or nondairy topping.

Serves 8.

Variations

You can play with the flavors in this pie by altering the amounts of cinnamon and nutmeg, adding ⅛ tsp. cloves, or cutting out the spices. You can also vary it by using dark instead of light corn syrup or by altering the amounts of white or brown sugar.

CHAPTER 29

Wednesday, June 20, Early afternoon

KAREN BURNETT

How did Granny know us all so well? Or was it strictly by inspiration that she had given us the directions she did? Before we made the drive to the cemetery, Carrie approached Tom and me to tell us she had spoken with Michael and Marco the evening before. I could barely believe it when she reported that, although they were not fully mollified by the stories she'd told and the documents she'd shown them, Michael was ready to offer the opening prayer at the graveside service. He told her, "You may not see me at church, but I'm not a heathen. I do pray, and I'll be happy to pray for Granny." What a giant step that was!

The small ceremony at the cemetery could hardly have gone better. At Granny's written request, Steve conducted, Michael offered the opening prayer, and then the little children sang again. There was no Wendy Nguyen to accompany them this time, but Emily and Alex sang along to help them stay on key, and they sang all three verses of "I Am a Child of God." When they finished, Tom dedicated the grave.

Then we watched as the cemetery attendants, with the men of the family assisting, fastened Granny's casket into its vault and lowered the vault into the space prepared for it. We each filed by, tossing in a flower and a handful of earth, and then we returned to our cars and headed back toward the stake center and the family luncheon.

As we drove, I said a small prayer of thanks. I had finally realized how inspired Granny Adelaide's odd lunch request had been. I now knew that even if no one recognized the dishes on this menu, the lunch had been a great focus for the family's worst overfunctioner, giving me something worthwhile to do during a difficult and stressful week. I silently thanked my late grandmother-in-law for her wisdom and insight concerning me.

The cultural hall was ready when we got there, tables and chairs set up with tablecloths and small bouquets, piping hot food, cold salads, and chilled melon slices neatly arranged along the kitchen-side wall with all the proper paper goods—thanks to Steph's friends and mine. Another table held two big punch bowls, one filled with fresh summer lemonade and one with ice water. A third table was set up for dessert. I recognized several of my coco-nutty pies, cut into eighths, and plates of Pavlova ready to serve.

The sisters in my Relief Society had outdone themselves, and I sent grateful thoughts to the twenty-plus women who had given up some of their precious summer vacation time to help with this meal. Many of them had also been in the chapel with us today, ready to "mourn with those that mourn." The great wisdom of our Heavenly Father showed in all this, and I could hardly have felt more gratitude.

As Terry stood to offer the blessing on the food, I thought of the meal I had helped to prepare just a week ago, only hours before Adelaide died. It seemed I'd come through quite a circle in the past week, and I knew there had been some astonishing growth along the way—for me, yes, but even more for my husband and for many of our family. It was a journey of hope and healing, entirely appropriate for followers of Christ.

I pondered my own lack of faith the week before when I saw the challenges this week had presented to us, and I realized once again that no challenge is too great for the Lord. It amazed me what He had accomplished this week, even softening some very hard hearts.

Terry closed his prayer, everybody said amen, and the line formed behind Marco, who happened to be standing at the far end of the buffet table. It was time to see how well Granny's plans had worked. I swallowed hard as I got into line.

*   *   *

EMILY BURNETT

I watched the relatives line up at the buffet table—light and darker ones, California and Texas family, full siblings and half siblings, plus some others whose relationship to me I didn't even quite know how to figure.

(Was Marco my half uncle? What was little Sofie to me, anyway?) Granny Adelaide was one of the few parts of our lives we all had in common, and maybe hunger was another. During happy and sad times, good and bad times, everybody eats. I guess Granny must have had that in mind when she'd made such a big deal of this funeral-slash-reunion lunch my mom had been struggling with all week.

The food smelled awesome. I took my place somewhere way far back in the line and waited while others filled their plates, and I slowly made my way toward the serving table. A few minutes into the trip, Sofie found me and took my hand. I caught her mom's eye and waved across the room. Aunt Carrie nodded, giving her approval, and just like that, Sofie became my lunch partner. I could have had less cool lunch buddies. In fact, I *have* had less cool lunch buddies many times at school. Come to think of it, nobody I know is much cooler than Sofie. I held her hand tightly as we approached the table.

Sofie and I were almost at the end of the line, but there was still plenty of food left when we got there, and I was glad Mom had asked the ladies from the ward to help because she was able to sit down and eat with the rest of us.

As we reached the table, I kept Sofie in front of me and helped her dish up the foods she wanted, trying to make certain she got some of the healthier stuff as well as the yummy-looking foods she asked for. By the time we had filled our plates, I thought Aunt Carrie would be okay with Sofie's lunch. Sofie seemed okay with it too, so I guessed I'd done a pretty good job. I carried both our plates as we made our way across the room, looking for two empty chairs together at a table somewhere.

As we passed other tables, I heard people talking, and I hoped my mom could hear them too. Like at one table we passed, I heard someone say, "Um, these tacos are delicious. Aren't these like Mom used to make?" Then another voice said, "Maybe. I'm not sure, but this slaw? The kind with cabbage and chili? That's Mom's slaw recipe. I'd know it anywhere." At another table somebody said, "I think this is the same corn casserole my mom used to make for holidays." And an older woman's voice answered, "Yes, it is. Mary saved the recipe."

Someone said something about the green beans, and another voice said, "Nobody made green beans like Aunt Judith did." Everywhere people were talking and eating and really enjoying the food, but wherever there were people who remembered my Grandma Judith, they remembered her food too, and I knew my mom had done what Granny Adelaide had meant for her to do.

Maybe it was part of what Granny had planned from the beginning, or maybe it was just natural after sharing some food they remembered, but it wasn't long before family members started sharing memories of Christmases past or summer vacations or other things they remembered from way back when.

My dad told about going to the hospital to see the new baby when Carrie was born. I guess in those days they had a nursery where they kept the babies during a special viewing time, and visitors could stand at an outside window to look in at the little ones. Anyway, my dad's dad had lifted Steve up so he could see in the window, then he said, "Look, Steve. That's your new little sister over there." Then Steve said, "Oh no, Dad, let's not take that one. There's a really cute one over on this side." Dad said Uncle Steve must have thought they were at the baby store and could pick any one they wanted.

Steve told about a Christmas when Mary gave him her favorite My Little Pony—the pink one. He didn't really want a pink pony, but he knew how much it had meant to Mary to give it to him, so he didn't want to hurt her feelings by giving it back.

Carrie teased my dad with a story about a time he had tried to beat some guy named Billy in a game of one-on-one hoops and had ended up taking a fall that peeled all the skin off his shinbone. Then Dad teased Carrie about how, when she was a toddler, she'd wait by the refrigerator until someone opened the door. Then she'd reach inside and grab the ketchup bottle and run down the hall with it, giggling. She didn't ever eat it or anything. She just wanted to grab it and run. They called her the Ketchup Snatcher.

Dad told a story about a family camping trip to a nearby lake that ended early after the third visit to the hospital emergency room, and then Uncle Steve told about a time he remembered camping in the tall redwoods near Santa Cruz. The Texas relatives got some family stories in too. I especially liked the one about playing around the monument to the five-foot-long pecan they keep in the park in Seguin. They claimed it was the world's largest pecan for more than twenty years until a bigger nut was found in Missouri. I wondered who the bigger nut was (tee-hee), and then I thought how I want to see that when I finally get to visit Seguin— maybe next summer!

While people were talking, Sofie and I went to the dessert table to grab the last two pieces of Mom's special coco-nutty pie before somebody else got away with them. Mom's pie is scrumptious! There was some Pavlova left for anyone who wanted seconds, so I didn't feel too bad about getting our firsts. We quietly ate our pie while the family entertained us with more shared memories.

I think the family pictures were Rocio's idea. Here was everybody all dressed in Sunday best, together for the first time in bunches of years, and why not get a picture? Some relatives were slow to agree, and my Aunt Mary insisted she had to go check her hair and makeup before anybody could make her pose for a picture, but it wasn't too long before Dad, Aunt Mary, Uncle Steve, Aunt Carrie, and Uncle Michael were all lined up together in front of the plain church wall. Everybody who had a camera got it out, and the group posed for several sets of photos. Turns out I was still carrying my camera from when I planned to go to the summer choir concert, so I took pictures of them too.

Then it was my dad who insisted that Tina, Mandy, and Marco join them too, and everybody shot more pictures. I looked at them, seeing how different and how much the same they were, and realized this must be the first time ever that all eight children of the grandpa I had never met were together in the same place at the same time. I felt grateful they were together now, but I also felt very selfishly glad that my sisters and brother and I had grown up together and knew each other—that there hadn't been any big split to divide our family the way my dad's family had been divided.

Then just as that picture was breaking up, Aunt Mary suggested we get one with everybody, the whole family. Mom found one of her counselors from the kitchen to come in and shoot it for us, and we all lined up against the wall. I made sure Sofie was in front of me—I wanted to have a picture with the two of us together—and then we stood there, saying "cheese" over and over and over again while every person with a camera passed it to Sister Christensen and showed her how to use it. She must have taken at least thirty shots with fifteen different cameras, including mine.

After the last of the pictures were taken, people started picking up plates and cleaning off tables, and I knew the lunch was over. I wondered if Granny had been there to hear the stories people told or to see her grandchildren all standing together for their first family pictures ever. I knew Mom had done a great job with the meal, and I hoped Granny was pleased with the way everything had turned out.

About then Sofie said she wanted a drink of water. I went to get one and realized someone had already taken the water pitchers back to the kitchen, so I told Sofie to wait where she was and I went to the kitchen to fill her cup. I was just going in the door when I heard people talking and realized my dad and my Aunt Carrie were alone in the kitchen, standing by the sink. Remembering the last conversation between those two where I had eavesdropped, I hesitated by the door, unsure whether to go in or not.

That's when I heard my dad say, "I don't think I remember your married name, Carrie. What's your last name now?"

Carrie said, "Juanarena. I'm now Carolyn Juanarena."

"Juanarena?" Dad asked. "You mean you married a—"

Aunt Carrie swelled up like a puffer toad. "A what, Tom? A good, decent Latter-day Saint? A loving husband and father? A good provider and caring man? Is that what you meant to say?"

My dad looked sick. His voice sounded small when he said, "Actually, I was going to say 'a Juanarena.' I played college ball with Felipe Juanarena. He was a good man and a great offensive lineman. I just thought maybe your husband had some relatives around here."

Carrie pushed her lips together, and then she slowly spoke. "It seems I've been guilty of a harsh and unfair judgment, Tom. Can you forgive me?"

Dad smiled. "Sure, sis. I've given you plenty of cause to feel defensive. Your Carlos sounds like a good man, and I hope to get to meet him someday soon."

They hugged each other, and I coughed loudly to let them know I was there and then went in to fill Sofie's water cup. When I left a half minute later, Dad was asking about how far it was to Waco and when would be a good time to visit. I took that as a hopeful sign.

*   *   *

KAREN BURNETT

The lunch was coming to an end, and I felt pleased with the way it had turned out. I hoped Granny Adelaide was pleased with it too. Much of the cleanup was done, and people were starting to pick up their coats and talking about who rode with whom when my son-in-law, Jason, stood on a chair and whistled loudly to get everyone's attention.

"Hello, everybody? Hello?" he said. When things quieted, he spoke again. "Just letting everybody know, a bunch of my buddies took the day off work so they could come to the funeral. They're going to celebrate having the afternoon off with a pick-up football game at the elementary school. Anybody who wants to join in is welcome."

There was some murmuring and then one of the women—I didn't see who—asked, "Is this coed? Can I play too?"

"Maybe, if you're feeling brave," Jason said, and it was clear he was bragging.

"So do you play namby-pamby two-hand touch?" Marco asked.

"No way, man. This is strictly tackle, no pads."

"I'm in," Marco said.

"Oh, then I'm out," the same woman's voice said again. "You guys go have your ridiculous male bonding ritual by yourselves."

"Who's playing?" Michael asked.

"Just some guys I know. We've got a group of about twelve to fifteen men who usually join us—"

"But is Tom going to be there?" It was Michael again.

"You betcha," my husband said. "Wouldn't miss it."

"Then I'm in," Michael said. "As long as I'm on the other team and get a chance to hit that guy."

"Yeah, me too," Marco said.

Terry looked at his wife and got her nod before saying, "I'll be there," and then Jeff chimed in as well.

I shuddered, knowing what it's like when the men in my family start hitting the football field—and each other. At least they sounded excited about it. They were all talking about the upcoming football game when I went to the kitchen to load the leftovers into the back of my car.

Pavlova

The national dessert of Australia and New Zealand

3 egg whites
1 ½ C. confectioner's sugar
½ tsp. vanilla
1 tsp. vinegar

1 tsp. cornstarch
4 Tbsp. boiling water
Unsweetened whipped cream
Fresh fruit

Directions

1. Beat egg whites, sugar, vanilla, vinegar, corn starch, and boiling water for 15 minutes or until very, very stiff.
2. Dump the meringue out onto a baking parchment or brown baking paper. You can shape it into a heart, square, oval, or free-form.
3. Bake in moderate oven (325–350) for 10 minutes, then reduce oven to slow bake (about 275–300) for another 45 minutes.
4. *Do not disturb* the Pavlova. Turn off the oven and let the dessert cool where it stands with the oven door ajar for 2–4 hours.
5. When the meringue is cooled through, remove it to a serving tray and frost only the top with unsweetened whipped cream.
6. Arrange fresh fruit slices or small berries in a pleasing pattern atop the cream. Cut into chunks or slices for serving.

Serves 4–6.

CHAPTER 30

Wednesday, June 20, Late afternoon

KAREN BURNETT

I WAS AT THE FAMILY computer in the upstairs hallway, recording my thoughts about the day, when Steph called up the stairway, "Hey, Mom! We've decided to finish off the next-to-last Pavlova. Want some?"

I barely hesitated. "Sure, honey." Okay, so I'd have to deal with it in July. It still felt worth it today.

I finished my entry and joined the other women in the dining room. Carrie was there, along with Candi and Sofie. They had come over shortly after the funeral when Sofie asked to "play with" Emily and Buster. So adorable! We sat down at the table, my daughters joined us, and we finished off the last of the dessert in companionable silence.

I guess I was more silent than companionable. After a couple of minutes, Steph put her hand on my arm. "Are you worried about them, Mom?"

I faked a smile. "How did you guess?"

She shrugged. "Maybe because I'm worried about them too?"

"Them who?" Em said. Then she looked at our faces and said, "Oh."

"Michael looked positively murderous," Carrie said.

"Tom seemed ready to take him on." I savored the delicate meringue and rich whipping cream while I hoped my husband wasn't out getting himself killed. It had been a long time since college football.

Emily, sage that she is, said wisely, "You know, guys are like that. They kind of have to beat each other up once in a while."

"Well, they're not like women. That's for sure." Melissa downed the last bite.

We lapsed back into silence. It had been nearly two hours since the men had loaded up their gear—but no pads—and headed for the elementary school. I couldn't help remembering the year when the annual Christmas bowl had landed both my husband and son in the emergency room, and there had been other injuries at other times of year. Although most injuries weren't serious, Tom had once worn a finger brace for two weeks, and Brian had needed stitches to close a gash in his eyebrow.

Today Michael had left here with blood in his eye—metaphorically speaking. Who knew what could happen under those circumstances? Whatever it was, I was glad the aunts weren't here to see it. They had gone to visit an old friend of their mother's they had met at the service, so they were spared the wait and worry.

"The guys should be getting back anytime now," I said to no one in particular, and everyone looked at the clock.

We were picking up the dishes a few minutes later when we heard the car pull up, and we rushed to the front door. It looked like a scene from a war movie. Tom had a swollen lip and a huge red bruise across his cheek. Michael sported a lump on his jaw that was already turning dark, and he was supporting Jason, who limped on a skinned knee and squinted through two black eyes. Marco had two scraped knees and a bloody elbow. They were leaning on each other, helping each other into the house, staggering like walking wounded—and they were laughing, bragging up a storm.

"You should have seen Marco run for the touchdown!" Michael declared as they neared Carrie.

"It was amazing!" Jason agreed. "One of the best runs I've seen in years."

"No question about it," Tom announced. "You guys beat us fair and square, six scores to five."

"And that's even counting that questionable run you made just before we called the halftime break," Michael said.

"Nothing questionable about it," Jason declared. "Tom was an NCAA athlete back in his college days, and he can still run—even though he isn't quite as fast as he used to be."

"Not too shabby," Michael agreed. "Pretty fast for an old guy anyway."

"Who are you calling old?" my husband challenged him.

"You, Grandpa!" Michael retorted, but they were grinning as they threatened each other, and I knew the old grudges had suffered an ignoble death on the football field.

"Any of that pudding stuff left?" Jason asked.

"What?" Melissa asked him. "You're becoming a pudding fan now?"

Jason shrugged. "It was good."

"It's Pavlova," I said, "Meringue, not pudding. We finished off the last cut one, but there's another one left. You guys get cleaned up, and the table will be ready for you when you're ready for it."

"Sounds like a deal," Michael said, and the four of them headed for the back porch sink while Emily took the girls into the backyard and Steph helped Carrie re-set the table.

The teasing and bragging continued as the men sat down to eat. I sat for a few minutes, listening to the various accounts of the game, until the ringing telephone called me away. Moments later I was back with the phone in hand. "Excuse me, guys." They quieted. "Rocio is on the phone. She's invited the whole family to come to Granny's for a traditional *Tejano* dinner tomorrow."

Michael was the first to speak. "Mama Rocio makes great tamales."

"The best," Marco agreed, "and carnitas, frijoles, the works."

"She mentioned it to us earlier," Carrie said. "Tina and Mandy and I all agreed to help. We'll be cooking most of the day tomorrow, but that's what we always do when we put on a feed. It will be the best Tex-Mex you ever ate, I promise."

"Well, shall I tell her we'll be there?" I looked at Tom, who nodded. Neither of us mentioned the subtext—tomorrow was Tom's fiftieth birthday.

"Jason? Will you and Melissa join us too?"

"What d'you think, Mel?" he asked his wife.

"Sounds good to me," she answered.

"Then sign us up for three more," Jason said, "since Mel's eating for two now."

I told Rocio we'd be there and gave her a rough head count. Then I asked what I could do to help. She said we could host everybody this evening with the leftovers from the funeral lunch, and the Texas family would host us all the next evening. She acted like it was an even deal, but I knew I was getting a break. I told her we'd check with the aunts when they returned and we'd get back to her.

An hour later, when the aunts had returned and the football mob had diminished, I went back to my journal to add a final note:

It's hard to believe how much has changed in only a week. I know it's partly the goodness of Granny Adelaide and her love for each one of us that has brought us through the past rough days and has given us so much hope and forgiveness, but it's also the goodness of our Heavenly Father.

Granny didn't pray, really. It was more like she had frequent, loving chats with God. I've wondered many times during these past few days if she didn't sit down and orchestrate this with Him, planning the hour of her death so she could get the most mileage possible out of the time when she could bring us all together. I never would have believed the changes, just in Tom alone, if I hadn't seen them myself. Add in what has happened with Rocio, Michael, Marco, and the rest, and it's nothing short of miraculous.

It's amazing and humbling, and I'm so, so grateful.

I closed my journal and shut down the computer, knowing we had indeed seen miracles and wondering if there might still be more to come.

Pasta Carbonara

½ pound bacon, cut into small pieces
4 eggs, room temperature
¼ C. heavy cream at room temperature
1 C. grated Parmesan cheese

16 oz. dry fettuccine pasta
¼ C. butter, softened
¼ C. fresh, chopped Italian parsley
ground black pepper to taste

Directions

1. Cook bacon until crisp. Drain on paper towels.
2. In medium bowl, beat together eggs and cream until just blended. Stir in cheese and set aside.
3. Cook pasta according to package directions. Drain and return to pan. Toss with butter until the butter is melted. Add bacon and cheese mixture, and toss gently until mixed.

Variations

For lactose intolerant guests, replace heavy cream with soy or almond milk (almond is heavier but adds a slight almond flavor), and serve the Parmesan separately, to be added at the table, or serve with other cheeses. Any kind of pasta may be substituted for the fettuccine. Regular parsley may be substituted for the Italian variety. For an even tastier alternative, replace parsley with fresh basil, or a part-parsley and part-basil mix.

CHAPTER 31

Wednesday, June 20, Early evening

EMILY BURNETT

THE RELATIVES WERE SCHEDULED TO arrive at any minute, and we were ready for them. Right after she got off the phone with Rocio, Mom had realized that there weren't quite enough leftovers for everyone, so she got Steph in the kitchen to cook some bacon while she boiled most of a big can of spaghetti from our food storage. And just before the relatives arrived, we had creamy pasta carbonara—enough to feed everybody, with leftovers on the side. We had Aunt Shirley's pumpkin bread. There were even a few Snickers-doodles left in the cookie jar, so there was no shortage of treats, but while we were waiting for the men to come home, Mom made four more coco-nutty pies, just to be certain we had enough dessert.

I had a plan of my own too. As we were leaving the funeral, when I was thinking about Granny and Dad and everything that had happened in the past week, I got an idea, and it just felt right, so with Mom's permission, I downloaded my camera to her computer, and then I sent everything electronically to a local one-hour photo center. Then I got Mom to let me drive her car—with Steph riding along, since I'm still on a provisional license—and I drove over to the photo center to pick up family pictures.

I had helped our ward's Primary activity days coordinator when the girls decorated simple picture frames for their families, and I still had a few left, at least one per family. When the kids came, I'd have something fun—and I hoped memorable—to do with them.

Just before six, the van and another car pulled up and the relatives piled out. Then came Steve and Cathy, Mary and Bill, and some of the other relatives. While the grown-ups were visiting and talking about the food, I rounded up all the little people and took them up to my room, where we got to work on my plan. In another half hour, when they called us in to dinner, I swore the kids to secrecy and gave them their final instructions, and then we all went in to dinner.

There's nothing quite like my mom's bacon-and-eggs pasta. The other stuff was good too, and then we all had coco-nutty pie for dessert. It took a few minutes to clean up after dinner, and then we sat down around the living and family rooms, just to visit. That's when I said, "The kids and I have been working on something special. Give us a couple of minutes, and we'll be right back."

Dad said, "I wonder what this is about," but nobody objected.

The kids and I went up to my room and every child, or pair of siblings, picked up the framed photo of our whole family together that he, she, or they had decorated for their families. As a last-minute brainstorm, I led the kids in singing "Families Can Be Together Forever" while we came down the stairs and into the living room. Then the kids presented the family pictures to their parents.

There were lots of gasps and "ohs" and even some tears, so I was pleased with the way it all went. This was turning out to be one of the best family reunions ever.

* * *

Late evening

STEPHANIE BURNETT

Our family gathering was over, and we'd enjoyed the last of the cookies and Mom's coco-nutty pie. The Texas family had all gone back to Granny Adelaide's house, and the other relatives from around the county had gone home. Aunt Carrie was thrilled to tell us that Michael and Marco had cancelled their hotel room in town and agreed to stay overnight with the rest of their group.

We were cleaning up in the kitchen when my cell phone rang. I thought the number looked familiar but didn't really recognize it. I answered, and the person on the other end said, "Hi, Steph. This is Matt Kerrigan."

My pulse picked up a little. Of all the guys who had ever shown interest in me, Matt is the only one who had ever tempted me to break my own two-date rule. I'd experienced my first minor heartbreak when I was in high school when the only boyfriend I'd ever had broke up with me the same week Grandma Judith had her biggest-ever psychotic break. She died a few months after that of unrelated causes, but sometime during those awful months, I had decided that I would probably never marry. Who would want to put a husband and kids through what Judith's family had suffered? And since I was likely to lose all my marbles someday, just the way she had . . . well . . .

Then I'd had my talk with Mom, and I'd begun to wonder whether the two-date rule (three dates max, if I'd been out with someone else in the interim) was really such a great idea.

So here was Matt on the line, and we had already dated twice. I hadn't been out with anybody else since then either. All of this pondering took me about one and a half seconds. Then I said, "Hi, Matt. How are you?"

"I'm doing great, thanks. I'm sorry I wasn't able to come to your grandma's funeral. I couldn't get off work, but I wanted to be there to support you."

"Thanks, Matt. That's very sweet."

"So are you doing okay?"

"Yes, I am. She was my great-grandma—not that that makes a big difference, but she was past a hundred years old, and she said she was ready to go. That kind of makes it easier."

"Yes, I guess it might. Listen, Steph, I wanted to see if you have plans for the special fireside program tomorrow evening. If you're feeling up to going, well, I'd love to pick you up? Say, around seven?"

I paused. Was I ready to break my own dating rules? I decided to jump first and think later. "That sounds great. You've got my cell number, so you may want to check a few minutes before seven, just to be sure I'm here at the house. We're going to have dinner with my Texas relatives, and I could still be over there."

"In Texas?"

"Oh no! Sorry! They're here in town for Granny's funeral. They're all staying at her house, so we'll be having dinner there, and I could still be over there at seven." I hoped that weird explanation hadn't confused him even more.

"Okay. That sounds good. I'll call you." There was an awkward pause when neither of us said anything. Then Matt said, "Well, have a good time with the relatives, and I'll see you tomorrow night."

"Excellent. See you then, Matt."

I put the phone down and hummed as I helped Mom with the last organizing in the kitchen. Then I went upstairs to my room and spent a little while looking through old journal entries, remembering how and why I had made my dating rules and trying to decide what it meant that I'd broken my own rule for the first time ever.

I already knew I was no longer afraid of ending up like Grandma Judith. I was simply made of stronger stuff than that. If it turned out that I developed the same kinds of problems she had, I could always learn from her example, just as Mom said. Besides, since Granny Adelaide's death, Dad had turned up records that showed Grandma Judith's illness going way back, even back younger than I am. Maybe that meant that I'd never be as bad as she was even if I did get sick. Maybe I didn't need to be afraid of getting close to someone. Maybe I could even marry someday and have babies of my own.

Wow, that was a revelation! I'd never been the kind of girl who went gaga over guys or spent hours looking at bridal magazines or cooed at every baby that went by. I was into my schooling and my career plans. But now? I was still excited that I had the possibility of publishing as an undergrad, and I still wanted to make the best of both my academic and future professional careers, but I had been surprised to discover that I felt a little melty over the beautiful babies my unknown aunts had brought to us this week. Sofie was darling, and who could resist little Tommy? Maybe there was some maternal instinct in me after all.

Uh, scary! Even more frightening was the realization that I was having all these thoughts after making a third date with Matt Kerrigan. Was he inspiring all these crazy ideas? Or did he just happen to be reaching out to me at the time when memories of Granny Adelaide proved that I didn't need to fear my future? I had to think a little about that one. Although I didn't like thinking that Matt had inspired this line of reasoning—I didn't ever want to be that dependent on another human being—I now felt braver than I'd ever felt before. At least brave enough for a third date. We could take it from there.

* * *

KAREN BURNETT

It was late, and everyone else had gone up to bed when I found Tom in the office, reading through some of the cards and letters he had found among his mother's things. He looked up at me with tears on his face.

"Is it that bad or that good?" I asked.

He swallowed hard. "Both, I guess."

I sat down beside him.

His voice was so rough. "Dad wrote some of these cards."

I couldn't help being startled. "Your dad wrote?"

"Several times. Cards, letters, sometimes a letter along with a card . . . I never had any idea."

"And your mother never let on?"

"Not so much as a clue. In fact, she always told us he never called, never wrote, never sent anything to us that wasn't court ordered."

"Do you think she was lying on purpose? Or that she just didn't understand?"

"Who can guess? It was always tough to know what Mom was thinking. Or why. Maybe she was afraid that if we knew Dad was in touch, we'd want to be with him. I can't begin to fathom what she may have been thinking."

I decided not to follow that. "What did your dad have to say?"

Tom shrugged. "Lots of things. One early letter talked about how he would be coming back to visit and to make better arrangements for the family. Then there was one that said he was sorry he hadn't been able to arrange visitation rights. One letter expressed his sorrow for the way he handled his first marriage in getting into his second, the loss of his covenants and his temple blessings. He even bore his testimony of the value of all he had lost. Another from a couple of years later apologized for leaving me with so much responsibility . . ." Tom dropped his head into his hands. "Karen, if I'd known this then . . ." His breath caught in a sob.

I stroked his face, taking care to avoid the side he had injured playing football. "You didn't know, sweetheart. You couldn't have known. But you know now, and that means that finally, you can let it all go."

"But I should have . . ." His voice broke on a sob. "I should have known. I should have realized—"

"Shhh, Tom, shhh," I soothed. "What's done is done, and there's never any going back. You were twelve years old! What did you know about what motivates men and women? What matters is the family you have now—especially those you're just getting to know."

He seemed to respond to that. "Granny had quite a plan, didn't she?"

I smiled. "She was always a smart old bird."

"Indeed," he said. I could see Tom's resilience kicking in. The strength that had helped his twelve-year-old self through such shocking and heartbreaking circumstances was reasserting itself now. Tom's backbone straightened as I watched.

"You're going to be okay, you know," I assured him.

"I know," he said. "Especially with you around to help." He kissed me. "I love you, Karen. I really appreciate the way you've helped me through this past awful week, dealing with the past awful me."

I kissed him back. "My pleasure," I said. The cuckoo clock in the office chimed eleven. "So, handsome, are you ready to go up to bed? If you play your cards right, I might even make it worth your while." I batted my eyes.

Tom chuckled. "Then happy birthday to me," he said and turned out the office light.

Pork Tamales

Authentic Mexican or *Tejano* (Tex-Mex) style

TAMALE FILLING:
1 ¼ pounds pork loin
1 large onion, halved
1 clove garlic
4 dried red chili pods
2 C. water
1 ½ tsp. salt

TAMALE DOUGH:
2 C. masa harina
1 can (10.5 oz.) beef broth
1 tsp. baking powder
½ tsp. salt
⅔ C. lard or vegetable shortening
1 package (8 oz.) dried corn husks
1 C. sour cream

Directions

1. Place pork into a dutch oven with onion and garlic, and add water to cover. Bring to a boil, then reduce heat to low and simmer until the meat is cooked through, about 2 hours.
2. Use rubber gloves when removing stems and seeds from chili pods. Place chilies in a saucepan with 2 C. water. Simmer uncovered for 20 minutes, then remove from heat to cool. Transfer the chilies and water to a blender and blend until smooth. Strain the mixture, stir in salt, and set aside. Shred the meat and mix in 1 C. chili sauce.
3. Soak the corn husks in a bowl of warm water. In a large bowl, beat the lard with a tablespoon of the broth until fluffy. Combine the masa harina, beef broth, baking powder, and salt; stir into the lard mixture, adding more broth as necessary to form a spongy dough.
4. Over corn husks, spread the dough to ¼- to ½-inch thickness. Place one tablespoon of the meat filling into the center. Fold the sides of the husks in toward the center and place in a steamer.
5. Steam for 1 hour.
6. Remove tamales from husks and drizzle with remaining chili sauce. Top with sour cream or mix sour cream into the chili sauce.

Variations

1. Substitute chicken or beef for the pork, or make a vegetarian filling with various kinds of squash, corn, beans, etc. (Don't overcook!)
2. For sweet tamales, add 2 Tbsp. brown or unrefined sugar to the masa

dough. Add sweet corn, raisins, chopped dates or nuts, or pineapple. Put a blob (2–3 Tbsp.) of the sweetened dough into a corn husk and steam with the rest of the tamales. You may want to add something to the wrap on these tamales so you can tell the sweet ones from the outside.

Enjoy!

CHAPTER 32

Thursday, June 21, Morning
Tom Burnett's Birthday

THE BURNETT FAMILY HOME

TOM AWAKENED EARLY. IT WOULDN'T matter what the rest of the day brought him. This week had given him some of the finest gifts he'd ever known. Last week he'd had one sister, Mary. Today he had four. He had known one brother, Steve. Now there were two more. He had felt nothing but hatred in his heart for a woman named Rocio. Although they were hardly the best of friends today and he still regretted the way his father had handled his private affairs—emphasis on that last word—he had made peace with a woman whose strength he was learning to admire. Just before she left yesterday, she had told him of how she had made sure his father's ordinances were all in order. She had also been sealed to her husband a little more than a year after his death. Tom had a feeling he and Rocio could build a lasting peace.

Then there were the blessings he'd already known that had been reemphasized to him by the events of this last difficult week. Karen lay beside him in the bed, still sleeping soundly, still beautiful even after twenty-five years and four births. He had always loved her, but he had never appreciated her more than he did today, and he knew that feeling would only intensify as the years passed and life threw them still more tough-to-catch passes. With Karen at his side, he was running for the goal line. He knew one day they would cross it together.

He smiled and touched her shoulder. "Morning, sweetheart."

She came awake, yawning and stretching. "Ummm. What time is it?"

"Almost seven."

She rolled over and kissed him. "Happy birthday, handsome."

He wrapped his arms around her. "It's feeling like a very happy birthday."

Karen stretched and settled against her pillow. "Remember how the kids sometimes used to wake you on your birthday? If it was a weekend or a day off, they'd come in singing the Spanish birthday-morning song you taught them from your mission. I don't mind sleeping in a little on birthday mornings, but I kind of miss the singing."

Tom pulled her against him and began to sing softly, "*Estas son las mañanitas, que cantaba el Rey David . . .*" He smiled, remembering the way his children used to sing them awake at some early hour. "I know what you mean," he said. "I miss it too."

"I dreamed about Granny last night," Tom said then, keeping his voice neutral.

Karen, who had heard him recount the dreams of the past week, sat up against him, worry written on her features. "Was it another of those frightening dreams?"

"No, not at all. I was eight or nine, and Granny was teaching me how to ride a bike. It was pretty much the way it happened in real life, except the place was different. You know how dreams can change things."

"Yes, I know. Go on."

"Well, she was teaching me to ride, and I kept falling over and catching myself with one foot on the ground. Finally Granny said, 'You're never going to ride until you let go and keep both feet up, Tommy. Just go. You'll be fine.' Then I put both feet up on the pedals, and I rode. She stood beside the sidewalk clapping for me."

Karen smiled. "She knew you were going to be okay," she said. Then she stroked the uninjured side of his face. "You are, you know. You're going to be okay now."

"Yeah," he said, leaning in to kiss her. "Yeah, I know."

*   *   *

Thursday, June 21, Midmorning

KAREN BURNETT

The most special gift for Tom's birthday was the long e-mail from Brian. We hadn't expected it, since his P-day is Monday, and that's usually the only time we get any correspondence from our missionary. But he wrote that, given the distress in the family over Granny's death, President Bettencourt had made an exception and allowed him to write a long, chatty e-mail for his father's birthday. He said he was only missing the exercise period for the day and that he'd promised to get right back into the daily round of classes with the other elders just as soon as his e-mail was complete.

It was long and thoughtful, and it really put a smile on his father's face. Brian remembered all the times when Tom had been there for him when he was little—the tree house they'd built together, the hours his dad had spent teaching him to throw and hit when he went out for Little League, even the time Tom had spent teaching him to ride a two-wheeled bike. That memory brought tears to my husband's eyes, especially after his dream of Granny Adelaide.

Brian's long letter had ended with his love and his wishes for a beautiful day. The rest of the gifts our family presented to Tom at breakfast were thoughtful and welcomed. I was especially pleased, and I think Tom was too, by the family photo that Emily had saved for him and put into a frame she'd decorated with small items that reminded her of her dad. Tom's eyes were brimming and his voice slightly rough as he told Emily, "I'm going to keep this on my desk at the office so I can look at it many times a day."

"We love you!" I said as our breakfast birthday party drew to a close, knowing I was representing a much larger "we" than had ever wished him a happy birthday before.

* * *

Thursday, June 21, Evening

STEPHANIE BURNETT

Dinner was delicious. I've never tasted better tamales—in fact, I've never tasted the sweet kind before—and the rest of the meal was equally fabulous. I got to help at the end and learned a little more about how an authentic Tex-Mex kitchen operates. The big surprise of the evening was the gorgeously decorated birthday cake the Texas women presented as dessert, together with some Mexican-brand coconut ice cream. I asked them who told them it was Dad's birthday. In fact, no one had mentioned it, but Carrie had been going through old family records recently and she remembered. Imagine that!

I'd love to know more about *Tejano* cooking. Aunt Tina and Aunt Mandy have invited me to come out to spend some time with their families and get to know them all better. Maybe one day soon I will, if I can figure out how to fit it into my academic life, which seems to get busier every day.

Matt should be here to pick me up any minute now. I'm so looking forward to this date. I've never felt so excited or hopeful about a simple date to a fireside. I've already decided that, whether or not I think Matt is "the one," I'm going to accept another date if he asks me out again. I'm ready—ready to have a boyfriend, ready to think about the future, ready to date with the possibility of marriage in mind.

As for the rest, I have an appointment scheduled next week to talk with our family doctor, and I'm ready to do whatever he tells me is best for dealing with the occasional depression and for dealing with whatever may come in the future. I want to be healthy, and I'm ready to do whatever I must to make that happen.

I got on the computer this morning and looked up some credible medical websites. Learning a little about what causes chemically induced depression and a little more of what is known about schizophrenia has really helped me too. To me, that's ironic. I never thought that learning more about mental illness would make me feel more free of it, but that's exactly what has happened. As usual, my mom was right.

This past week has taught me so much, and I couldn't be more grateful. It's time to trust myself, time to move on. The future looks bright, and I've never felt so hopeful.

* * *

Friday, June 22, Midmorning

EMILY BURNETT

Aunt Carrie called a few minutes ago to tell us they were in Stockton and well on their way. She'll call again when they're safely home in Texas.

I had barely hung up the phone when Ms. Nguyen called. She was just getting ready to leave town to go see her family for her summer vacation, but she wanted to talk to me before she left.

She said she was really impressed with all the songs we sang at Granny Adelaide's funeral. She asked me some questions about the words, like, "How about this line: 'and angels are coming to visit the earth'? Do you mean that literally?"

I felt kind of awkward answering all those tough questions when I really would have liked to pass them off to the missionaries, but I did the best I could, trying to answer with what I thought was true.

Then Ms. Nguyen asked something about the Book of Mormon and how we pronounced the name *Nephi*. I asked her what she knew about the Book of Mormon, and much to my shock, she said she had looked up the missionaries at the end of Granny's funeral service and had asked them for a copy. She had already read through 1 and 2 Nephi—even the parts that quoted Isaiah—and was starting on the Book of Jacob. I asked her what she thought of it.

"It's interesting," she said, "very different from what I expected."

I didn't know whether that was good or bad. Then she said, "Emily, when I get back after my visit, and before school starts up again, I'm going to start having the missionary lessons. I'm hoping you will be able to come when they teach me."

I said, "Just a minute, Ms. Nguyen. Hang on," and then I went to ask my mom, who was right there in the kitchen making lemonade. She said exactly what I expected her to say. I got back on the phone and said, "Ms. Nguyen, that will be cool. Mom says I can come there when the missionaries teach you, or you can come here anytime you want and the elders can teach you here at our house."

Ms. Nguyen said, "Thank you, Emily. I will consider that," and then told me she needed to go so she could get to her parents' place before dark since she was missing a headlight, so we said good-bye.

Like, wow. Ms. Nguyen is going to have the missionary lessons. And she's reading the Book of Mormon too! I wonder if Granny knows what has come from her funeral plans.

Water Punch

2 Tbsp. citric acid*
1 quart water

2 cups sugar
2 Tbsp. pure lemon extract

Directions

1. Cook ingredients until all are dissolved. Cool.
2. Refrigerate mixture until ready to use.
3. To serve, pour concentrate into an additional four quarts of water and ice, for a total of five quarts.
4. Garnish with lemon and lime slices.

*Citric acid can be found at most pharmacies or natural food stores.

Variations

You can add ½ cup orange juice to the finished punch to give it an added citrus boost, or experiment with 1–2 tsp. orange extract as well as the lemon extract in the recipe. Be sure to remove citrus slices before storing leftover punch in the refrigerator. Left in the punch, the citrus skins will add an unwanted bitter taste.

EPILOGUE

Tuesday, July 3, Midmorning

KAREN BURNETT

IT'S BEEN ROUGHLY TWO-AND-A-HALF WEEKS since Granny died. It almost seems we've begun a whole new life. Part of that life is happy. Carrie called this morning, asking for the recipe for the punch we served at Granny's funeral lunch. We had a great visit, just as if we'd been chatting for years, and it was a pleasure to send her the recipe. Of course, part of our new life is sad too. Aunt Shirley is putting Granny's house on the market, and I have moments when I miss Granny so much it hurts even to breathe. But I'm too happy and far too grateful to spend much time grieving.

Tom conducted family home evening last night, and it was all about plans for a reunion in Texas next June. If all goes as we're currently planning, we will leave here right after Emily finishes her senior year. We'll fly or drive out to Texas and will have a big reunion in the parks around Waco. Tom is inviting Mary and Steve and their families to join us, and they're thinking about it too. Then if everything still looks good, we'll leave Emily there with Carrie and her husband, Carlos, for the rest of the summer.

She will be able to spend some time with the little ones and some time working in the restaurant, building her savings for college. Em is so excited, and it thrills me to see Tom enjoying his plans to be with his extended family, the family he didn't even acknowledge a month ago.

Emily is excited about so many things these days. Wendy Nguyen is progressing quickly with her missionary lessons. She came to our ward's block of meetings last Sunday and had another lesson here yesterday. The elders say she is golden. Emily could hardly be happier.

Steph seems happy too. I think she's been out with Matt Kerrigan three or four times since the funeral. He is a fine young man—ambitious, handsome, faithful—and it will be fine with me if she wants to bring him into the family. Melissa did well with Jason, but Stephanie never seemed very interested in dating until now. I hadn't realized why until she called me aside for that talk. It's good to see her so interested in someone who also seems seriously interested in her. Her article for publication is coming along well, and she seems happier than I've seen her in years.

And speaking of Melissa, she and Jason are scheduled for a sonogram on the eighteenth, two weeks from tomorrow. They've invited me to come, and I surely plan to be there. They talked about whether they wanted to know the baby's gender yet or not and decided it will be a surprise whenever they find out and they'd really rather know now. They haven't decided on names yet, but they've already agreed that, if it's a boy, they want a first name that will go with the middle name Thomas. Zachary Thomas Kingsley is the current favorite.

Tom is thrilled. I think he's as excited about this baby as he was when we were having Melissa. It's another testimony that our Heavenly Father loves us at both ends of our mortal lives. He was certainly with Granny Adelaide when she was making plans to go home again, and He is with us all now as we plan to welcome a newcomer. Yesterday I was shopping for some new socks Em needs for girls' camp, and I spotted a cute little yellow one-piece bodysuit, newborn size, with a picture of the Earth as if taken from outer space and the phrase, "Hi! I'm new here." I picked it up and put it in my cart. It made me happy to think of dressing a sweet little newborn in it and cuddling it close, holding my first grandchild.

And why shouldn't we be happy? When I married Tom, I didn't realize how much his past had left him emotionally crippled. He is a happier, healthier person today, and he is facing life with so much more excitement and energy; it's wonderful to witness. I married a good man, but I have an even better one now. Granny did this for us, and I bless her memory every day.

Mostly I'm grateful to our Savior. It was Granny's plan that started me hunting for recipes and brought all these changes in our lives, but it was His Atonement that made it all possible. Because of Him, we have the recipe that lets us move forward, trusting that each day can be better than the last. That's the message and the hope of His Atonement and the recipe that feeds us all.

About the Author

Susan Aylworth adores her husband, her children, her many grandchildren, and good jam. She loves well-written books of all kinds and enjoys writing fiction, poems, and plays. She enjoys cooking and likes creating her own recipes or improving on the recipes she finds.

Susan started her first "book" at the age of nine. Now a novelist and playwright with deep roots in the West, she was born in Mesa and raised in northeastern Arizona near the Four Corners, eventually attending college in Utah. She and her husband, Roger, have raised their seven children in Northern California, where she recently retired from teaching writing and literature at a state university.

Previous works include a series of novels set in fictional Rainbow Rock, Arizona, and a play about Hamlet's mother. Her first book for Covenant was *Right Click*, published in 2009. Find her at www.susanaylworth.com, www.susanaylworth.blogspot.com, or www.facebook.com/susan.aylworth.author. Follow her @SusanAylworth.